PLAYING FOR THE
Devil's
FIRE

PHILLIPPE DIEDERICH

PLAYING FOR THE

Devil's

FIRE

PHILLIPPE DIEDERICH

CINCO PUNTOS PRESS
WWW.CINCOPUNTOS.COM

LIBRARY OF CONGRESS CATALOGING-IN-PUBLICATION DATA

Names: Diederich, Phillippe, 1964- author.
Title: Playing for the Devil's Fire / by Phillippe Diederich.
Description: First edition. | El Paso, TX : Cinco Puntos Press, [2016] |
Summary: Thirteen-year-old Boli lives in a small pueblo near Mexico City, a landscape destroyed by drug crime, where one day a severed head is found in the plaza, then Boli's parents leave town and are not heard from, then a washed out masked wrestler turns up and Boli hopes to inspire the luchador to set out with him to find his parents.
Identifiers: LCCN 2015024951 | ISBN 9781941026304 (paperback) | ISBN 9781941026298 (hardback) | ISBN 9781941026311(e-book)
Subjects: | CYAC: Coming of age—Fiction. | Criminals—Fiction. | Mexico—Fiction. | BISAC: JUVENILE FICTION / Social Issues / Violence. JUVENILE FICTION / Social Issues / Drugs, Alcohol, Substance Abuse. JUVENILE FICTION / Social Issues / Emigration & Immigration. | JUVENILE FICTION / People & Places / Mexico.
Classification: LCC PZ7.1.D54 Pl 2016 | DDC [Fic] —dc23
LC record available at http://lccn.loc.gov/2015024951

Book, illustration and cover design by Antonio Castro H.

FOR FINN

1.

It was a hot Sunday morning when we discovered the severed head of Enrique Quintanilla propped on the ledge of one of the cement planters in the plaza.

Father Gregorio had just finished mass. His congregants shuffled slowly out of Nuestra Señora del Socorro. The men, dressed in pressed polyester slacks and shirts and shiny cowboy boots, put on their western hats and gathered in groups while the women waited under the ovals of shade cast by the small bay trees near the fence.

Mosca, Pepino, and I ran to the opposite side of the church where the ground wasn't paved and the hard dirt was perfect for playing marbles. Mosca had been bragging all morning about the devil's fire marble he'd won the day before from some kid in his neighborhood. The devil's fire was a legend—*el diablito rojo*. None of us had ever seen a devil's fire marble before. I thought it was a myth, one of those lies older kids tell to tease the younger ones. But Mosca was one of the best marble players in Izayoc. And he wasn't a liar. If he said he'd won a devil's fire, it had to be true. I wanted to see it. Pepino wanted a chance to win it.

Mosca was my best friend. His real name was Esteban Rodríguez, but he was short and tough and fast and had big round bug eyes like a fly. That's how he got the nickname. He didn't always come to church because he didn't have a mother and his father left town after the brick factory closed, crossing over to *el Norte*. Now he worked at a meat plant in Kansas.

Pepino moved quickly around Mosca and patted my shoulder. "Make your line, Boli."

That's what they called me: Boli. It's short for *bolillo*. Since my parents own a bakery, I guess it makes sense. I don't mind. It's better than my real name Liberio, which is so old fashioned.

I marked a straight line on the dirt with the heel of my shoe. Pepino tore a branch from a bush and started to draw a circle, but Mosca stopped him. "I'm not playing for the *diablito rojo*. Just so you know."

Pepino dropped the stick. "You chicken or what?" He was older than Mosca and me. He had bushy eyebrows and small eyes and a big fat nose like a potato, but we called him Pepino, I'm not sure why. He didn't play marbles anymore. I guess he was coming out of retirement because of the devil's fire.

"*No chingues,*" Mosca said. "I'll play, but I'm holding on to the *diablito* for a while."

I couldn't blame Mosca. I'd hold on to it too, maybe forever. When you won a marble like that, you had to hold on to it for a bit, let the news spread. How else were you going to build a reputation?

"*Entonces,*" Pepino said. "At least let us see it, no?"

"It's in my house."

"Liar."

That's when we heard a woman scream.

We ran to the front of the church. The men were making their way across the street to the plaza. The street vendors had abandoned their carts at the center of the square and gathered around one of the planters that divided the plaza into the shape of a cross. The man who sold the lottery tickets raised his head over the crowd and yelled, "It's *el profesor* Quintanilla!"

This was Izayoc, which in Nahuatl means the place of tears. It was just a small pueblo in a tiny valley in the Sierra Nanchititla. Even though we were only a few hours west of Mexico City, where the State of Mexico meets the states of Michoacán and Guerrero, we were hidden from the world by a pair of huge cliffs, El Cerro de la Soledad at the south and El Cerro Santacruz in the north. Nothing ever happened here.

Until now. This was one of those moments everybody would talk about for months, maybe years. I wasn't going to let it pass me by. I ran after Pepino and Mosca, but just as I was about to cross the big iron gate of the church and cross the street, my mother grabbed my arm.

"Liberio!" She pulled me back to her side. "Where do you think you're going?"

"To see. It's *el profe* Quintanilla."

"This is not for your eyes." Her voice seemed to splinter into a zillion pieces. My sister Gaby was standing behind her, an arm around my grandmother who was looking up at the sky, her face covered by a black *mantilla*. My mother and Gaby were staring at my father. He was standing in the middle of the crowd. He turned and gave us a sad nod: up and down real slow as if relaying a secret message, letting us know it was true, that it was *el profe* Quintanilla's head.

And then, just like that, my mother released my arm and covered her mouth with her hand, her fingers trembling over her painted lips.

El profe's head had been severed clean across the neck, just over the Adam's apple, so there was very little neck. His black hair was slicked back the way he used to wear it in class when he taught us civics and lectured on history or marched us in parade before the flag on patriotic fiestas. Except for the big black flies buzzing and crawling into his nostrils and ears and his open mouth, he looked just like when he was alive, his glazed eyes staring up at the empty bell towers of the church across the street.

He looked sad.

The men removed their hats. Everyone crossed themselves.

My father shouted, "Someone get the authorities."

Ignacio Morales, the big fat man who owned the Minitienda, a small grocery store near my house, flipped shut his cell phone and shoved it back in his pocket. "Captain Pineda's not answering."

"He's probably sleeping it off," one of the street vendors said.

Father Gregorio, still dressed in his elaborate chasuble, came forward and carefully plucked a folded piece of paper from *el profe's* mouth.

"What is it, Father?" Don Ignacio asked.

"A note."

"Well?"

Father Gregorio lowered his head and read the note in a trembling voice: "He talked too much."

2.

The gate at the Secundaria Vicente Suárez school was closed.
The groundskeeper sat on a chair inside, his big straw hat pushed
back on his bald head, his arms crossed. He smiled, showing us
his rotten teeth. "Haven't you heard, *niños? El Profe* Quintanilla is
dead." He slowly ran his thumb across the front of his neck from
ear to ear. "They cut off his head."

Classes were cancelled for three days. I ran home, changed
out of my uniform, grabbed my shoeshine box, and went to the
Minitienda to meet Mosca. Three days without school meant
three days to polish shoes and earn some cash. The *feria* was
coming to Izayoc in a few weeks. Mosca and I had to make some
serious money.

A lot of us hung out at the Minitienda on Avenida Porvenir,
one of the old cobblestone streets between my house and the plaza.
Don Ignacio was cool with that. He didn't have a problem if we
brought bottles to redeem the deposits or just hung out on the
narrow sidewalk in front of his store, even if we didn't buy anything.

I set my shoeshine box down and sat on the sidewalk when
Edwin Contreras walked up. He was seventeen, fat, and wore

clothes that were too small for him. He was always hanging around: all talk and no action. That's why he got the nickname Zopilote, the vulture.

Zopilote's parents owned Dos Caminos, a big open restaurant with a palm-thatched roof. It was on the outskirts of town near the new highway. On weekdays, it was popular with truckers, and on the weekends people from Izayoc would spend the afternoon there drinking and eating seafood *cocteles* and grilled meats.

"What's up, *pinche* Boli? No work?"

"At least I work, no?"

"Take it easy, *güey*. I was just saying. You look bored. Where's your girlfriend?"

"Shut up."

He laughed and walked into the Minitienda.

Zopilote was a fool. His father resented him because he never helped with the restaurant, but his mother gave him money. I actually felt sorry for him. He was always alone. Everyone laughed at him behind his back, but he didn't seem to care. He was a jerk, always acting like he was too good for the rest of us.

He came out of the store with a *caguama* of Carta Blanca and leaned back against the wall. The big bottle looked huge in his hand. "Too bad I'm wearing sneakers, otherwise I'd ask you for a shine."

I glanced at his shoes.

"They're the new Nikes," he said and took a long drink of his beer.

"They're fake."

"What are you talking about?" He looked at his shoes and turned his foot to examine the logo. "My mother got them in Toluca."

"Real Nikes don't have that stitching around the logo like that."

"Bullshit." He turned to the side, holding his beer between his arm and chest, and texted someone on his smart phone. Then he grinned at me as he put the device back in his pocket. "It's the latest model. You can't get them around here. Or even in Toluca."

A group of girls was walking toward us on the opposite side of the street. They were still in their school uniforms—blue skirts, white blouses and tall white stockings, their black hair in braids and ponytails. They stopped to look at the fabric in the window of Telas y Novedades Virgo. The store belonged to Bonifacio Cruz. All the girls in town, including my sister Gaby, bought material there to make their *quinceañera* dress. My father always said Don Bonifacio had a sweet deal. Unless people were willing to make the trip to Toluca, they had to buy from Don Bonifacio.

"Check it out." Zopilote pointed to the girls with his beer. "Here they come, Boli. Get smart." He stepped away from the wall and squinted. "*Ay güey*, that one looks like Ximena."

It was. Ximena Mata and her best friend Regina Martínez and three other girls from the *secundaria*. Ximena was a princess. She never braided her hair like the other girls. She kept it loose so it sailed across her face whenever the wind blew. She had high cheekbones and sleepy eyes. I swear that was what drove us all crazy. That, and how she wore her stockings rolled down and always kept her uniform blouse unbuttoned down to the middle of her chest.

"That Ximena's a real doll," Zopilote said. "Look at how she swings her hips when she walks. "*Qué nalgas*, no?"

Then we heard the pounding of a deep bass at the opposite end of the street. A late model black Ford Expedition Max with pitch-black windows and spinning silver rims was coming slowly down the hill.

Zopilote gawked. "That's a fine truck right there. One day I'm gonna get one just like that, but red with gold rims. Or a pickup."

The sound of the *cumbia* got louder as it got closer. When it passed, the bass shook all the windows on the street.

"For real, *cabrón*. You all think I'm wasting my time, but I'm making friends in important places. That's how it's done. You'll see."

I had never seen the truck in town before. As a matter of fact, only Don Bonifacio had one like it, but his was a Suburban. It was green and old and he didn't even drive it anymore. This was a brand new Ford with California plates and wide, low profile tires. It was so low to the ground, the bottom almost scraped against the cobblestones. When it reached the girls, it stopped. The girls pushed each other and laughed, covering their mouths with their hands. Ximena smiled. She never smiled.

"I bet you they pick up those whores," Zopilote said.

The girls jostled and giggled, but Ximena was a statue, staring straight at the side of the truck. I wished to God I could see who was inside. The whole scene made my stomach shrink.

Then the Expedition started moving again. The girls made a tight circle and watched it bounce slowly down the hill.

"*Pinches putos*," Zopilote said. "If I had a *troca* like that, I'd be taking those girls on a joyride to the countryside." He took a long drink of the big bottle and moved his hips forward and back a couple of times. "You know what I mean?"

"Who was that?"

"Who cares?"

The girls split up. Ximena and Regina started up the hill toward us.

"My father says the new highway's going to change our little town," Zopilote went on because that was what he did. He talked and talked and didn't care if anyone listened. "As a matter of fact, my *jéfe* says he's going to expand the restaurant and might even open a hotel right there where the new highway meets the road into town. But don't tell anyone. It's a secret." He took another long pull at the bottle. "It's a time of prosperity. If we play it right, we're gonna be rich. You'll see, *cabrón*. Pretty soon you'll see me in a new *troca* just like that one. Or maybe a better one *Ya verás.*"

Regina held on to Ximena's arm as they came up the block. Both girls were older, seventeen. Regina was friends with my sister Gaby. She was talking, but Ximena didn't seem to be listening. Ximena was like that. She had this look as if she couldn't be bothered with what was happening around her, but not in a bad way. It was as if she belonged in a different world and was waiting for life to take her there.

I had a thing for Ximena. I'd had it for a couple of years, ever since I was in fifth grade and she was in ninth. We were paired together on a school-wide history project about the Niños Héroes. When the teacher complimented us and named our group one of the winners, Ximena turned in her seat and locked eyes with me. I smiled. She kissed the palm of her hand and blew, sending that invisible kiss straight to my heart.

"They're coming." Zopilote was all excited. "You know Ximena has a badass crush on me. She's just a little shy."

Regina waved as they crossed the street. "*Hola,* Boli."

"What's up?" I said. "It's nice that they gave us some time off to mourn *el profe,* no?"

"Can you believe it? *Pobrecito.*" Regina covered her mouth. "Gaby said you were there when they found his head."

"It was pretty gross."

Ximena turned her eyes away. She reminded me of a cat.

Regina said, "He was my favorite teacher."

"Who was that in the *troca?*" Zopilote asked.

Regina shrugged. "A couple of guys."

"*¿Gringos?*"

"*No, qué va.*"

"It had California plates."

"I didn't notice," Regina said. "They said they're from Uruapan."

"Yeah, I bet," Zopilote said.

"What are you saying?"

"*Ya,* it's not your fury I want, *mi amor.*" Zopilote pressed the beer bottle against his chest. "It's your love."

"I'd rather be dead," she said.

I laughed. Ximena rolled her eyes. Regina released her arm. Ximena walked into the store.

"Don't be cruel," Zopilote said.

Regina turned to me. "Why do you hang out with this idiot?"

"I'm not. I'm waiting for Mosca."

"Maybe we'll see you later," she said. "Tell your sister I said hello."

Zopilote watched her go into the store. "She likes me."

"You're crazy, *güey*."

"You're too young to understand these things."

"Seriously, *pinche* Zopilote. It's like you live in your own world."

"Chill out, Boli. When you're ready to learn about life, let me know. I'll be happy to give you lessons. *Gratis.*"

Then the girls came out of the store. Zopilote and I watched Ximena's smooth brown calves shining in the sun as they walked up the street.

A few minutes later, Mosca showed up.

"What happened? Where's your box?" I asked.

"I'm done." Mosca nodded at Zopilote. "There was a group of men drinking at El Gallo de Oro. I shined all their boots. A hundred pesos."

"You're rich, *enano*," Zopilote said.

"Who's talking to you, *pinche puto*?"

"It's a free country, no, *güey*?"

"So I'm free to break your face?"

Zopilote laughed. "You and what army, *pendejo*?"

Mosca stepped back and raised his fists. "Bring it on."

I'd been friends with Mosca since the second grade. I'd never seen him back down from a fight. Most of the time he won, but sometimes he lost. He wasn't a troublemaker. But for some reason, maybe because he was short or just because he was Mosca, people liked to pick on him.

"Come on." I grabbed his arm. "I've wasted enough time here."

"No, Boli." Zopilote set his beer bottle on the ground. "Let him try, see how he likes it."

We walked away.

"Chicken."

We stopped. "Watch out," I said. "I'll let him go."

Zopilote raised his fists. "I'm not afraid of him."

"Just pray I don't find you walking alone when Boli's not there to save your ass," Mosca said.

"I didn't ask him for help." Zopilote curled his fingers and waved his hand in an obscene gesture. "*Mocos güey.*"

Mosca tore away from me and charged. Zopilote's face twisted. He jumped back. Mosca stopped and laughed. "Yeah, that's what I thought, *cabrón.*"

"Guess what?" Mosca said as we walked away. "They put up new posters for the *feria* announcing the wrestling."

"For real?"

"They're all over the wall of the old brick factory."

"So who's coming?"

"El Zorrillo de León, Subministro Fox, Ruddy Calderón. And guess who else?"

"Don't tell me."

"El Hijo del Santo!"

"Bullshit."

Mosca crossed his thumb over his index finger and kissed it.

Last year at the fair, the wrestling matches had been a joke. All the wrestlers were nobodies, amateurs from the provinces. But now it was not only El Zorrillo de León, but also Ruddy Calderón. And El Hijo del Santo. That was huge. He was the last of the good guys. A real *luchador.* A legend just like his father Santo, *el enmascarado de plata*, the silver-masked wrestler.

"But there's one thing." Mosca grabbed my arm. "The tickets are super expensive."

"With a lineup like that, they gotta be like a million pesos, no?"

We turned the corner. A group of boys was running up the street. It was Raúl Guerrero and three other boys from the elementary school.

"What do you think's up with them?" Mosca asked.

"They probably want to play you for the devil's fire," I said.

"Yeah, they wish."

They stopped in front of the butcher shop where Raúl's uncle worked. Two butchers came out on the sidewalk, their white aprons covered in blood. Raúl pointed to where he'd come from. One of the men nodded and gestured toward the plaza and went back into the shop. Raúl and the boys ran up the sidewalk and crossed the street to meet us.

"We found a body," Raúl said. He was panting and out of breath.

Mosca shoved him. "Liar."

Raúl crossed himself. "I swear to God."

Mosca and I looked at each other. We had to be thinking the same thing: the body of *el profe* Quintanilla.

"We're on our way to get Pineda," one of the boys said.

I grabbed Raúl's arm. "Where is it?"

He pointed east. "The Flats. In the weeds right before you get to the dump."

Mosca and I ran as fast as we could. The dump was just outside town at the end of a long field where we played soccer and where they set up the *feria* and the circus whenever they came to town.

The dump was always smoldering, but there were never any flames, just a long line of whitish smoke that rose like a thin string up to the sky. Most of the time the wind blew the stink away from town. But when there was no wind or in winter when the wind swept up from the east, they could smell the rot all the way to the top of Santacruz where Mosca lived.

The field was deserted except for a few dozen vultures and crows pecking at scraps and circling the sky over the dump. By the dry weeds, a pack of stray dogs growled and barked at each other.

We made our way across the dusty field. The dogs raised their heads, waited, then scampered away, their tails between their legs.

It was not the body of Enrique Quintanilla. It was a woman.

She was lying face down. And she was naked. She was missing the
fingers of her right hand—just had five red stumps with white
bits of bone at the end. But there was no blood. It must have been
what the dogs were biting at. She had long black hair. Her skin
was pale and tight against her swollen body. It had a weird shine
to it like oil. Flies were crawling all over her back and ass and
between her legs. It stank of rotten eggs and shit.

It was the first time either of us had ever seen a naked woman.
We just stood there, hands over our nose and mouth, staring at the
strange nakedness, at her ass and arms and her wide thighs.

"She's...dead, right?"

I nodded, but I really had no idea.

"Who is she?"

"I don't know," I said. We were breathing fast, sweating,
staring.

"You think we should turn her over?"

"What about Pineda?"

A group of men and women were heading toward us from
the row of small wood and cardboard houses that lined the field.
The dogs kept watch from a short distance, waiting.

I don't know if it was because the woman was naked or
because she was dead or if it was the foul stench of rot that mixed
with the burning trash that came and went with the breeze, but
suddenly I realized something really ugly was happening. A fire
burned in my throat. This wasn't like when we found *el profe*
Quintanilla's head. This was worse.

Just as the group arrived and gathered around the body,
Captain Pineda's little Chevy turned off the road and bounced
up and down as it cut through the field, its lights flashing like wet
fireworks. When he arrived, he pushed everyone out of the way.
One of his men covered the body with a white sheet. He waved us
off and ordered the women to take us away because this was unfit
for children. Then he picked up a rock and threw it at the dogs.

3.

I knocked on the door of my grandmother's bedroom. I was always the one who had to get her to come to dinner. It was never easy. I opened the door slowly. She was sitting in her rocking chair, facing the open window, a Superman blanket over her lap. "Abuela?"

"Yes, *mijo*?"

"Mamá told me to come get you. Jesusa's serving dinner."

"I'm not hungry. *Gracias*."

"Come on."

"Thank you, but I'm not hungry."

"*Ay*, Abuela. You know she's just going to tell me to come back and tell you that you have to come."

She was rail thin. Her white blouse hung on her bony frame like a blanket. She had small dark eyes and thin lips. Her translucent skin was crisscrossed with wrinkles like cracks on dry earth. She wore her long gray hair pulled back into a bun set with a big ivory comb.

"Abuela, *por favor*."

This was how it was. She didn't like coming to the table. She didn't eat. She just sat in that rocking chair all day, staring out the window, dreaming of who knows what because the window looked out to the small patio where there were just a few plants in pots and cans and a few rows of laundry line where our maid Jesusa hung our clothes to dry.

"Abuela?"

She nodded slowly and raised a delicate hand. "Be an angel and help me up then."

We walked into the dining room together. Jesusa came out of the kitchen. She was a small, dark Indian woman from the sierra in Oaxaca. She'd been with us since before I was born. She was quiet and rigid and didn't let me get away with much. Somewhere, though, in all that toughness, there was a little soft spot. She went around the table and served soup and *quesadillas* and green salsa.

No one spoke. Even Gaby didn't say a word and she was a chatterbox. She brought home all the gossip and always went into painful detail about everyone and everything.

Something was going on.

I thought my parents were angry. I thought maybe if someone said the wrong thing, they would lash out. It was so quiet I could hear our spoons touch the bottom of the plates, my father's slurps. They were the same sounds we made at every meal, but they were amplified by the silence—the chewing and swallowing. Even the fabric of my father's sleeve as he reached across the table for a tortilla made a soft noise like a sigh. I closed my eyes. For a minute, I thought I even heard my mother's heartbeat.

"She was jealous," Abuela said suddenly. "She was jealous about my date with Carlitos. That's what started it."

My father glanced at my mother.

"But it was not my fault. Father arranged the whole thing," Abuela went on, "because Carlitos is the son of Jorge Tizapa. He runs the terminal at the end of the port. It's true, they are very wealthy. But I do not care for him." She pouted. Then she nodded and whispered, "He's a dandy."

"Mamá," my mother interrupted. "Please, not tonight."

Abuela ignored her and looked at me as if I were someone else. "My father thinks he can control me."

"Esperanza," my father said. "*Por favor.*"

"What?" She stared at my father. "What ever happened to that boy from Xalapa, what was his name?"

My mother tapped her fingers against the table real slow like the second hand on a clock: tap, tap, tap, tap. I guess she'd had enough. But I don't think my *abuela* had any clue of the tension in the room. She went right on with the tale of her sister's unchaperoned adventure in Veracruz in the 1950's. We'd all heard the story a dozen times. When she finished, she placed her hand on mine and smiled. "How is it at the university?"

She was crazy. Ever since my grandfather died, she'd been forgetting things and talking of the old days as if they were happening right now. That's why we ended up moving into her house. We used to live in a big house near the highway, but she refused to move in with us so my father sold it and we moved in with her. Her house was just like a lot of the other houses near the plaza: old with thick walls and small rooms, a patio in the center and iron bars on the windows. It wasn't bad. Gaby and I had our own bedrooms, but we had to share the bathroom with Abuela. The living room and dining room were connected through a big archway where all the family stuff like pictures of my first communion, Gaby's *quinceañera,* my parent's wedding photos, and an old black and white picture of my grandfather with his big mustache were displayed with my grandmother's collection of porcelain saints and a big pink conch shell sculpture my mother bought as a souvenir from one of our vacation trips to Acapulco.

Abuela always refused to eat. She only drank coffee with milk and sugar. Most of the time she asked to be excused so she could return to her room. And the only time she ever left the house was on Sundays when we went to church. I liked her because she laughed. In her old age she'd discovered a secret joke that made her happy. I hoped that when I got old, I'd find the same joke because most of the old people I knew were always cranky and mean.

"I didn't tell Papá that I had already met Dorian," Abuela went on. "He was taking photographs on the *malecón.*"

Dorian was my grandfather. He started the bakery, Panadería La Esperanza, which now belonged to my parents, and where Gaby and I worked whenever we weren't in school.

My mother sighed and rolled her eyes. She tapped her fingers against the table: Tap. Tap. Tap.

"I was with Isis," Abuela went on. "We had just had a nice *café* at La Parroquia and were taking a stroll along the Plaza de Armas. It was a beautiful afternoon. The military band was playing in the gazebo. When we came to the *malecón* we saw Dorian with his big camera on a wooden tripod. The boy who was helping him was someone Isis knew. His sister worked as a maid at her house."

"Mamá," my mother complained. "Please, your food."

Abuela stared at her plate. "But I'm not hungry."

"Not again." Tap. Tap.

Abuela shrugged and turned to Gaby. "I would just like a coffee with a little milk, please."

"You have to eat something, Mamá. You're skin and bones. Please."

"But I am not hungry. A nice little coffee would do me well."

Tap. Tap. "Jesusa!"

Jesusa came into the dining room. "¿*Sí señora?*"

"Bring Doña Esperanza a coffee with milk."

"Liberio," my father said. "I need you at the *panadería* for the next couple of days."

"But I have to—"

"You have to nothing."

"Papá, I need to shine shoes."

"The only thing you need to do is be at the bakery. Lucio needs help."

"But the *feria's* coming and—"

"Liberio." His tone was firm. "I am not asking you. I am telling you. I need you there. I gave Leticia the week off."

"So? She works at the register. All I ever do is clean."

"Don't talk back to me."

Jesusa came out of the kitchen with a cup of *café con leche*. Abuela's eyes followed the cup as if it were filled with gold.

"You're the man of the house," my father said. "You need to take your responsibilities seriously. You need to spend more time helping around here instead of hanging out with that Esteban, shining shoes like a common street boy. You're not poor."

"But I need to make money. El Hijo del Santo's going to wrestle—"

"Please, Liberio," my mother said. "Do as your father tells you."

"Maybe if you paid us—"

"¡*Ya basta!*" My father slammed his spoon against the table. "The *panadería* puts the food on our table and the clothes on our backs. You're doing your part, Liberio, and that's final."

"It's not fair."

"Life is not fair." He waved his finger. "It's about time you realized that."

"But Papá—"

"End of conversation."

"He was taking a photograph of one of the large freighters," Abuela said.

Gaby grinned. I couldn't tell if she was trying to make me feel better or rubbing it in.

"He allowed us to look through the camera," Abuela went on. "We had to cover our heads with a black cloth. The image appeared on the glass. It was very clear, but it was upside down."

My mother actually smiled. "How's your coffee, Mamá?"

Abuela glanced at her cup, at my mother, and then her eyes wandered around as if she'd been pulled out of a dream. "Good. It's always good."

My mother reached across the table and placed her hand over hers. "I'm glad."

After my parents left the table, I looked at Gaby. "What's their problem?"

She shrugged and turned to the living room. She had her priorities. Her *telenovela* was going to start.

Later that night, I was lying in my bed reading *Super Luchas,* my favorite wrestling magazine, when I heard my parents in the living room. I slipped out and tiptoed to the end of the hallway. My father was sitting in the big chair where he always sat. My mother was standing, leaning against the couch.

"I don't understand, why her?" my father said.

"That girl was a tramp, Alfonso."

"*Por favor,* Carmen, don't call her that."

"I'm not saying she got what she deserved. It's a terrible tragedy. But—"

"But what?"

"Quiet down, you're going to wake up the children."

He lowered his voice. "Rocío Morales was a human being. She was a lovely girl. She did not deserve the judgment of the community. And certainly not this—"

Rocío was Leticia's cousin and the daughter of Ignacio Morales. She was real pretty. She always dressed like a model in a magazine and smelled of perfume. My mother never liked her, probably because she didn't go to mass and hung out at the *cantinas,* La Gloria and even El Gallo de Oro.

"Leticia said she was seeing a man from Michoacán."

"That's impossible," my father said.

"Oh, and how would you know?"

"No, no. I don't. I just thought she was seeing someone else."

"She probably was. I'm sure she slept with half the town."

"Enough, Carmen. Besides, I don't see how all this is connected."

"Alfonso, you need to wise up, *mi amor.* What happened to

Enrique Quintanilla was not just any crime. Enrique was too much of an activist. Did you think we would be immune forever? The whole country is infected."

"What I'm saying is that we don't know anything for sure. Nothing like this has ever happened before."

"And until six months ago we didn't have a four-lane highway passing by our town, going from the coast, through Michoacán, and straight into Mexico City. If I didn't know any better, I'd say the governor built the damn thing to make it easier for his *amigos* to do their dirty business."

My father shook his head. "In the morning, I'll go see Ignacio and offer him our condolences."

"*Dios mío*, I can't imagine how he must feel. Alfonso, if something like that ever happened to Gaby—"

"No, don't think that way. After I see Ignacio, I'll go to the municipal building and see if Captain Pineda has any idea what's going on."

"I'm worried for the children," my mother said.

"They'll be fine."

"I'm sorry?" She stared at him. "Two murders, and Rocío Morales. Just because you—"

"Carmen, please. Stop."

"And there's no school for the next two days."

"They'll be at the bakery."

They fell silent. My father stood and went to the end of the room and poured himself a drink.

"You're staying up?" my mother asked.

"I don't think I can sleep right now." He took a drink and whispered, "Poor Rocío."

I hurried back to my bedroom. I lay on my bed and closed my eyes and tried to sleep, but all I could see was the naked body of Rocío Morales laying in the weeds and the smell of burning trash. But now, knowing it was her, remembering how pretty she was, like the women in the old Santo movies, with big *chichis* and round *nalgas,* thick fleshy legs and lips so red and shiny they looked electric. Something strange twisted deep in my stomach like I had to piss a fish.

4.

After my grandfather died, my father took over the *panadería*. I guess
the plan was for Gaby and me to take it over from him eventually.
The bakery was on a street between our house and the plaza. It was
a small storefront with a big open room in the back where we did
the baking. Two walls were lined with shelves for the sweet rolls.
At the center was a big square bin where we dumped the *bolillos*. It
was the only bakery left in Izayoc that still baked bread in a wood-
burning clay oven. The oven was like a brown igloo covered in soot.
My father said it was the oak and hickory that gave our bread its
unique flavor. I loved the smell of the fire. Early in the mornings
when Lucio got the fire going, you could smell the sweetness of the
bread and the sour spice of the smoke from blocks away.

Working at the bakery wasn't so bad. Ever since Gaby and I
were little we were given chores there. We'd spent so much time
there it was like a home away from home. I was usually stuck with
cleaning. I swept the sidewalk out front, washed the tall windows
and the big round aluminum trays and tongs the customers used
to pick out their bread. I also carried in the firewood and helped
Lucio with the baking.

Lucio was old and skinny. He kept his long gray hair bunched up into a net and wore his pants below his waist just like Cantínflas. He told me once he'd spent most of his life in the gutter until my grandfather rescued him. But my *abuela* always referred to him as a stray, *un perro callejero*.

My grandfather defended Lucio. He said it was better to teach a man to bake bread than to just give him a *bolillo* every other day. Lucio stuck with it. He was very faithful to our family.

The next day, Gaby and I went to work at the *panadería*. She attended the register, and I wiped down the displays. After I cleaned the front and set out the second batch of *bolillos* in the bin and *pan dulce* on the racks, I went to the back with Lucio. It was like a barn back there, but with a tiled floor and thick walls. There were no windows, but it had a long door that we always kept open to let the light in and the smoke out.

On a corner we had stacks of flour sacks, a big pile of firewood, and three long shelves with jars and cans with sugar, honey, yeast, cartons of eggs and all the other ingredients Lucio used to make the bread. By the door, near a small counter, Lucio had placed a small altar with a little statue of the Virgen de Guadalupe and a pair of *veladora* candles which he kept lit all day long.

Lucio was preparing dough for the mid-morning. I sat on the side of the long wood counter and watched him work. His thin arms moved like a wave, forward and back, his whole body leaning over the dough. One hand punched in under the dough while the other one pulled at the top, over and over. He said it made the crust crispier and the inside of the bread fluffier.

After a while he stopped and gave me the signal. I took a handful of flour and sprinkled it on the counter and on the blob of dough, which looked like a dead body.

"Did you hear about *el profesor* Quintanilla?" I asked.

He nodded and got back to work, leaning over the counter with all his weight, in and out, turning the dough little by little. "And the girl too, *¿que no?*" Lucio said without stopping his work.

"She was Leticia's cousin."

He nodded again and glanced at the neighbor's chickens, four brown hens that always wandered in and scratched and pecked relentlesly at the ground.

"You know, I saw her."

"¿*La niña*?" He reached over the counter and turned off the little transistor radio he had hanging on a nail.

"Mosca and I went to the dump. She was naked."

"Pass me the stick."

It was one of his baking tools. It was just like a small broomstick. He rolled it over the dough to flatten it into a long thick blanket. Then he grabbed a plastic spatula and in a few swift moves, cut the blanket into sections.

"It was scary," I said.

"I can imagine."

"Who do you think killed her?"

"God knows." Lucio moved quickly, his hands rolling the flat little blankets into rolls and stacking them on one side of the table. "There are bad people in this world."

"But why would anyone kill her?"

He finished stacking the rolls and tapped the side of his head with his index finger. "You'd be surprised how many people have problems up here."

"I guess."

"I noticed they're going to have wrestling at the *feria* again this year."

"Yes." I chased the chickens out the door. "Did you see who's coming?"

He laid out the rolled chunks of dough, each piece just bigger than his hand, then made a small indentation with the stick over each piece and placed them in a metal tray.

"El Hijo del Santo," I said.

"Didn't he retire?"

"Not anymore. It's on the *carteles* all over town."

"Did I ever tell you about the time I met Mil Máscaras?"

He had told me the story a million times. He grabbed the long wooden pole with the flat end that looked like a big oar and slid it under the metal tray and carried it to the clay oven.

"I was an assistant to one of the grips at Estudios Churubusco, and one day Mil Máscaras showed up." He slid the tray into the round oven. "When I walked by him, he grabbed my arm and told me I was too skinny, that if I ever wanted to wrestle, I had to build up my muscles."

"Did you want to be a wrestler?"

He finished with the last tray and set the pole down. "No, qué va. That wasn't my thing." He smiled and leaned against the table. "But all the other boys did."

"Who do you think was better, Santo or Mil Máscaras?"

"An eternal question, ¿que no? I think most people will tell you Santo."

"I think Santo, for sure."

He shrugged and clapped his hands. "Ándale. Stop wasting my time. Let's get back to work. Fetch me the flour and some water."

I took one of the big sacks of flour from the side and dragged it on the floor.

Lucio helped me lift it to the counter. We poured the flour, the eggs, and the cinnamon and baking powder into one of the big mixers. When Lucio turned it on, he bobbed his head up and down and gyrated his hips, dancing to the sound of the mixer's motor.

Later, my parents arrived at the panadería. We had just pulled out the bolillos from the oven and placed them on the cooling racks. Lucio was preparing conchas. I rolled a rack of bolillos into the store. I wanted to see what was going on. Enrique Quintanilla's wife Yolanda and Rocío's father Ignacio were with them. I placed the rack of bolillos by the bin in the center of the store, but my father waved me away. "I'll take care of that. Go help Lucio. Stay in the back."

I did as I was told. Lucio was busy spreading icing on the little mounds of dough for the *conchas*. I turned back and pushed the door open just a little. The rack of *bolillos* blocked most of my view, but I could see my father leaning against the counter. He was looking at my mother. She was on the other side by the register with Gaby. I couldn't see Don Ignacio's large body or Yolanda.

"Absolutely useless." It was Ignacio's deep voice. "That man's an embarrassment to Izayoc."

"He never had to do anything," my father said. "He's just a figurehead."

"True," Ignacio said, "but it doesn't solve anything."

"I just want to know that something is being done." Yolanda moved forward. I could see her black blouse. She set her purse on the counter blocking my view of Gaby. "They haven't even found my husband's body, *por el amor de Dios.*"

"What we need is professional law enforcement, someone who has experience with this kind of thing." My father leaned forward and massaged his temples. "We cannot allow this to go on."

"Absolutely," Ignacio said.

"This is exactly why Enrique and I left Acapulco in the first place," Yolanda said. "Things there were so bad, you couldn't go out anymore. You couldn't trust anyone. Not even your friends."

"Savages," Ignacio said.

My mother waved across the counter. "It will be the death of this country."

"We need to stop them." Ignacio's voice filled the store. I looked back to see if Lucio had heard, but he was busy, leaning over the table taking care of the sweet rolls, painting them with *piloncillo* honey.

An old lady and her teenage daughter walked into the store. Everyone fell silent.

"*Buenos días,*" she said. Her daughter picked out one of the big round trays and a pair of tongs.

"*Buenos días,* Señora Velasco." My mother smiled and touched Gaby's shoulder. She went around the counter to help them.

"My condolences, Yolanda," the woman said.

When the old lady and her teenage daughter left, my mother glanced at my father. "We can't just stand by—"

"Please." My father ran his hand through his hair. He bowed and stooped as if he'd dropped something on the floor. "We all agree, Carmen. The question is how—"

"In Acapulco," Yolanda said, "no one did anything about it."

"But we can't fight them ourselves," Ignacio said.

My mother caressed the back of Gaby's hair. "Think of the children."

Ignacio turned away. My mother grabbed his arm. "I'm sorry, Ignacio, I didn't mean—"

"It's not your fault, Carmen."

My father said something I couldn't hear, but suddenly Ignacio stepped back and pointed at him. His voice boomed, "And who's to say they're any better than that idiot, Pineda?"

"We could also reach out to Senator González Parral."

"Alfonso, *por favor.* They're all crooked." Ignacio smacked the counter with the palm of his hand. "Every single one of them."

"*Entonces,*" my father turned. "What would you suggest?"

"My daughter's dead. She was my only daughter, not my—"

"Ignacio!" My father glanced at my mother and back at Ignacio. He reached out and his hand disappeared behind the rack of *bolillos.* He said something to Ignacio I didn't get. I pushed the door open a bit more. They leaned closer together. Their voices were small.

"...outside help..."

"...a peaceful town...."

"...our problems...the federal police...Toluca."

Then Yolanda began to weep. My mother pulled a box of tissues from under the counter.

A man and a woman walked in and everyone paused. The

man tipped his hat at my parents and waited by the door, looking up and down the street, like he was keeping guard. The woman took a tray and tongs and filled a tray with *bolillos* from the bin, which was weird because anyone else would have taken the fresh ones from the rack.

She walked up to the counter.

My mother smiled. "*Buenos días.*"

The woman nodded. My mother rang her up and Gaby put the *bolillos* in a brown paper bag. The woman stepped outside and marched up the street. The man followed her.

"I've never seen them before." My father stepped outside and looked up the street. Then he walked slowly back to the counter. "I know everyone who comes here. We cannot let this happen to our town."

His tone reminded me of when Enrique Quintanilla would lecture us in the parade grounds at school, the big flag dancing and waving with the wind, red and green against the blue of the sky, making flapping sounds like applause. I don't remember exactly what *el profe* said, but we all swelled with pride. I remember feeling then that—no matter what—Izayoc was my home. It was the place I would defend with everything I had, the same way the Niños Héroes had defended Chapultepec Castle and the honor of the Republic.

My father said, "I'll go to Toluca in the morning. I'll get help. I'll alert the federal police and Senator González Parral."

"It's worth a try," Yolanda said.

"But no one must know what we're doing," my father said.

Then I felt a tap on my shoulder. Lucio was standing behind me. He gestured with his hand for me to get back, then pulled the door closed.

"What?"

He pointed at the sacks of flour. "We have to stack them and clean this pigsty."

"But—"

"Otherwise we'll have rats."

"Or mice," I said because six months ago when the *panadería* was closed, my father decided it was time to get rid of the mice in the bakery. We came in after mass and tucked our pants into our boots and began removing the sacks of flour one by one. At first we only saw a mouse or two scurrying for cover. They were the dark gray ones that are like field mice and not ugly like the big brown rats we see in the garbage dump or the open sewers in the neighborhoods on the other side of the highway. We removed things one at a time. The mice seemed to multiply as they lost their hiding places. Pretty soon there had to be hundreds of them running around with no place to go. We stomped them, Lucio and my father whistling and yelling the way people yell at the *cantinas* when the mariachis play happy songs. The three of us marched and danced over the little guys until they were all dead.

"Mice, rats," Lucio said. "Call them what you want. We don't want them here. Everyone knows if there's one, there will be more. A lot more."

5.

It was still dark when Gaby and I walked to the *panadería* the following morning. My parents had already left for Toluca. The roosters crowed and the loud diesel engines of the trucks barreling down the mountain on the new highway sounded like a distant parade. Some of the streetlamps didn't work so the road was a mix of light and dark patches. It hadn't rained in months, but the morning dew on the stones made the narrow street slippery. My dog Chapopote, a black mutt I had adopted a few years ago, followed us for a couple of blocks. Then he got distracted with a smell and trotted off.

When we came home that evening, my parents hadn't come back. We tried my father's cell phone, but there was no answer.

We sat down to dinner. Abuela came to the dining room without protest. There was no one to give her a hard time about eating her food. Jesusa brought her a cup of coffee right away. Abuela smiled and thanked her and even asked her to sit with us, calling her Susana.

Gaby sat at my father's place. She didn't say anything. She just dug into her *enchiladas* as if she hadn't eaten for days. Jesusa returned from the kitchen with a plate for herself and took my mother's place at the table.

"*Buen provecho,*" she said. It was the first time she'd ever sat with us at the big table.

Then Abuela started. "I wasn't impressed by the fancy camera. Dorian said he had studied with some man Castillo, who had photographed *la revolución* with a plate camera alongside Casasola." She told us it didn't impress her that he and another man named Turok had been commissioned by the government to make an important photographic document of Mexico. Or that he was half *gringo.* But she cared that he was handsome, rugged. She cared for him a lot more than she cared for the other man Tizapa. "Dorian was no dandy. I can tell you that."

When Abuela stopped talking to sip her *café,* Gaby turned to Jesusa. "Did you hear about Rocío Morales?"

Jesusa set her fork down and her black almond eyes grew round. "And Enrique Quintanilla. Everyone is scared. People said he talked too much about what was none of his business, *pues.*"

"What did they say?" I asked.

"*Pues,* Hortensia, the one who brings the tortillas, she said people are moving into town. They're building big houses in Montes de Oca. And up in Santacruz too."

Santacruz was Mosca's neighborhood. It was at the top of the mountain north of town, just past the creek and the old highway. When you drove into town from the west on the old highway, the first thing you saw was the giant white metal cross at the highest point of the mountain. The people there were poor, but not dirt poor like the real *gente pobre* from the neighborhoods like Montes de Oca. Or further past the trash dump and the Flats on the other side of the new highway where Lucio lived. I guess Santacrúz was an in-between place, a sort of between us who had some money and those who were really poor.

Abuela laughed. "I was surprised to find out he was interested in me."

Jesusa smiled at her, then she turned to Gaby. "Any news of your parents?"

Gaby shook her head. "Mamá said it might take them a couple of days."

"Lucky," I said.

"Lucky how, you fool? They're working."

"Yeah, but Toluca rules."

"Whatever." Gaby rolled her eyes. "And just because they're not here you can't just go around goofing off. There's school tomorrow."

"I'm watching a movie tonight."

"I'm watching my *novela*."

"Don't worry," I said. "My movie's not on 'til eleven."

Jesusa turned to Gaby. "¿*El dolor del amor?*"

After dinner, we all sat together on the big couch. My father had reupholstered it last year in bright orange fabric he got from Don Bonifacio's store and covered it with thick transparent plastic.

Personally, I wasn't interested in the soap opera, but there was nothing else to do. Besides, I wanted to stay up in case my parents arrived. I wanted to ask my father for a loan for the wrestling tickets. I figured I could pay him back by working at the bakery.

When the *novela* was over, Gaby went to bed. Abuela and Jesusa stayed up with me to watch *Santo contra el rey del crimen,* the quintessential Santo movie. It was an old black-and-white wrestling movie. True. It didn't have the best action, and it didn't have a lot of fighting compared to the other ones, but I could relate to the plot. I mean you get to see Santo when he was a boy, like my age. People forget that he had to come from somewhere. He was fighting against injustice since he was a kid. I totally got that. Even as children we have to face bad guys, bullies, big kids, drunks, whatever. But Santo, he was lucky. His father had the mask and passed it down to him.

I guess that's what I always liked about these movies. They weren't about heroes with supernatural powers. They were about real people. They gave me the feeling that I too could be like Santo. I guess deep down I was hoping that one day my father would reveal some kind of secret identity he could pass on to me, giving me the responsibility of fighting crime. Maybe I would find myself in a situation where I had to save Ximena from the bad guys, from Zopilote or whoever. Then she would fall in love with me, just like the women always fall in love with Santo.

6.

At recess, I met Mosca in the schoolyard by the swings. He was surrounded by a group of boys who wanted to see the devil's fire. Word had spread about the *diablito rojo*. For now, Mosca was the king of the marble world.

Mosca held up a fist. Then he turned it and slowly opened his hand. There, in the center of his palm, was the little red sphere: *el diablito rojo*. It was bright red and iridescent with a soft swirl of yellow at the center. It was beautiful. It didn't even look like a real marble. It glowed like a jewel, like fire.

"You see it, *cabrones?*" Mosca said as if daring anyone to cross him and deny that he had won the legendary marble.

Then someone said. "Let's play for it."

Mosca closed his hand into a fist and shoved the marble back in his pocket. "You wish."

"What's the matter?"

"You chicken?"

Mosca laughed. "I'm not afraid of any of you amateurs. I'm going to keep it until I find a worthy adversary. Besides, what's the point of playing for your common marbles? What do I get if I win?"

"*Ya*, Mosca, don't be so dramatic."

"That's not it, Chato. If you win, you get the devil's fire, but if I win, all I get is your common *agüita* and *perico* marbles. I have thousands of those."

"Money." Pepino pushed through the crowd and came face to face with Mosca. "How much is it worth?"

Mosca grinned. "Plenty. I don't think you can afford it."

"A hundred pesos."

Some of the boys sighed. Mosca didn't flinch. "Maybe."

"You think about it, *enano*, because I'm not going anywhere. I'll be right here whenever you're ready to lose the little red rock."

Pepino nodded at Chato and Kiko. They were like the three stooges—Chato with his flat face and crossed eyes and Kiko, who looked just like Kiko from *El Chavo del ocho* with his buckteeth and fat cheeks. And Pepino. Those three were inseparable.

"I'll let you know," Mosca said.

Pepino turned as if he was someone important and marched away with his friends.

Mosca and I sat in the shade.

"You gonna do it?" I asked.

"For a hundred, I don't think so. But I'll bet you anything he comes back with another offer. Pepino hates to lose."

"And if you lose?"

He shrugged. "I'll be the guy who played a marble against a couple of hundred pesos, no?"

"*Pinche* Mosca, you're smarter than I thought."

"It's all about reputation. I mean in the end, the devil's fire is just a stupid marble, no?"

Across the yard Ximena was leaning against the chain link fence, talking to some guy I didn't recognize. He was older, tall, and wore a clean white cowboy hat with a green, white and red band.

Mosca nudged me. "What's the matter?"

"Nothing." I didn't want him to know I had a thing for Ximena. I would never hear the end of it. I kicked at the dirt.

"My parent's aren't back from Toluca. I have to go to the *panadería* after school."

"Ah, don't worry, we'll shine shoes on the weekend."

"It's not that. It's just that they should have been home by now. Or at least called."

"Take it easy." He nudged me with his elbow. "You know how it is in Toluca. They're probably having a good time."

"But they could call, no? They always call."

"Boli, you worry too much. Let them do their thing. Enjoy your freedom."

Now Ximena had her hand up on the fence, and the guy on the other side had his hand in the same place, their fingers touching. It looked as if they were kissing.

7.

My parents were still not home. Gaby was flushed, pacing back and forth in the living room with her arms crossed. "It's not right," she said. "Something must have happened."

"Something like what?"

"I don't know." Her voice was quiet. She chewed her thumbnail. "I've tried Papá's cell phone over and over, but it goes directly to voicemail."

Jesusa walked out of the kitchen, wiping her hands on her apron. "Is it possible they had car trouble?"

"And? What does that have to do with his cell phone?"

Jesusa smiled, but it was a strange smile, as if she was trying to convince herself. We all knew there was nothing wrong with the car. Besides, Gaby had called my parent's friends in Toluca. No one had heard from them.

I could see the fear in Gaby's eyes. I tried calling the number myself, but all I got was my father's deep baritone: "This is Alfonso Flores, please leave a message after the tone and I'll call you back. *Gracias.*" Those were his last words, because when we tried to call him later, the voicemail didn't even come on.

That night and the following day, I was in a daze. The anxiety was like a puzzle I couldn't solve, like something had broken and I was the one who was supposed to fix it. It didn't make any sense. Why hadn't they called?

After school, I met Gaby at the *panadería*. We closed early and went to see Captain Pineda. The municipal building was across the street from the plaza, perpendicular from the church. It was a two-story old stone and concrete building with a long arcade in the front with big arches where food vendors sometimes set up. On the second floor it had big windows with balconies. Everything around the plaza was like that: old stone buildings with red-tile roofs and wrought-iron bars on the windows. Like the church. It dated back to the 1600s. But the municipal building was rundown. The paint had faded and the political posters from the last election were peeling off the walls.

Pineda's office was upstairs. The only person in the room was a secretary—a heavy-set woman—sitting behind an electric typewriter. Her hair was made up in a large bun just like some of the women in the old Santo movies.

When Gaby told her we wanted to see Captain Pineda, she slowly raised her eyes, spread her fingers in front of her, and studied her nails. "He's busy."

"It's important."

The woman glanced back to a door with a small plaque: Capitán Efraín Pineda del Valle. "He's in a meeting."

Gaby took a place near the open window and sat with her back straight, chin up. "We'll wait."

The thing was, it was Gaby's fear that kept fueling my own. Whenever her voice cracked or her eyes widened, I shivered. It reminded me that something was wrong. I guess I was trying to convince myself that this was normal, that they would turn up at any moment with a perfectly logical explanation. Then Gaby would sigh and it would all come back to me: they're gone. What if they don't come back? And then, what if instead of *el profe's* head it was my father's—and instead of Rocío's naked body, it was my mother's.

The same picture of Benito Juárez that was in the civics textbook we used in *el profe* Quintanilla's class hung on the wall of the office. Next to it was a color photograph of the President. And, at the end of the wall near the door to Pineda's office was the same calendar with Tania Rincón in a bathing suit that Lucio had hanging in the back of the bakery.

The smell of fresh tortillas came and went with the soft breeze that blew in through the open windows. It caused the papers on the empty desks to flutter. The man who sharpened knives and scissors around town whistled the tune that announced his arrival in the plaza. Someone kept revving the engine of a Volkswagen Beetle. A woman yelled an obscenity and a radio played a *ranchera*. It was strange how the sounds of the plaza were different than the sounds from school or those at the *panadería* or at home. It was the same town but different sounds. At home it was mostly dogs and roosters, sometimes a television. In the *panadería*, it was people and cars and the squeak of the machine in the *tortillería* across the street.

I walked to the window and stepped out on the balcony. The treetops blocked my view of the plaza, but I could see Father Gregorio in the side yard of the church talking with Chucho, the *mayordomo* who took care of the grounds. The church looked like a sculpture with its ornate empty bell towers and the big central cupola. During the revolution, the people of the town had to melt the church bells to make ammunition. A hundred years had past and they still hadn't replaced them. Father Gregorio joked that Izayoc was the only town in Mexico where mass was not announced with tolling bells. But my father and the men of the town saw it as a source of pride. They said everyone needed to remember the sacrifice the town had made. They were proud that in all its history Izayoc had never been occupied by an army, federal or revolutionary.

At the other end of the plaza, a worker swept the sidewalk in front of Los Pinos restaurant with a reed broom. The man who sold fruits and vegetables and *chicharrón* had parked his cart by a bench where he lay asleep in the shade. A boy and a girl sat on the planter where we had found *el profe's* head. No one was shining shoes.

Father Gregorio crossed the churchyard and met a well-dressed man in a black western hat at the entrance of the church. They shook hands. Father Gregorio opened the door to the church, allowing the man to pass. Then he followed him inside.

Behind the buildings across from the plaza, the mountain rose tall and steep like a brown monster. My eyes followed a narrow road which climbed up the side of the cliff to the neighborhood of Santacruz, but I couldn't make out Mosca's house from here. Above the neighborhood of unpainted concrete houses I could see the giant cross, white against the gray sky. It looked like rain.

I went back to my seat and waited. Gaby had her hands folded on her lap, her fingers moving one over the other like she was counting minutes.

Every now and then we heard voices coming from Captain Pineda's office. Someone laughed. They seemed to be talking about food somewhere, perhaps Los Pinos, and about a car, and something about the importance of a civic association that would allow and support progress. It made me think of my father. He always talked of progress for Izayoc. I tried not to think about him and my mother, that they had had an accident on the highway. That they might be dead.

Suddenly Gaby stood and marched past the woman's desk and into Pineda's office. I was right behind her.

Captain Pineda sat to one side of his desk, smoking a cigarette. Behind the desk was a man I'd never seen before. He was young, tall, light-skinned and wore big reflective sunglasses pulled up on his head. He was leaning back on the chair, his legs stretched out, boots resting on Pineda's desk, a white cowboy hat on his knee.

Pineda plucked the cigarette out of his mouth. "What is this?"

A man standing by an open window, a hand lost inside his black leather jacket, glanced at an older man on the other side of the room and moved toward us, but the man behind Pineda's desk raised his hand and stopped him. He stepped back to the window and peeked out at the street.

Then the secretary from the front room stomped in. "*Perdón, Capitán*. I told them you were busy."

Gaby lowered her head and glanced at the floor. "It's just that we were waiting for two hours." Her voice was a tiny squeak. I could tell she was doing everything she could to keep the pieces from falling. "I thought you were finished."

"So? This is a private office," Pineda barked. "You don't just barge in like that. Do you understand me?"

"It's about my parents." Gaby's lower lip trembled. It gripped my chest, squeezed so hard I couldn't breathe.

"I don't care if it's about the President of the Republic," Pineda said. "There's a protocol."

Gaby touched her eyes. "I'm sorry."

"Your business will have to wait until I'm finished with these gentlemen."

"No, no, Efraín." The man with the reflective sunglasses gestured toward Gaby. "Come in, please. Tell us what's going on, *señorita*."

Pineda waved at the secretary, who gave us an ugly look and walked out. The man behind the desk eyed Gaby up and down like he was appraising an animal he was about to buy.

"My parents went to Toluca three days ago and we haven't heard from them," Gaby said softly.

"Poor creature," the man behind the desk said. "And you miss them, no?"

"It's not that. They should have come home by now. Or at least called. And with everything that's been going on, *¿usted sabe?*"

Pineda waved. "Three days is nothing."

The man behind the desk leaned to the side and eyed Gaby's

legs. Then he smiled to the man by the window. "How do you see it, Pedrito?"

"Like for the races."

"That's what I was thinking. A jet-plane, no?"

"*Simón.*" The man by the window laughed.

My stomach burned. At that moment I hated Pineda and all the men in the room. I wanted to grab Gaby's hand and pull her out. Run away. Go home. Find my parents.

The man behind the desk ran his index finger back and forth across his chin. "What's your name, *linda?*"

Gaby looked away, then at me and back at the man. "Gabriela Flores."

The men looked at each other.

"Flores, Flores." The one behind the desk nodded. "Perhaps your father kept company with the wrong people, *mi amor.*"

"No," Gaby said. "He's nothing like that. He's a family man, a hard worker."

"People respect him," I said.

The man behind the desk chuckled.

"Rumor had it, your Papi liked to play around," Pineda said.

"That's a lie," Gaby cried. "And what do you mean, liked? What happened to him?"

The man behind the desk waved. "Don't mind him. He's just upset because he's not getting his way. Isn't that right, *gordo?*"

Pineda turned away. Gaby clenched her hands and pressed them against her chest. "Please, did something happen?"

The man behind the desk shook his head real slow. "I know nothing of them, *linda.* But I do know that no man in this world is completely innocent."

"Maybe we can call someone in Toluca," I said.

Pineda laughed. "Like who?"

"I don't know, the authorities," I said.

Gaby took my hand and pulled me close to her side. "Maybe there was an accident."

"Maybe they just wanted to get away from you two brats."
Pineda took a long drag from his cigarette. Everyone except the
man behind the desk laughed.

"*Por favor,*" Gaby pleaded. "Help us."

"No, no," the man behind the desk said. "Don't worry,
Gabriela Flores. I'll look into it for you. I'll make sure Pineda
here gets off his fat ass and makes some inquiries on your behalf.
We'll find your parents." Then he turned to Pineda, "Right,
gordo?"

Captain Pineda shoved the cigarette back in his mouth and
turned away.

"I said, right, *gordo?*"

Pineda grinned. "Sure, *efectivamente.*"

The man behind the desk smiled at Gaby. "Joaquín Carrillo, at
your service."

Gaby nodded. "*Mucho gusto.*"

"If I need you," Joaquín said. "Where can I find you, Gabriela
Flores?"

"At the Panadería La Esperanza."

The man by the window leaned out and signaled someone
in the street. He nodded and turned back to the room. "*Señor*
Joaquín. They're ready."

"Very well, *linda.*" Joaquín grabbed his hat from his knee and
pulled his feet off the desk. "You can leave now. And don't worry.
I'll come looking for you. I promise."

Gaby and I walked out. Half a dozen peasants from the
adjacent *pueblos* crowded the room. The secretary who had been
painting her nails was typing something. No one spoke.

On the first floor, people had gathered outside the tax office.
One of the beggars who always hung around the plaza made his
way past us. Outside, a gentle rain fell. The sharp smell of dry
earth seemed to rise from the ground. The vendors slowly moved
about covering their carts with blue tarps, others pushed them
under cover of the municipal building's arcade. At the end of the

block, a brand new gray double cab Chevy pickup pulled out and turned down on Calle Virtudes.

"Maybe we should go to Toluca and look for them," I said.

"That's a stupid idea." Gaby crossed her arms and looked at the darkening sky. "Who would help us?"

I didn't know. I was just as lost as she was, but I guess I wanted her to tell me something I could latch onto, something that would make sense. "What do you think he meant?" I asked. "About Papá?"

"Nothing," she said angrily. "Men. They're all the same."

"Yeah, but do you think—"

"Stop it, okay? Just shut up." Her face was flushed, her eyes red. We crossed the plaza and headed home in the rain.

8.

My parent's absence was everywhere: the empty places at the dinner table, no one telling me to turn off the television and do my homework, the afternoon silence that had replaced my mother's voice as she sang her favorite Luis Miguel songs.

I didn't get it. Sickness, death, suffering, they happened to other people. We were healthy, law-abiding people. We believed in God. We went to mass on Sundays. We were good, He took care of us. My parents never did anything to hurt anyone. They didn't deserve this. None of us did. It wasn't fair.

Deep down, I had this feeling that I would come back from school and find them at home, joking and laughing as if nothing had happened. Like it was all a bad dream. But every time I felt sure of it, Gaby broke the trance and reminded me that something horrible was happening to us.

"I'm going to have to take care of the bakery," she said.

"What about me?"

"You'll have to help after school."

We were sitting in the living room. Behind Gaby, I could see my parents' wedding photograph on the wall, the image of my mother staring at me, smiling.

"Every day?" I asked.

"What do you think?"

I leaned my head back on the couch and closed my eyes. I didn't want to keep seeing that picture of my mother. I kept hearing her soft voice telling me everything was going to be fine, that life was a long road and all we had to do was learn to avoid the potholes. But when I opened my eyes and saw her picture, her eyes, her smile, it made me angry. I wanted her here, in the flesh.

We had spoken with the Federal Police headquarters in Toluca and checked the hospitals. We had made I don't know how many declarations, but no one had any record of them, not by name or description, dead or alive. It was as if the earth had swallowed them up, car and all. If this was a dream, I told myself, I will open my eyes and everything will be back to the way it was.

It wasn't.

"Are you listening to me, Liberio? This is important."

"Gaby," I said. The ugly truth crawled like a rat up my throat. "I'm scared."

She tilted her head to the side. Her lower lip trembled and her eyes turned narrow. She put her arms around me and held me like she never had, the way my mother always did. Her perfume smelled just like hers, her hair against the side of my face, her earring pressing painfully against my cheek.

I took a deep breath and held it. *Mamá, Mamá,* I thought over and over as if I might have some magical power. But nothing happened. I was in the same place with the same horrible truth. Why was this happening to us?

"Señorita Gaby," Jesusa's voice interrupted our sobs. She stood by the archway that separated the dining room from the living room, a big plastic bag in her hand. "Viviana from across the street dropped off this bag of *tamales.* She said if we need anything to please knock on her door."

They had all been doing that. All our friends and neighbors had been stopping by the house, bringing food, giving us advice, telling us everything was going to work out. They offered untangible help, as if their words could change things, bring back my parents. But we were lost. Helpless.

Gaby nodded and wiped her eyes with the back of her hand. And for a moment there was this strange heavy silence that seemed to press all the emptiness forward.

"What should I do with them?" Jesusa asked.

"I don't know." Gaby's face twisted with terror. "I don't know what to do."

Jesusa set the bag down and placed her hands on Gaby's shoulder. "We're going to be fine, *señorita*," she whispered. "You'll see."

But we weren't fine. Too many days had passed. Something bad had happened, and no one could deny it, not Jesusa, not Father Gregorio or even Pineda. The not-knowing twisted my insides. If they'd had an accident, I wanted to know. If they were dead, I wanted to give them a mass and bury them in the cemetery next to my grandfather. I wanted to know that they were there. Not knowing just fed that helpless feeling like I was falling into a dark empty hole.

I worked at the *panadería* every day after school. On Saturday afternoon after closing, I fetched my shoeshine box and met Mosca at the Minitienda and we went to the plaza. It was just starting to get dark. Peasants from the nearby *pueblos* sat on the iron benches and leaned against the cement planters watching the parade of young people. Everyone was decked out in their best clothes—pressed shirts, cowboy hats—walking around the plaza. The girls moved in small groups, their arms laced together, giggling, the boys marched quickly, their eyes darting around like they were trying to find something.

A boy carrying a long pole with packages of pink cotton candy circled the children playing in the gazebo. The man selling *nieve* from a pushcart rang his bell. The whole plaza smelled of grilled corn and perfume.

I checked the corners and the area around the benches where most of the shoeshine boys worked. There were only two. The night had promise.

"Why don't you take the plaza?" Mosca said. He knew the best places to shine shoes. "I'll take the side streets and the restaurants. Then we'll hit the *cantinas*."

"For real?" We both knew there was more money to be made in the plaza.

"Sure. You need to catch up. I don't want to go to the wrestling alone."

Mosca took off toward Los Pinos restaurant. I slung my box over my shoulder and walked around the plaza, my eyes down, scanning the ground looking for shoes to shine. It's not about dirty shoes because you'll never find dirty shoes on a Friday or Saturday night. It takes an eye, and it takes experience. You just have to be on the lookout for the expensive shoes. You have to read people, find the person who's begging for a shine but doesn't know it yet. Sometimes a guy who's making the moves on a girl will get his shoes shined just to show off. Insecure guys who walk too fast will get their shoes shined because they want to look like they're doing something, like they have some place to go. It's all about personality. When you recognize one, you have to move in with confidence—but not too aggressive. Sometimes you just make eye contact and nod at the shoes. Sometimes you ask if they want a shine. Sometimes, with the right person, you can just set your box down and, almost automatically, they'll set a boot on your box. No words.

As the evening turned to night, families and old people and most of the peasants trickled away and were replaced by a crowd of young men and women. Lovers embraced on benches. A few *conjuntos* strolled along, looking for customers. Accordions and guitars filled the gaps of conversations and laughter. Later, after the *cantinas* closed, it would be men alone or in pairs, drunk, swaying, singing their pain into the night.

I stopped by a group of teenagers hanging around one of the planters. They were passing around a bottle of Anis Mico and getting cocky. I moved on. When I came around the corner across the street from the municipal building, I saw Ximena and Regina with a group of men. Everything about them screamed money: hats, sharp clothes, gold chains and bracelets, boots made of fine skins—shark, snake, caiman. And real Nikes.

I was too close to turn away. I lowered my head and walked quickly, but when I looked up Regina locked eyes with me. "Boli." She stepped away from the group. "Where you off to?"

"You know, working."

"No news of your parents?" she asked quietly.

I shook my head.

"I'm really sorry. But I'm sure they'll turn up soon, no?"

"Sure. I hope so."

"Is Gaby okay? I've tried calling her like a million times."

"She's busy with the *panadería*."

"*Caray,* I don't even know what to say. I can't imagine—"

I forced a smile. "It's okay."

"¡*Ey!*" It was the same man who'd been sitting behind Pineda's desk. Joaquín. "Bring the boy over."

I wanted to walk away, but I also wanted to stay. I wanted to be close to Ximena. I wanted to know what she saw in this guy—the big gray truck? The polo shirt with NEW YORK in big letters? The tiny gold AK-47 hanging from a chain around his neck?

"He's working," Regina said.

"Can he talk?" Joaquín asked.

"I can talk," I said.

Ximena leaned against Joaquín, her cheek resting on his shoulder. My heart did a dance.

"I know you." Joaquín waved his finger at me. "Pineda's office, no?"

I nodded.

"Did you find your *mami*?"

I shook my head.

"What a shame."

Regina stared at me. She looked worried.

"*Entonces,* you're doing the shoe shine thing, *¿o qué?*"

"That's right." I glanced at his shoes, Nikes with no laces.

"No. I don't need one, but you know who does—Piolín." He waved his friend forward and pushed him toward me. "Piolín, get a shine on those crusty boots of yours, *cabrón.*"

Piolín was Pedro, the one who had been wearing the black leather jacket in Pineda's office. He looked older than Joaquín. He was skinny and ugly. He wore a silk shirt that had the Mexican seal of the eagle eating the serpent, a big cowboy hat and a giant gold belt buckle embossed with the image of a *Cuerno de Chivo.* His boots were of multiple leathers, all exotic. I had never seen such fancy boots.

"You got the clear stuff?" Pedro asked.

I nodded and set my box down.

He placed his boot on the platform at the top of the box. "You better not mess'm up, *cabrón.*"

Joaquín laughed. "*Ese* Piolín. He paid fifteen hundred dollars for those stupid boots." Then he addressed me. "You think they're worth it?"

I nodded and squatted in front of my box. I took out my creams, cloths and brushes, and got to work. I applied a thin coat of clear cream to the boot. Because of the different colors and leather, I couldn't use any color, just the clear. I worked quickly. When I was done, I tapped at the bottom of the toes and started on the other.

Someone made a joke about when they were in the plaza in Uruapan.

Regina looked at me with an expression I couldn't place: pity, sadness. She was difficult to read. Ximena too. I guess that's the thing about girls: mystery.

I worked the rag over and around the boot, giving it a nice

clean shine. Then I brushed it lightly with my best brush. I tapped
his foot and looked up.

Pedro glanced at the boots and grinned. "*Ay cabrón*, they're
like new."

Everyone stopped talking. Joaquín examined the boots. "Not
bad. Now let's see how you do with these." He set one of his
Nikes on top of my box. "Make them sparkle."

I had never shined sneakers. I had no idea how to start. They
were fake leather and plastic. I knew some of the other shoeshine
boys in town used paint to work on them, but I didn't have any
paint.

"*Andale, güey.* What are you waiting for?"

I pulled out the clear and got to work. Everyone came around
to watch. Ximena placed her hands around Joaquín's shoulders.
I was their entertainment. I had no clue if the shoe would shine
or turn dull, because sometimes the grease can scratch the plastic,
leaving it cloudy. If that happens the shoes are ruined for sure. You
can never fix that. But I had to do something. I applied the clear,
just a light coat. I worked quickly, dabbing grease, rubbing it onto
the shoe, spreading it over the white parts of the sneaker. I focused
on that. There was nothing else. Ximena was not there. It was just
this Nike shoe and the boom of the music in the stereo of the
truck blending with the *conjunto* at the other end of the plaza and
all the laughter. I thought of the tickets to the wrestling. With
every stroke of my hand and the smack of the rag, I thought of El
Hijo del Santo. I kept saying it to myself: *Santo, Santo. Santo.* That
was it for me. After I earned enough for the wrestling tickets, I
was going to quit shining shoes. I wanted to get out, escape.

I glanced at Ximena, at Regina. She turned away. Then one of
the men said, "¡*Ey*! He's checking out your girl's legs, Joaquín."

Everything stopped. The men who'd been in the background
moved closer. I kept working at a furious pace, leaning into the
shoe, smacking the rag and running it back and forth along the
back, sides and top of the sneaker. I was sweating. I dropped the

rag and grabbed the brush without missing a beat. I was non-stop, my hands moving so fast I couldn't even see them. Then someone said something about the girls Joaquín had in Uruapan, and everyone laughed.

"You talk a lot of shit, *carnal,*" Piolín said.

"It's true. Right, Joaquín? Remember that short girl. She dyed her hair blond and was trying to show off, saying she was a *gringa* or something?" the man said.

Joaquín laughed. "You remember the strangest things, *pinche* Barajas."

"And the strangest girls," Piolín said. "Remember Ursula? She wanted Joaquín so bad, she said she would do anything."

Barajas whistled. "That's how God makes them, no?"

"And what about in Houston?" Joaquín said. "La Tania whatshername."

They laughed. I looked at Ximena. She was looking away from them like she didn't care. Then Joaquín took her chin in his hand and turned her face so they were eye to eye, lips to lips. "But don't worry your pretty little face, *mi amor,*" he said softly. "None of them compare to you. It's only you and me now." He turned to his friends. "You get that, *pinches putos?*"

They all nodded and their laughter died away real fast. Ximena grinned. Regina stepped back and leaned against the truck. Somehow I had this feeling that she too wanted to escape, only she didn't know how.

"What are you looking at?" Joaquín barked.

"Nothing," I said. "I'm done."

Joaquín inspected the Nikes. "Not bad. Are they real clean?"

"Yeah."

"Really clean?"

"As clean as they're going to get," I said.

"Clean enough to lick?"

Regina stared at me, her eyes wide. Afraid. Ximena was the way she always was, sad, disinterested. Waiting.

"I guess," I said.

"Then do it."

"Do what?"

"Lick them, *cabrón*."

I forced a smile.

"*¡Ándale, güey!*"

I put my brushes and grease away in the box.

"You wanna get paid, no?" His friends surrounded me, all of them looking down. Behind them, Regina shook her head, her lips forming a silent no.

I closed my box and stood.

"What's this?" Joaquín pushed his chest out, his hands resting on the sides of his waist.

My skin was on fire. I leaned down to grab my box, but Joaquín pushed his foot down on it.

"What do you say?"

I straightened up, swallowed hard. Held it down. "About what?"

"About cleaning my boots, *cabrón*."

I looked at Ximena, at Regina.

"Don't look at them. Look at me." Joaquín poked me on the chest with his finger. "What do you say?"

"Nothing."

A couple of his friends laughed. "*Ya, chíngatelo*, Joaquín."

"No." He raised his hand. "What do you say?"

"I don't know." I was a raging inferno. "What do you say?"

"Me?" he grinned. "I'd say, how much?"

"How much what?"

"How much do I owe you, *cabrón*?"

Everyone exploded in laughter.

"Thirty for the two," I said without missing a beat.

He pulled out his wallet and held out a hundred-peso bill.

"I don't have change," I said.

"Keep it."

I stared at the folded bill pressed between his long fingers embellished with golden rings. Every single voice in my head told me not to take it. Then he dropped it. I watched it float to the ground like a kite in a windless day. It landed between his shoe and my box.

He smiled. Then I glanced at Ximena, standing beside him, looking at me with her sad cat eyes. I hated her. I hated her more than anything in the world. No. I hated Joaquín more.

One of the men smacked Pedro on the back. "Come on, turn that shit on the stereo off and call the musicians over. We need a good song."

"Yeah, *el corrido de Joaquín Carrillo*."

"You wish," Pedro waved to the musicians at the end of the plaza.

I glanced at the hundred pesos and back at the men. I was invisible again. Only Regina was looking at me. She nodded and mouthed the words: *Take it.*

I picked up my box, grabbed the money and walked away. I kept walking all the way to my house, the hundred-peso bill crumpled in my fist. I kept seeing Ximena and Joaquín. I was burning out of control. I wanted to hurt. Kill.

When I turned on my street, Chapopote came trotting toward me, his sloppy tongue dangling from the side of his mouth, his tail wagging. I ran at him and kicked him in the side with all my rage. He yelped and ran off. I chased him, my shoeshine box rattling against my side. I couldn't catch him. I unlocked the gate and set my shoeshine box outside the front door.

The light in the living room was on. My parents! I ran inside thinking of the surprise in my mother's face, her eyes, her smile. But it was only my *abuela* and Jesusa watching the stupid *novela*.

9.

On Sunday morning Abuela, Gaby and I went to church. At one
time, maybe like two hundred years ago, the church must have
been a grand old place. It had been built with huge volcanic rock
and the wall behind the altar was like a pirate's treasure, all gold
and jewels. But the pews were scratched up and the ceiling and
walls were stained from leaks and mildew.

The church was crowded. All the places in the front were
taken so we had to sit near the middle, which was great. With my
parents, we always sat in the front. I hated that. Father Gregorio
had a way of making eye contact with me whenever he talked
about good and evil. I knew he was addressing everyone, but
it always felt as though he were talking only to me. And when
he paused to prepare the communion vessel, he stared at me as
if the communion—and sometimes the entire ceremony—was
being performed just to save my soul from the terrible sins I had
supposedly committed. But the truth was that I wasn't much of
a sinner. I mean, I did curse but never as much as the other kids,
especially Mosca. He had a real mouth. I just told a few innocent
lies. I guess my worst sins had to do with Ximena.

There were like twenty or thirty newcomers sitting up front. Well-dressed families—old people, grandparents, couples, kids. They were just regular people, but they looked different. Some of the men kept their sunglasses on. The women had their hair done real fancy. They wore a lot of gold. You could almost smell their money over the incense. I didn't see Joaquín or his friends from Saturday night.

Father Gregorio focused his mass on how we all need to strive for what he said is the inner person, which is Christ, or something like that. He spoke unusually slow and quoted Saint Paul over and over. But the main point was that carnal life is a passing stage of the inner life. Or something. It was a sad mass. His voice was deeper than usual. At one point he reminded us of Enrique Quintanilla and Rocío Morales. He said death was the ultimate sacrifice, and their souls were now with Him. Then he asked us to pray for them and their families. He said we were a community of believers, that we were all the children of God, and had to trust the Lord's plan and not question his motives for the things that happen to us.

He didn't mention my parents, which made me wonder if he knew they were missing. My father and the priest were good friends. Papá would sometimes visit him during the week or meet him at El Venus for coffee where they would talk about things that my father said had nothing to do with religion. He said there was a lot we could learn from listening to educated men like Father Gregorio.

I scooted down on the pew and stared at the washed-out paintings of the fourteen Stations of the Cross on the church walls. I felt sorry for Christ. He was always so sad. I suppose he had good reason. In some of the paintings, people helped him with the cross, but in the end he was going to die. He knew it, and I guess they knew it too. It was like Jesusa always said about life, that it's a journey of burdens and suffering that ends in death. Our journey was to live and suffer and die. It's what Father Gregorio was always talking about.

To me, it's more about the help we get along the way. Looking at the paintings, I wondered if the people helping Christ on his way to Mount Calvary were really helping him. I mean, weren't they actually helping him die? Wouldn't it have been better if they had helped him escape?

Once, I mentioned this to Mosca. He laughed and said Jesus had to die, otherwise he wouldn't have been able to resurrect and become *the* Jesus Christ, and if that had been the case, there would be no Catholicism. "Besides," he'd said, "it's all a fairy tale made up by the priests. All they wanted was to enslave the Indians and steal the gold of the Aztecs."

I wasn't the best Catholic, but I did fear God. And Father Gregorio. I mean, what kind of life would we have if there were no heaven? It would all be meaningless. We would be here only so we could die. What would be the point of that?

After mass, Father Gregorio came to where we were lighting *veladoras* for my parents at the feet of the Virgen de Guadalupe.

He bowed to my *abuela*. "Any news of Alfonso and Carmen?" he asked Gaby.

"We're praying, Father." Gaby's voice had an edge to it, as if she were about to lose control. "But it's been a week."

Father Gregorio rubbed his chin and watched my *abuela* light her candle. "I'm sure there is a good reason for their delay."

Abuela didn't answer. She dug around her purse for change to place in the box for the *limosna*.

"And how are you holding up?" He ruffled my hair like he used to do when I was in catechism.

"Fine, I guess."

"Sometimes adults make mistakes too," he said.

"What mistakes did they make?" I asked.

Father Gregorio's blue eyes faded. I couldn't tell whether he didn't want to tell me something, or if he'd just said one of those things adults tell children when bad things happen so they won't feel afraid. Like when my *abuela* started talking about Veracruz all the time, my mother told us she was just a little sick with nostalgia. I asked her if it was something she had to go to the doctor for, and she looked at me exactly like Father Gregorio looked at me now. Like she had made a leap and fallen and now didn't know how to get back up. Then she said it was one of those things everyone has to live with when they get old.

"Don't worry," Father Gregorio said. "I'm certain they'll turn up soon. There has to be a logical explanation for this. Have faith."

"This church," Abuela said and pointed at the ceiling, "is falling apart."

The cupola was marked with brown stains, peeling paint and patches of bubbling plaster. "Maintenance for such an old building is terribly expensive," Father Gregorio said.

"Why do we fill a collection basket every Sunday?" Abuela pursed her lips and turned back to the Virgen.

"Father," I said, "do you really think my parents are okay?" I really wanted to ask him if he thought someone had cut their heads off like they had done to *el profe* Quintanilla, but I guess I wasn't that brave. I was scared to find out they had died. I wanted to know. But I didn't want to know so I could hold on to the hope that they were okay. And yet, not knowing was scary. It left me with an empty feeling just like the time Ximena blew me that kiss in fifth grade.

Father Gregorio leaned his head to the side. "Trust in God, *hijo*. He has a plan for all of us."

"We've called the hospitals and the *procuraduría* in Toluca, but no one knows anything," Gaby said.

He nodded. "Have patience. The Lord is on their side."

"Sure," Gaby said. "It's not your parents that disappeared."

"Please, I'm here to help. Gabriela—"

But Gaby turned and marched away without letting Father Gregorio finish.

"I can't blame her. She's heard too many empty promises," Abuela said and followed Gaby out of the church.

"And what about you?" Father Gregorio said.

"I have faith, Father, at least for now. But I'm scared. The new people in town, with their big trucks and gold chains, I have a bad feeling."

"You've been watching too many *lucha* movies, Liberio."

"I just don't want my parents to end up like *el profe* or Rocío."

"*Hijo*. Why would someone want to hurt your parents?"

"I don't know, Father. I don't know why anyone would want to hurt anyone, but look at how Rocío Morales ended up. My father always said she was a nice girl. She used to come to the *panadería*. Sometimes my father would even walk her home. Now she's dead."

He placed his hand on my shoulder. "I'll speak with Captain Pineda and see what he knows."

I lowered my head. His shoes were black and very shiny. I wondered who shined them for him.

"And listen to me, *hijo*." He ruffled my hair again. "When you're out in the streets, you might hear things about Rocío or *el profesor* Quintanilla or about our new neighbors. I want you to come to me and tell me what you hear, okay?"

I glanced at the big statue of Christ on the cross behind the altar. It was so real. I thought of the sadness that Christ had pressed on me since I was a little boy—all the cuts and blood and the horrible crown of thorns. But seeing him up there now helped me understand one thing: maybe my problems were not so bad. God could not be that bad. What I was going through was not nearly as bad as what His son had to suffer.

I left feeling a little better. Having Father Gregorio there was helpful. I trusted him more than anyone else in town.

When I walked out of the church, Mosca was waiting for me by the iron gate. "What took you so long, *güey*?"

"Nothing."

"Guess what? Pepino's offering a hundred and fifty for the game."

"For real?"

"Didn't I tell you?"

"So, you gonna do it?"

"I'm gonna wait a little."

"*Güey*, take the hundred and fifty."

"*Naranjas*. I'm going to hold out for three hundred, the price of my ticket to the *lucha*. How did you make out Saturday?"

"A hundred and seventy."

"Not bad."

My sister and Abuela were in the corner across the street. Gaby was eating *chicharrón* with lime and chile.

"*¿Entonces?*" Mosca nudged me with his elbow. "Any news of your parents?"

I shook my head. A man leaned out one of the windows of the municipal building and signaled someone below. A white double-cab truck with chrome wheels, the black Expedition with black windows and California plates, and the gray pickup were parked there one after the other like they were about to go on parade.

"You know," Mosca said, "maybe we should go to Toluca and look for them."

For a second it felt real, like we could do it. Like we could just hop on a bus and go find them. But the truth was like a rock, heavy and without pity. "What?" I said. Maybe I expected him to offer a plan, show me that we could really do it. "You and me knocking on doors all over the city? Just like that?"

"I don't know, Boli. I just wish I could help. Everyone here is scared to death."

"Scared *of* death is more like it."

He stared at me. I felt bad. He had his own problems. He didn't need to take mine on. I mean they were my parents. They were my responsibility. I had to find them.

I forced a smile. I think he understood because he nudged me with his elbow. "So a bunch of us are going to the Flats to play *fútbol*," he said. "You in?"

"I don't know." When he mentioned the Flats, all I could see was Rocío Morales' naked body lying in the weeds. "I have to walk my *abuela* home."

"Let Gaby do it."

"She has to go to the market."

Mosca looked at them. "*Oye,* she's all grown up, no?"

"What are you talking about?"

"Gaby. She's looking real good. You should put in a good word for me."

"Don't be gross, *güey.*" I punched him on the shoulder and ran across the street.

I took Abuela's arm. Gaby walked away, up Avenida de la Merced to the market by the bus stop.

Abuela and I walked along Calle Lealtad. When we came to the corner where there was a big bougainvillea spilling over a wall, she stopped to admire the purple flowers. Then she pointed across the street. "Look how pretty, a hummingbird!"

10.

The following week, Chato caught up with Mosca and me outside the main gate of the *secundaria*. "Hold up," he said. "Pepino wants to talk to you."

Just then a metallic green VW Golf with dark windows pulled up across the street. It had wide tires, silver rims, and was lowered down almost to the ground. The stereo played an American rap song—all bass, real loud, and lyrics none of us could understand but could tell were angry, full of attitude.

The music stopped and Zopilote stepped out. He wore a green polo shirt too small for him and a black leather jacket. A pair of thin dark glasses covered his eyes. And, although I would never admit it to him or to anyone else, even to Mosca, I thought he looked pretty damn cool.

He came around the car and leaned against the passenger side and crossed his arms. "What's up, *mis pendejitos?*"

We crossed the street and surrounded his car like a bunch of stupid goats.

Chato ran his hand long the front of the hood. "*Chingón.* It's so bad ass."

"Don't touch," Zopilote said. "I just had it waxed."

"You mean you waxed it, and now you have to take it back to its owner," Mosca said.

Zopilote grinned. "Laugh all you want, *enano*. But when you're walking home, I'll be cruising around in my chariot. I might even drive out to Coyuca del Rió, check out a flick, maybe that new *Avengers* movie that's playing right now."

"Where'd you get it?" I said. "Seriously."

"I got a job."

"Bullshit."

"It's for real, *hijo*." He dangled the keys. "And this was just my bonus."

Mosca laughed. "I didn't even know you knew how to drive."

"It goes to show you don't know shit."

Pepino and Kiko came running out of the school and moved around the car checking out the dark headlight covers, the rear spoiler, the black antenna, and even the little sticker of Tweety Bird on the back window.

"What's it like inside?" Kiko asked.

Zopilote opened the door and stepped aside. "Careful. I don't want your dirty paws all over it."

The seats were red and black leather. It had a cool-looking Blaupunkt stereo and massive speaker grills on the doors and in the back hatch cover. The dash was all shiny. It smelled real sweet like vanilla.

Zopilote waved at Ximena and Regina who were just walking out. "Let's go," he yelled. "Joaquín's waiting."

My eyes locked on the girls. Then I saw Zopilote's ugly smile. He leaned in and pulled the seat forward. Regina stepped in first. Our eyes met. She forced a crooked smile, her eyes blank, distant, as if she knew she was doing something she was not supposed to do, but was doing it anyway because she had to.

Ximena was different. She knew everyone was watching her. It was her big moment, getting into Zopilote's fancy car so she could be delivered to her prince. She said nothing and looked at no one. She just floated right into the front seat as if she'd done it a million times, pulling her skirt, folding it under her leg without revealing an inch of skin above the knee. She looked as if she belonged there, in that seat, in that car, with him.

Zopilote closed the door and waved us away. "Let's see, *chavos*, make way."

He cut around the front of the car. Before he got in, he glanced at me and smiled like he was the devil, as if he knew I was crazy in love with Ximena and was pushing and turning the dagger deeper into my heart.

The stereo blasted where the song had left off. Zopilote revved the car a couple of times so we could all hear the modified muffler growl like an angry tomcat.

Everyone moved aside, like the sea parting for Moses. The car inched forward real slow. Then it revved again and the tires spun, screeching against the asphalt. We backed away and watched it speed off, leaving us in a sour-smelling cloud of burnt rubber.

"*¡Hijo de su chingada madre!*" Kiko cried and wiped his mouth.

I looked around. Mosca had this weird sparkle in his eyes, as if something had been revealed, or promised, as if he too could one day have a car just like that one. Things were changing, and Zopilote was the first one to take advantage of it.

"I bet you it's that guy's car," Mosca said. "He just let Zopilote use it so he could pick up the girls."

I walked away. This thing with Ximena was killing me. I knew it was an impossible love. She was older than me. But it hadn't been my choice. She had been the one who smiled at me. And the kiss. She did it. She made this happen. I was doomed.

Mosca caught up with me and grabbed my arm. "What's the matter, *güey*?"

"Nothing." I tore away from his grip and kept walking.

"Hold on, Boli. Let's see what Pepino wants, no?"

I stopped at the end of the block.

Mosca ran back to where the guys were waiting. They gathered around him. I could see Mosca moving his hands, gesturing and pointing at Pepino, then at Kiko and Chato, and then back at Pepino. Then he nodded and came running back to where I was.

"Come on," he said. "They want to play for the cash."

"I can't," I said. "I have to go help Gaby at the bakery."

"Pepino says he'll pay three hundred."

"For real?"

"A ticket to the wrestling, *güey*."

"And if you lose?"

Mosca's face twisted as if I had just insulted his dead mother. "I'll never lose. Ever."

The crowd that had been hanging around under the patch of shade in the side of the street followed Pepino to where we were.

"*¿Entonces qué?*" he said. "You wanna lose now or later?"

Mosca looked at me. "Now, no? I'll make it quick, Boli. I swear. Then you can go help Gaby."

I smiled. "Let's do this."

We marched together to the *fútbol* field in the Flats outside town. That was the place where all the important games, fights, and duels took place.

I knew one thing for sure: No one in the history of Izayoc had ever played marbles for three hundred pesos. Even if Mosca lost the devil's fire, his reputation would be solid.

The soccer field was south of the dump near the area where we had found Rocío Morales. It had real metal goals without nets. On weekends, when it was the season, teams from around the municipality played matches there. But the team from Izayoc had not won a game in my lifetime.

The field was mostly dirt with patches of dry grass and weeds and no trees. On the other side of the dump, past the highway, the hills grew again where the Montes de Oca neighborhood looked like a giant construction site with dozens of concrete-block and brick houses that never looked finished—unpainted and with long stalks of rebar sticking out their roofs and walls, the ends covered with glass soda bottles. The houses had been built along narrow dirt roads one after the other. All around, little *colonias* were sprouting up like gray encampments. Closer to the dump, clusters of small shacks of wood and tarpaper spread out all the way to the edge of the highway.

The wind was blowing hard, kicking up dust all over the Flats. A few boys from the *colonias* were flying homemade paper kites. They watched us for a while. Then they reeled in their kites and came running. They probably thought there was going to be a fight.

Pepino explained that the game would be played out between him and Mosca and Kiko and Chato, because they had each put up a hundred pesos. "And there's no interference from anyone," he warned. "Everyone has to stay back."

"What about Boli?" Mosca said.

"No. Just us."

Mosca wanted me to play for strategy. When we played together, we used our marbles to block our opponents or to set each other up for a shot. I suppose you could call it cheating, but that's just how it worked. Everyone did it.

Pepino was really hyper, pacing and pointing at things. "*Órale*, Kiko. Make the line here. Chato, draw a circle there."

"Boli holds the cash and the *diablito rojo*," Mosca said.

Pepino balked. "*Ni madres.*"

"He holds the bet," Mosca said. "You can trust him. Right, Boli?"

I crossed my thumb over my index finger and kissed it.

Pepino stared at me with wild eyes. It was like he was possessed. Then he glanced at his friends and nodded. They each gave me a hundred pesos.

Mosca pulled out an opaque white, orange, and blue oilie marble from his pocket.

"What's this?" Pepino said, "You're not playing with the *diablito*?"

Mosca shook his head. "I'm playing with my trusty *perico*."

Pepino frowned and spat on the ground. "Let's see the devil's fire then."

Mosca laughed. He dug the legendary marble out of his pocket and held it over his head for everyone to see, the little red ball shining between his thumb and index finger like an ember, a swish of yellow at its center. The crowd of boys shuffled and murmured like they'd seen the eye of God.

Mosca handed me the marble. I put it in my pocket with the money. I was so nervous I kept my hand in my pocket, my fingers fondling the money and the marble just to make sure they wouldn't disappear.

The four of them gathered where Kiko had drawn the line on the dirt. They played rock, paper, scissors to see who would go first. Pepino won.

As soon as they started, the crowd formed a wide circle around them.

I had never seen Pepino play before. He used a bluish cat's eye marble and put a lot of weight on his hand and pressed against the ground. His face was flushed. His hand shook. I thought he was nervous, but he was shooting real well. Maybe it was just his style.

The wind came in gusts, kicking up dust, our clothes flapping like little flags.

After four turns, Chato left himself exposed. Mosca shot and knocked his marble way out of the circle. "*Chiras pelas*," he called.

Pepino was flustered. His face was getting redder by the minute. But I knew he wasn't too fazed. Chato wasn't a good player. Everyone knew that. He must have come up with a hundred pesos so Pepino had to let him into the game.

Mosca shot and missed Pepino's marble. His *perico* ended up too close to the line of the circle. It was Kiko's turn. He knelt and aimed his marble.

"Focus," Pepino said. "This is our chance."

Kiko took a deep breath. It was quiet. Between the gusts, we could hear music coming from somewhere far up in the *colonias*. Kiko closed an eye, held his marble tight against the knuckle of his thumb. Then his clear green *agüita* shot across the circle toward Mosca's *perico*. It nicked it but didn't go far enough.

"*Pinche*, Kiko!" Pepino threw his arms in the air and stomped on the ground. "It was yours. What the fuck were you thinking?"

"It was a long shot," Kiko complained.

"If he knocks mine out, I'll kill you." Pepino was in a rage.

Mosca's *perico* was now in direct line with Pepino's blue *agüita*. Mosca knelt and shot quickly, almost without aiming. He missed Pepino's marble. When Mosca raised his eyes, I could tell he had done it on purpose. He was that confident. He wanted to beat Kiko first so he could face Pepino alone.

Pepino studied the position of the marbles. It wasn't an easy shot, but it wasn't impossible. When he aimed, his hand shook like an electric current was zooming across his body. He pressed down against his hand, his face red, his body shaking like an old man. He missed.

Kiko's marble was at the edge of the circle. There was no shot except to get back in the game.

Now it was Mosca again. He smiled at me. He knelt and shot quickly. His marble spun and knocked Kiko's green *agüita* out of the circle by about an inch.

"It's still in," Pepino cried.

"It's out," Mosca said. The wind had faded the circle making it difficult to tell where the line was.

"*Ni madres*. It's in." Pepino was sweating, shaking like a rabid dog.

Mosca glanced at me and shrugged, but then Kiko grabbed his marble. "No. Mosca's right. It's out."

Pepino looked stunned.

It was Mosca's turn. He had a decent shot at Pepino's marble, but it would need to be real powerful to knock Pepino's cat's eye out of the circle.

Mosca knelt and considered the shot. He leaned to the left and to the right. He bit his tongue, held his breath and shot. The marble flew like a bullet and smacked Pepino's with a loud clack. The cat's eye flew out of the circle by at least a foot.

"*Chiras pelas.*" Mosca grabbed his *perico* and stood.

Pepino froze. Even Kiko and Chato stared at him, waiting for something to happen. I thought this was it. Pepino was going to lose it and jump Mosca, but all he said was, "Rematch!"

"*Ni madres, güey.*" Mosca glanced at the crowd and back at Pepino. "We're done."

That was it. If there was going to be a fight, this was it. Pepino and Kiko and Chato stood mesmerized, staring down at the faded circle. The boys around us began breaking up, walking away, and already talking about Mosca's amazing skill.

A gust of wind blew over the field bringing a wall of dust. Mosca and I turned away and closed our eyes. After it passed, we walked across the field that was now a sandstorm, brown with dust and bits of trash from the dump.

When we reached the road and no one had jumped us from behind, Mosca put his arm around my shoulder and laughed. "We rule this fucking town, *pinche* Boli. You and I. We're the kings of Izayoc!"

11.

We celebrated our victory at the Minitienda with a couple of sodas. Ignacio Morales was still dressed in black even though it had been more than a week since they'd found his daughter's body. He was leaning over the counter by the scale, talking quietly with a couple of workmen. When we approached the counter, the men hushed up real quick and Don Ignacio waddled his huge body to the register.

"Any news of your parents, Liberio?" he asked.

I shook my head. He looked tired, sad. I thought it was because of Rocío. She was his only daughter. But when our eyes met, I realized it had to be something else. His whole face seemed to sag like it was melting or something. His eyes were dark and quick. I thought he was angry. But when we set our drinks on the counter, he waved us away. "It's on me, *niños*. Go on. Have fun, *pues*."

He walked back to the two men. One of them was Jesús Valdez, a stonemason. He'd done work for my father—and for just about everyone else in town. He was a drinker. Once I heard the people at the pharmacy talking of how they found him passed out on the street a few blocks from Taguería Los Perdidos.

Mosca stepped outside, but I lingered by the door for a moment. Jesús was saying, "…No. No, just that. No one knows anything."

Don Ignacio shook his head. "They leave us no option, do they?"

"Pay, leave or die," the other man said. "It's extortion."

Jesús stretched his neck and looked sideways at his companion. "Lupe García left. Took his family with him. Just closed his shop. Left everything. And Quintanilla's widow's gone too. But that I can understand."

"Genaro Jiménez and Everardo Rodríguez left last week. They both had a good business here," his friend added.

"They've come to me a number of times already. Now they want my store." Don Ignacio knocked twice on the counter. "I don't know what to do."

Jesús waved. "But just look at the alternative, *pues*."

"What did Pineda do about the leg?" Don Ignacio asked.

"He just came and got it with Francisco Monroy. They said they were taking it to the mortuary."

Don Ignacio ran his hand under his chin and scratched his sideburns. "And they didn't take photographs or interview witnesses, ¿*ni nada*? No investigation?"

Jesús shook his head. "And there was a good crowd there. They didn't ask any questions from nobody. Not that they would have talked. Everyone's afraid."

"They're afraid, or they're with them," Don Ignacio said. "Like that Pineda. Corrupt *hijo de puta*."

"They just took the leg and cleaned up the mess," the other man said. "That's all."

"*Ey*. They just came and picked it up and put it in a black bag and left. *Zas*, just like that."

"I wonder who it belongs to?" Don Ignacio said.

"You know how it is. Anyone who associates with them ends up, you know—"

"You're wrong," Don Ignacio interrupted. "Rocío was not involved with them."

"I didn't say she was," Jesús said. "It just seems some of the men she knew are all turning up, *ya sabe usted*, in little pieces. You don't just lose a leg like that, *¿que no?*"

Don Ignacio stared at Jesús and said nothing for a long time. He ran his hand back and forth along the back of his neck. He turned to the side and saw me.

"Hey!" He yelled. "Go on, you. Get out of here."

I joined Mosca on the sidewalk and drank my Mirinda.

"We have it made," Mosca said.

"Made how?"

"When word gets out about the devil's fire, other people will dare me to play for money. We'll keep going like this until we're rich."

"That's gambling, *güey*."

"Yeah, right. Who died and made you a saint?"

"I'm just saying."

"Well, don't get all high and mighty on me now. We just made three hundred *varos*."

"We?"

"*Simón*. You and me, *güey*. We're partners, no?

"*Chingón*," I said, but it came out flat. I kept thinking, *A leg*?

"What's the matter?"

"Nothing."

"*Güey*, we just won three hundred pesos and you're acting like we lost the game or something—" He stopped suddenly.

I turned away. A drunk stumbled out of La Gloria, a *cantina* down the street. He yelled something to no one, then he sat on the sidewalk and dropped his head in his hands.

Mosca put his hand on my shoulder. "I'm sorry, Boli. I forgot."

The workmen who had been talking to Ignacio Morales came out of the Minitienda and crossed the street toward the plaza.

I ran after the two men. "*¡Oigan!*"

They stopped.

"What happened?"

They looked at each other for a moment. They stank of sweat and mud. Jesús said, "They found a leg up by the old highway next to the junkyard, El Yonke Estaqui."

"What kind of leg?"

"What do you mean?" Jesús looked at his friend.

"Man or woman?"

"*Ah, pues.* A man's, of course."

"And just a leg?"

The other man nodded.

"But did it have like pants or a shoe or what?"

Mosca caught up with us. The men looked at each other. Jesús said, "I suppose it was blue pants, no?"

His friend nodded. "And a black shoe. Nice shoe, *¿verdad?*"

"Yes, dressy," Jesús said. "It was leather and polished real clean, like for church."

"What did Captain Pineda say?"

Jesús' friend shook his head. "*Ese gordo* is no good."

Mosca put his hand on my shoulder. "What's going on?"

Jesús tipped his hat, and the two of them walked way.

"Cut the shit," Mosca said. "What is it?"

"They found a leg at the Yonke."

"You think it's *el profe's?*"

"I was wondering if...if...maybe it's my father's."

"Boli..."

My stomach turned. I felt sick. "I can't remember what kind of shoes he was wearing."

"Does he have black ones?"

"Of course," I cried. "But I can't even remember how he was dressed."

"Then—"

"Everyone has black shoes!" I dropped my soft drink and ran away as fast as I could. Mosca called after me, but I didn't stop.

I was not going to believe it. Everyone owned a pair of black leather shoes. I shined them all the time around the plaza. The leg could belong to anyone.

I went to the mortuary. It was a small storefront a few blocks north of the plaza. Inside it was quiet and cool like the church. Everything was gray. There was a display of six big coffins with brass handles stacked one over the other.

A woman sat at a table, a painting on glass of Jesus and the Sacred Heart on the wall behind her. She smiled at me. "How may I help you?"

I was panting. "Is Señor Monroy here?"

"I'm sorry, he's not. And you are?"

"They said he picked up a leg by the old highway."

"I'm sorry?"

"A leg. He picked up a leg by the old highway, at the Yonke."

"I don't understand." The woman stood. She wore a skirt that came down to just above her knees and a tight blouse that reminded me of Rocío Morales.

I took a deep breath, but when I exhaled, it came out in short, painful sobs.

"Are you all right?" She motioned to the chair across her desk. "Sit. I'll get you some water."

"I just want to know about the leg."

"I'm sorry. I don't understand."

"Is there anyone else here?"

"Not right now. Saul went to the cemetery and Señor Monroy is out. He won't be back until closing. What's going on?"

I explained about the leg. She covered her mouth with her hand and then looked out the window for a moment. "Señor Monroy went out early this morning and hasn't come back. But that's not uncommon for him."

"So he didn't bring the leg here?"

She shook her head. "And I would know because I would have to unlock the back and do the paperwork."

"So maybe they took it to the municipal building."

"I doubt it," she said. "They don't have the facilities. They would bring it here. Unless they took it to Coyuca del Río or Toluca."

"Why would they do that?"

"I don't know. But there are facilities there. I mean, if Captain Pineda wanted to take it there in the first place. But you said a leg? Just a leg? Are you sure?"

I nodded.

"How strange. First a head. Now a leg."

I didn't know what to do, where to go. Mosca's idea of going to Toluca was so abstract. We wouldn't even know where to begin. And what if we disappeared? Where did people even disappear to?

I had to find them. I had to find out what happened.

I walked toward the plaza. I kept seeing my father walking with me after church on the way to the Flats to watch a game of *fútbol*. I could feel his heavy arm resting on my shoulder as we walked, his excited voice telling stories about his life, about how—since the age of six—he had to take care of the goats on his father's farm, and how hard work had pulled him out of poverty. "Just look at my brother and his stupid pigs," he'd said with a strange mix of pride and tenderness. "What kind of life is that?"

But I knew from my mother that marrying her had been his ticket out of the farm. He fell in love with the right woman, and she fell in love with him. That's how he left his family's farm in Coyuca del Río and came to Izayoc. That was how he became the *panadero* everyone loved. There was nothing wrong with that. He had nothing to be ashamed of. But he was too proud so I didn't tell him I knew any of this.

And I was proud of him. People always came to him for advice or to thank him for something he had done for them. He was a good man, a hard worker. Everyone said so. When I grew up, I wanted to be like him, loved and respected by everyone in town.

And then it came to me: El Centenario. It was a restaurant attached to the Metrópolis Hotel, by the old highway west of town. My father supplied them with bread. He delivered it himself twice a week. He'd said he was friends with the owner and sometimes stayed until late at night playing chess with him.

It was one of those restaurants no one mentioned much. I had never been inside. It was small and dark with red candles on the tables and mirrors on the wall. I suppose it was meant to look romantic. It even smelled like candy.

The man who claimed to be the owner shook his head. "I'm not sure what you're talking about." He was a big man, with big muscles and thick black hair combed back like Elvis Presley.

"Alfonso Flores. My father," I said and got on my tiptoes over the bar. "He brought bread and played chess with you."

"It don't ring a bell," he said and looked across the empty dining room to one of the waiters. "Beto, you remember an Alfonso Flores?"

The waiter, a small dark-faced man, came over and leaned against the side of the bar. "What'd he look like, *pues*?"

"Medium height," I said. "I guess average. He's thirty-eight and his hair's a little gray on the sides. He always wears a dark red jacket, the kind with the straps on the waist and neck."

The waiter touched his lip with the tip of his finger. "Had a little mustache?"

"Yes, yes. That's him," I said.

"Didn't he used to come in with *la niña*?," the waiter asked the owner. Then he pointed at a table in the far corner. "They always sat back there and ordered oyster cocktails and white wine."

"No. He brought bread and played chess." I nodded at the owner. "With you."

"With me?"

The waiter looked confused.

"I don't even know how to play," the owner said.

"But he came here all the time," I said. "I'm just trying to find him. I need help."

"Maybe it's someone else," the waiter said. A woman poked her head out of a door in the back and called him. He nodded at the owner and disappeared between the tables, his reflection on the mirrors flickering in the candlelight like a ghost.

"I'm sorry, *amigo*," the owner said. He looked concerned, with furrowed eyebrows and a sympathetic grin. "But what can I do?"

I walked out of the restaurant, wondering where his friends were. Where were all the people who loved him?

By the time I arrived at the *panadería,* Gaby was getting ready to close.

"What happened to you?" she said, her eyes red and puffy. I couldn't tell if it was from crying or sleeping. "You were supposed to be here after school."

"I had to finish a project in class."

"Don't lie to me, Liberio. *Por favor.* You're supposed to be helping. I have to go to the bank and the Telmex office and pay bills at the municipal building. I can't do everything alone, *¿entiendes?*"

"I'm sorry."

"Leticia had to go home early." She looked around the store. "I need you to help Lucio." She grabbed her purse, took out her keys and fiddled with the keychain. "Make sure you clean up. And don't forget to lock the back, okay?" She handed me the keys to the bakery. "Please don't lose them."

When she stepped out, she reached up and pulled down the metal shutter that rumbled like a freight train, and the store went dark.

I swept the front, locked the door and walked to the back. The place was a mess, but at least Lucio was already wiping down the counters. "Before you sweep," he said, "start with the wood scraps."

"I know, I know." I grabbed the broom and started at the corner where we usually piled the wood for the oven.

Lucio leaned over the counter and raised the volume on the radio. A woman's sad, high-pitched voice belted out a *ranchera*. The music reminded me of my mother. I was beginning to hate that music.

Lucio dumped all the leftover bread in a small plastic bin. Then there was a knock on the back door.

It was a group of about a dozen kids, all of them *niños pobres* like the ones who begged at the plaza and picked trash from the dump. Lucio let them inside and they formed a neat line along the wall. At first they were quiet, hiding their hands behind their backs, staring at me with their big dark eyes. They smelled of dirt and rot. One of the older boys nudged a younger one and they looked down at the floor, shuffled their feet.

"*Buenas tardes*," Lucio said.

They all spoke at the same time, saying they were doing well, thanking him, promising they had been good. One of the boys said his mother had been praying for Lucio.

Lucio ruffled his hair. "Tell her thanks." He wheeled the bin with the bread closer to the door and dropped three *bolillos* in the boy's bag. "There you go, *mijo*."

"*Gracias*, Señor Lucio. *Que Dios lo bendiga*."

Each kid told Lucio some anecdote of the good they had done. They updated him about their families. Lucio dropped a few *bolillos* into every bag. One girl even kissed his hand the way we sometimes kiss the priest's hand.

After the children left and he'd shut the door, Lucio saw me staring at him. "What?"

"You just give the bread away?"

"They're hungry." He wheeled the empty bin to a corner.

"But are we allowed to do that?"

"Allowed by whom?" He leaned over the counter and turned off the radio.

"I don't know, my father?"

"He knows. Sometimes he comes back here and helps." Lucio grabbed his *morral* and turned off the light in the storage closet.

"He never said anything about it."

"Why should he?"

"I don't know, he—"

"Listen, *mijo*. Your father was a good man. Don't think—"

"Was?" I cried. "You think he's dead?"

Lucio bowed his head. "I don't know, *mijo*. I don't know what to think anymore."

"I don't want him to be dead."

"No one wants that. Certainly not me, Liberio. Down here," he said and tapped his chest, "I wish there was something I could do. I just don't know what."

"Me too," I whispered. "I feel so…" I wiped the tears from my eyes. "…lost."

He nodded and rested a gentle hand on my shoulder. "Courage, *mijo*."

At least he didn't tell me to be patient or have faith or that everything was going to be all right. I went to the front and double-checked the locks on the register and turned off the lights. When I met him at the back door, he looked sad, guilty.

"You know," I said, "if Santo were here, he could help. He could find them."

"I know."

"Did you hear they found a leg by the Yonke?"

He nodded and switched the light off. Then he reached over the altar and extinguished the flame of the *veladoras* with his fingers. We stepped outside into the alley. It was getting dark. Dogs were barking across the street and further down the road.

"Do you remember what kind of shoes my father was wearing when he left for Toluca?" I asked.

"It wasn't his leg. Paquito told me it had to belong to a short man."

"But my father wasn't that tall."

"He was taller than most."

There was something gentle about the way Lucio said things. I had so many questions for him. I wanted to know more about my father. I wanted to ask him about what the owner of El Centenario had told me. Sometimes I felt as if I didn't even know him. My brain was flooded with so much information. And yet it was also full of holes. There were so many things I didn't get. And things I was afraid of knowing. It was so complicated I couldn't sort any of it out. I just stared at Lucio's dark eyes and his messy gray hair spilling along the sides of his old straw hat and the halo of the street light behind him. I wanted to hug him.

"Come on." He touched my shoulder. "We both need to get some sleep so we can be sharp in the morning."

When I got home, I went straight to my parents' bedroom and checked my father's closet. There was a pair of clean cowboy boots, plastic flip-flops, unused sneakers, and a pair of nasty, old leather *huaraches*. No dressy shoes, black or brown.

Maybe he wore brown shoes, not black. I sat on the corner of the bed and tried to remember his shoes. I remembered him wearing his boots at church. I remembered him in his sneakers. He'd gotten into a health kick a couple of years ago. Every evening after dinner he'd go walking with my mother, but it didn't last and the sneakers were abandoned in the back of the closet. And the flip-flops. I remembered him standing on the side of the lake in Tequesquitengo with his shorts and no shirt and flip-flops. And I remember him telling me the *huaraches* had belonged to his father. He'd said he kept them as a reminder of how poor they had been.

I had no memory of dressy shoes. It was as if someone or

something had erased the memories. And suddenly, I was gripped with a new and horrible fear: What if I forgot my parents? If they never came back, would I forget our vacations in Acapulco? And the time we went horseback riding in La Marquesa. Or when my father punished me by having me wash his car—and then, when he came out to help me, I accidentally sprayed him with the hose and we laughed together for like an hour. Would I forget my mother's smile and how she touched my cheek whenever I was sad? The way she calmed my father when he got angry at me. Or when she came into my room after Gaby and I had an argument and told me not to pay too much attention to how angry I was, but to focus on how much I really loved my sister.

And her smell. Oh, her smell. I was already forgetting her smell.

12.

The following Friday, I met Mosca outside the Minitienda so we could go shine shoes together, but I didn't want to hit the plaza again and have to deal with Joaquín and his friends. I suggested we check out the *cantinas*.

My father didn't allow me to go into the *cantinas,* especially El Gallo de Oro. It had a bad reputation. So we went into La Gloria, just down the street from the Minitienda. I was surprised at how small it was on the inside. I'd heard all kinds of stories about it, so I imagined a big place, kind of like Zopilote's parents' restaurant— big and wide open. La Gloria was dark with small brick columns and a cupola-like ceiling where cigarette smoke hung like thick blue fog. There was a long wooden bar at one end and a few square tables set around a broken fountain where someone had put a big stuffed toy, a panda with a black cowboy hat. It looked ridiculous.

I followed Mosca and avoided eye contact. The men sitting at one of the tables closest to the door sounded real drunk, arguing about an actor in a movie and whether he had been the same guy they had seen somewhere in Mexico City. They slammed their glasses and bottles against the tabletop. Everything about them was loud and exaggerated—their gestures, their laughter, their drunkenness.

The *cantinero*, a big ugly man with thick sideburns and a Pancho Villa mustache, kept his little beady eyes on us as we traveled from table to table.

"I'll take that side." Mosca pointed to the left. "You go that way and take the back."

I weaved between the small tables, pointing at shoes and looking for gestures from hands or eyes, watching for a nod. Sometimes the drunks smiled at me, but no one nodded. I thought of all the times Mosca bragged about shining shoes at the *cantinas* as if they were a goldmine. I was striking out big time. It was just me, the sound of drunks and the strange stench of stale liquor and Pino floor cleaner. Then, as I came around the jukebox, a tall man sitting alone gestured for me to come.

He was a gentle-looking man, about my father's age. He had light brown eyes, almost yellow, and his hair was slicked back with pomade. He had the dimples and lines of a person who liked to smile. A long thin scar ran from the bottom of his chin to the side of his lip.

He leaned back on his chair and stretched out his legs, exposing a fine pair of boots. I set my box down and got to work. The boots were of caiman leather and had the backside of the animal running along the front of the boot. At the top, a pair of claws gripped both ends so it looked as if the boot was half animal. They had to be handmade. I had seen all kinds of caiman boots before, but never like this, with such careful attention at how the leather and the animal blended into the boot. If I ever got rich, I thought, this was going to be the first thing I'd buy: a pair of custom-made caiman boots just like these.

I worked a combination of dark brown, tan and clear grease into the leather. I wanted to be faithful to the original color. The boots were not scuffed or mistreated, but they were dusty and had lost their luster. They were my first shine of the night. I was going to make it the best.

I glanced at the man as I worked, but he wasn't paying attention. He just sat, leaning back on his chair, his eyes fixed on the entrance of the *cantina*, one hand resting on the table, fingers loose around a shotglass of tequila. His other hand lay against his belt, just to the left of his stomach.

When I finished, he didn't look at me or at his boots. His eyes remained glued to the front. He smiled like a blind man—not looking but knowing—and reached into his pant's pocket with his fingers. That's when I saw the gun, a chrome-plated, *escuadra* automatic with a mother-of-pearl handle and the emblem of Mexico embossed in gold. He stretched his hand out and gave me a rolled-up fifty-peso bill.

I dug into my pocket for change, but in a deep mellow voice, he said, "Keep it."

Mosca was in the middle of the rowdy group we'd passed when we first walked in. He was squatting at the head of his box, leaning over, his arms moving back and forth with the brush, polishing a man's boots.

I stood a little ways away. There was no one else in the *cantina* that we hadn't approached. The men beside me were leaning forward, their heads almost coming together near the center of the table. They talked quietly of someone who was in prison somewhere. They had accents from the north, Nuevo León or Chihuahua.

"¡*Niño*!" The *cantinero* yelled. He was leaning over the counter, staring at me. "You done?"

I nodded.

"Go on then."

Outside it was a crisp night, cool and clear and very dark. I set my box down and leaned against the stone wall. A while later, Mosca walked out swinging his shoeshine box back and forth as if he was getting ready to throw it into the street.

"How'd it go?"

"Fifty *varos*," he said, and held up the bills. "And you?"

We crossed the street. "The same."

"See, didn't I tell you? Let's go to El Gallo de Oro."

"No. I'm good."

"We can clean up."

"That man had a gun, *güey.*"

"So? People have guns."

I stopped walking. "Maybe he was a policeman, you know, working undercover." I was thinking of my parents. If he was a cop, he might help me find them.

"*No chingues*, Boli."

"Why not, it's totally possible."

"You watch too many Santo movies."

"You watch them too, *cabrón.*"

A pair of headlights moved slowly down the road in our direction. Mosca looked at me. I was scared, not of the car, but the whole scene. I suddenly wished I'd never gone inside La Gloria.

The car making its way down the hill was a black Chevy Cheyenne double cab pickup with tinted windows. As it came level with us, it stopped. The driver's window slid down and we got a whiff of cigarette smoke and vanilla.

"What's going on, *¿muchachos?*"

"Nothing," Mosca said.

The driver was an older man with thick eyebrows. I didn't recognize him, but I'd seen the other two men hanging out with Joaquín.

The driver grinned and nodded toward La Gloria. "You been shining shoes in there?"

We looked back at the *cantina* with its narow awning, bright neon sign and a lone bulb illuminating the wooden door.

The driver pushed his hat up with the tip of his thumb. He wore a thick gold watch. Then he leaned forward and checked the rearview mirror. "Tell me, did you see a tall man in there?"

Mosca looked at me.

"Had a scar on his chin?" the man asked.

I nodded.

"Is he alone?"

I looked at Mosca, and then at the man. "I guess, yeah."

The driver smiled. He put his hand out the window. On his finger he had a heavy gold ring with the letter D embossed in cursive. We shook hands. When he let go, he left a piece of paper in my hand.

"What's your name, ¿hijo?"

"Liberio Flores."

"Thanks for your help, Liberio." He waved his index finger at me. "I'm going to remember you, amigo." Then he leaned back on his seat. The window buzzed up and the car moved slowly down the road toward La Gloria. On the right corner of the back window was a sticker of Tweety Bird.

Mosca and I stared at each other. Then I looked at the paper in my hand. It was a hundred-peso bill.

We walked quickly away and turned off on Calle Lealtad and didn't stop until we came to Avenida de los Recuerdos.

That's when we heard the gunfire.

The following morning when I walked into the kitchen Gaby stared at me as if I was a zombie in a Santo movie. "What happened to you? You look like you haven't slept in weeks."

"Leave me alone," I said.

Abuela took my hand. "What a marvelous day for a picnic. Glorious. I have always said, 'In Veracruz the weather conspires with love.'"

I rolled my eyes. Every nerve in my body was coiled up and ready to snap. I sat at the table and sunk my face into my hands. I kept seeing the silver gun in the man's belt, the man in the truck, smiling, all the gold, and the owner of El Centenario telling me he didn't know my father. It all merged into an intricate net— my parents, Rocío Morales, the leg, the gunshots at La Gloria. I wanted to erase everything.

Jesusa served me a plate with a couple of *molletes* with extra cheese and a glass of orange juice. "How do you feel, *pues*?" She placed her hand on my forehead.

"I'm fine."

Gaby gathered the stack of folders on the side of the table. The papers looked important, like official documents with stamps and seals. She shoved them into her school bag. "I need you at the *panadería* before noon. No excuses today, okay?"

"Am I going to have to be there all afternoon?"

"Yes." She mocked me, tilting her head from one side to the other. "You're going to have to be there all afternoon. It's Saturday."

"It is Saturday!" Abuela announced like she'd just discovered a treasure. "Everyone is invited. We will drive together to the park. My mother has hired musicians. It will be a memorable party. I only wish I would have known ahead of time so I could invite Dorian. But I suppose that is how things go sometimes."

"Would you like some more coffee?" Jesusa asked Abuela.

"But they're setting up for the *feria*," I said. "Mosca and I—"

Gaby raised her hand. "Enough, Boli, I don't want to hear it. I need you at the bakery. We've been through this, right?"

"But—"

Jesusa smacked my shoulder and waved a stubby finger at me. "Your dog did his business in the patio again. I'm not cleaning up after that beast."

"God, why can't I get a break?" I cried.

Jesusa served Abuela another coffee. The old lady took the cup in both hands and held it up to her nose and smiled. "In La Parroquia, the tradition is to tap the side of your cup with a spoon if you want the waiter to come and add milk to your coffee."

"For the tortillas and the milk." Gaby handed Jesusa a few folded bills. "And please, please go to the market and buy some vegetables for the next couple of days."

Jesusa nodded. Gaby took her bag with the documents and was out the door.

"It all happened on the same week," Abuela continued. "You would have never guessed it from the weather."

Jesusa served herself a cup of coffee and sat. Her black almond eyes were on me. She knew. Or she didn't know, but worried about something that was written all over my face.

I wanted to find out what happened at La Gloria. It had something to do with Joaquín and the new people in town. I was sure of it. Even Father Gregorio couldn't convince me it wasn't true. It was the same people: Joaquín's men. No one in town flaunted their wealth like that—all the gold. The guns.

"We stayed," my *abuela* went on with her monologue.

Jesusa walked out of the kitchen.

"I don't know, there is something about the sun and the humidity and the soft breeze with its sweet smell of jasmine and bananas. Dorian always says the wind brings the smells of New Orleans to Veracruz." She laughed and set her cup down. "I thought it was only a romantic notion. But when I think of it, it could be possible, no? I mean why not?"

"Abuela," I said, "is Veracruz really that great?"

"*Ay,*" she rolled her eyes and flailed her thin hands back and forth across the table as if she were trying to swat a fly. "It's paradise, *mijo*. Everyone knows everyone. Society in Veracruz, well, we have our place. You would love it."

Maybe she was on to something. Maybe it was that place where everything was peaceful, where people were nice to each other, where it was all palacial buildings and neat coffee houses like the ones she always talked about. Maybe it was the kind of place where no one ever disappeared.

Jesusa came back into the kitchen tossing her long braids to the side and flicking the wet off her shoulders. "It looks like the rains are finally here."

13.

No matter how hard we tried, Mosca and I couldn't find any evidence that there had been a shooting. There were no signs at La Gloria. No bullet holes or marks on the walls, inside or out. No blood. Not even a sign of fear in the eyes of the men drinking there—or the *cantinero*. No one was talking about it. It was as if it had all been a dream: the tall man with yellow eyes, the gun, the truck, the gunshots. It was too weird. And no one was talking about my parents anymore. It was as if everything was back to normal in good old Izayoc. But it wasn't. It was getting worse. A bunch of stores and businesses had closed. People were leaving town. There were fewer students at school. And at night, people stayed home. A strange, eerie silence had descended on us like a steady rain. No one was talking about that either.

I had been marking a calendar with the days my parents had been gone. I had this vague idea that I should have a deadline of some kind, that at some point I would come to a number and somehow finally accept that they were gone forever. But every morning when I drew a line across the little square of the day, I felt the same fear I'd felt the day they failed to return from Toluca.

I wondered if they'd be enough days in my life to get over their disappearance.

The arrival of the *feria* changed everything. It was huge. Tents and tarps and vendors and mechanical rides were set up all over the Flats. The dusty, stinky field was now a colorful, magical city. Suddenly, our sad fearful town turned into a giant party.

The entrance to the *feria* was crowded with stalls selling food and drinks and novelties. Vendors stepped out from under the blue tarps and called out their products and waved for people to come closer. The smell of corn, perfume, baked sweets, anisette and vanilla was all over the *feria*. A man with a dark face marked with lines from years in the sun held a snake in each hand at arm's length, away from his body. "I have been bitten hundreds of times," he declared in a strong voice that carried over the small crowd surrounding him. "But their venom cures me. It cures me from every malady that can attack the human immune system. Snake venom cures anything and everything."

Mosca nudged me. "Yeah, but does it give you a hard on?"

"What I tell you is not a lie," the man continued. "This ancient cure was born deep in the forests of Chiapas. It is the secret of the Lacandon people and was passed on to me by my great grandfather, Chilam Balam. People," he cried, "I am a hundred and two years old."

The crowd gasped.

He squeezed the head of the vipers. They opened their mouths revealing a pair of thin white fangs and curled their bodies around the man's arms all the way to his armpits. "I personally milk the venom from my snakes to make available to you vials of this miracle cure at the reasonable price of seventy pesos. But today being opening day, I am willing to sell the first hundred vials for the low price of fifty pesos. Fifty pesos will buy you a vial that might save your life. I ask you, good people of Izayoc, is your life worth fifty pesos?"

People shuffled toward the table where a woman in a white

muslin dress with colorful embroidery handled the sale of the vials of venom from a small wooden box at her side.

We walked on, past a man who sold plastic fish that sharpened scissors and knives of all types. Past a fat woman who peddled a cream made from the crushed pearls of oysters from the bay of Campeche. It could erase spots, warts, moles and imperfections of the skin caused by age.

"This cream is a miracle of nature," she said from behind a table full of opened oysters shells and brown jars of cream. "It will lighten your skin. It will make you beautiful. It will change your life. I guarantee it. Beware of imitations."

Then I saw Ximena. She was with Joaquín and Regina and some of the men who always hung out with them. They were decked out like cowboys, with shiny shirts, tight jeans, long pointy boots and hats. They strutted around as if they owned the *feria*. The men led the way, Ximena and Regina following a few paces behind, their heads bowed, eyes combing the dirt.

Joaquín paused by one of the games where you throw darts and pop balloons. He missed two of three. He kicked the dirt. Then he pulled out a silver pistol from the back of his belt and aimed at the boy behind the stand. The boy covered his head with his hands and ran. Joaquín and his friends laughed. Then he raised the weapon over his head and popped off two shots in the air. But it was so noisy in the *feria*, no one even noticed.

"Did you see that?"

Mosca shrugged and followed my gaze to Joaquín and his men.

Ximena took Joaquín's hand and leaned against him, the side of her face against his arm. He turned and their lips met for eternity.

I didn't want this. I didn't want Joaquín's shit. I didn't want to see Ximena with him, with anyone. Why did he get to have everything?

"Check it out." Mosca was all wound up. "Did you see her? She kissed that *güey*, tongue and all."

"And?" I was about to vomit. "What about it?"

"Nothing." He stared at me as if there was a big red neon sign on my face announcing my broken heart.

We watched the fireworks, but the vibe had changed. The grotesque image of Ximena moving under the embrace of that reptile, their tongues in each other's mouth, kept reeling in my mind like a merry-go-round. I hated my life.

We left the *feria* and walked in silence until we came to the crossroads of Avenida de los Recuerdos and Calle Martirio where we heard someone call my name.

It was Junior Espinoza, Pedro Casas and Eduardo Zúñiga, friends from school. Junior's father was a mechanic who sometimes worked on my father's car.

"Boli!" Junior caught up with us at the corner. They were breathing fast, sweating. "You're not going to believe what we saw."

"My parents!"

"No, *güey*, your sister."

My hope crumbled. But then a wave of panic shook me. I envisioned Gaby as Rocío Morales.

"She was with one of those men. They were getting real cozy, *güey*."

"One of the guys from Michoacán." Pedro shoved Junior to the side. "They were going at it real heavy, *cabrón*."

Junior nodded.

"And she was into it," Pedro said sarcastically.

"I'll break your fucking face—"

"But it's true," Junior said. "I swear."

"Liar."

"We saw them. They were up by your house, on the corner of Calle Corta and Avenida de los Recuerdos. They were pressed against each other. He had his hands all over her back." And in case that weren't enough, Junior mimicked the maneuver, his hands caressing the air to give me a visual.

Pedro said, "Kissing real heavy."

"Then they got into his *troca* and drove off," Junior said.

"And how do you know he was one of them?" I wanted to defend my sister, her integrity, her purity.

"Well, because—" Junior said.

"He had one of those big silver buckles," Pedro said. "And the *troca*. No one drives a big Chevy truck like that around here. And besides, I've seen him hanging out with the same guys that hang out with Ximena and Regina."

"It's true, Boli. I swear. Eduardo said he saw you at the *feria* so we were coming to tell you."

Mosca put his hand on my shoulder. "You okay, Boli. I—"

"She's old enough, no?" I shrugged Mosca's arm off. "What she does is her business."

Mosca stared at me like I was crazy.

But I couldn't fight this. It was too much. I just nodded and walked quickly away.

At home, Jesusa was in the living room watching one of the *novelas*. "How was it, *pues*?"

My eyes caught the photograph of Gaby in her elaborate *quince* dress, the bouquet of flowers on her lap, her hair up in curls and waves and an elaborate silver tiara. She looked like a beauty queen. But her eyes were dark and shiny like when she was a little girl.

"Liberio," Jesusa said, "what's the matter?"

I marched into my room and slammed the door. I couldn't hold it anymore. It wasn't just about my parents and Gaby, it was everything. It was Pineda and Joaquín, Zopilote and the green Golf and how he smirked at all of us as if he owned the town. It was Izayoc because it wasn't Izayoc anymore. It was the man with the caiman boots and all the others. Yes. Who didn't want to be like them, with money and power and guns? They could do whatever they wanted. I could do nothing.

14.

After we closed the *panadería* on Saturday afternoon, Gaby slung her purse over her shoulder and dropped a bomb. "I'm going out tonight. I need you to stay at home and take care of Abuela."

"Tonight? You can't. It's the wrestling—"

"Too bad. I have plans and Jesusa's going to Coyuca del Río. Someone has to take care of Abuela."

"Why don't you do it?"

"Listen, fool. I work all week. I open and close the *panadería*, do the shopping for the house and pay all the bills. I deserve a night off."

"Gaby, please. I can't miss the *lucha*. El Hijo del Santo's going to be there. Please. I've been waiting for this all year."

"Grow up, Liberio."

"I beg you."

"I already made plans with Regina."

I grabbed her arm. "Can't Abuela stay home alone just this once?"

"Seriously? What if she burns the house down or something? Someone has to stay with her."

"Gaby!"

"Please, Liberio, spare me the drama, okay?" She tore her arm away. "You went out last night. It's my turn to have a night off." She stomped on the ground the way my mother used to do whenever she lost her patience.

"Oh, so just because you wanna get all cozy with some guy—"

"What?"

"You think I don't know? Everyone knows. Junior and Pedro saw you last night with one of those *pendejos* from Michoacán."

She slapped me on the back of the head. "Don't be vulgar. What I do is my business. Francisco and his friends are businessmen. They're going to bring jobs to this Godforsaken *pueblo*. Open your mind, you dope."

"Are you blind? Can't you see their cars? Their guns? Those guys are bullies. They—"

"¡*Ya*! I don't want to hear it. And you better do as I tell you." She waved dismissively and marched off toward the plaza.

I ran home. Jesusa. She was my only chance.

"I can't," she said flatly. "My *comadre* is giving birth. She needs me. Her cousin is on his way to pick me up." She set her vinyl overnight bag—a hand-me-down from my parents—beside the front door.

"Please, Jesusa. I beg you. I'll do anything you want. I swear. I'll clean all of Chapo's turds and make my bed. I'll wash the dishes every day."

"If I could I would, Liberio, but Magdalena needs me. I'll be back tomorrow night."

We heard a horn outside.

She took her bag. "There's *chilaquiles* in the oven and a container of pork stew in the refrigerator."

I grabbed her arm. "Please, Jesusa. Please. I'm begging you. Please."

The driver honked again. She stared at me, her dark eyes unyielding. I released her and she was gone.

"I wonder—" my *abuela* said when I walked into the kitchen. She was wearing makeup, rouge on her cheeks and pink lipstick. She had her hands cusped around a large cup of *café con leche*. "If the weather holds, we might go on the boat to the Isla de los Sacrificios like Dorian wanted. "

"What's the matter with your lips?"

Her smile twisted and she brought the tip of her fingers to the side of her mouth. "Jesusa did it for me."

But none of this was her fault. It wasn't fair. I reached across the table and touched her hand. "It looks good, Abuela. Really."

She smiled and turned to the window. Maybe she thought it was a mirror. "*Gracias*. I thought it would look nice for the picnic. You think Dorian will like it?"

"Of course he will." But honestly, I was just hoping there would be a Santo movie at midnight because this was going to be the worst night of my life.

After dinner Abuela settled back into her room. Then Mosca arrived.

"What do you mean?" he said. "We've been planning this for months."

"I know, but Gaby went out with her stupid boyfriend."

"So?"

"I can't leave my *abuela* alone."

"*Puta madre*. Of all the nights. And with one of those *pendejos* too. I can't believe it." Mosca paced across the living room. "Can't you take off for just—"

"She's not well."

"Just for a little while."

"I can't, Mosca."

"It's only a couple hours, *güey*. You said she was getting better."

I looked at her bedroom. She was getting better, in a way.

"Gaby won't even find out."

"It's not that," I said. "What if something happens?"

"What's going to happen, *güey*? You told me all she ever does is sit in her room and dream of Veracruz."

It was true. It wasn't as if she ever needed anything. We were the ones who were always pulling her out of her room to eat or go to church or watch television. If it weren't for us, she would probably never leave her room.

"Why do you let Gaby push you around like that, *cabrón*? It's El Hijo del Santo, Ruddy Calderón, El Zorrillo de León, Subministro Fox. *Güey*, you're gonna miss it."

Mosca was right. This was a once in a lifetime opportunity to see the best in *lucha libre*, and Gaby was spoiling it for me because of some stupid date. Besides, Abuela had been having good days lately. Sometimes she almost seemed normal.

"Hold on a sec," I said and knocked lightly on the door to her room. "Abuelita, it's me, Liberio."

"Come in, *hijo*. Come in. Dorian went to Xalapa on business. I'm just here sewing."

She was sitting in her rocking chair like she always did, the old Superman blanket on her lap and staring out the window like there was something in the darkness of the little patio. Her face had the same expression of longing I had seen so many times before, only a little brighter because of the makeup.

"Abuelita?"

"Is that you, Camilo?"

"No, it's me, Liberio. Your grandson." I placed my hand on her shoulder. "Is there anything you need?"

"*No, muchas gracias, mijo.*"

"Abuelita," I said. "I'm going to go out to the fair for an hour, okay?"

She stared out the dark window where our reflection was distorted, our faces melting with the raindrops.

"Jesusa and Gaby are out. You think you'll be okay by yourself for a little while?"

"Of course, *mijo*. I will just sit here and watch the sunset."

I squeezed her shoulder and gave her a kiss on the forehead. I caught our reflection again and she smiled.

Chapopote walked in the rain with us for a couple of blocks and then sauntered off in the darkness. We crossed the *feria* bypassing all the vendors and rides and went straight to the big canvas tent they'd set up for the *lucha*.

The makeshift arena was just like the one from last year's *feria*. Inside the tent, folding metal chairs with the Corona logo on the backrests had been set in rows. A string of lights on the ceiling illuminated the ring. It wasn't the Arena Coliseo, but it was better than a couple of years ago when they had a rickety ring made of plywood and vinyl and not a single chair. Halfway through the *lucha* schedule, the whole thing collapsed.

We found seats on the third row, close enough that we could smell the stink of sweat and blood from the canvas. The place filled up quickly. Pretty soon people began to clap and whistle, trying to get the event started. Finally, a short man in a black suit stepped into the ring to announce the first match: El Zorrillo de León against Ruddy Calderón.

Zorrillo wore his trademark black mask with white trim around the mouth and eyes. He had a black fur cape. He looked just like the skunk from the cartoons.

Ruddy had on a yellow and red mask with fake yellow hair and a black cape. When he climbed into the ring, only a handful of people cheered. He was a nobody.

Zorrillo was a *técnico*. *Técnicos* were all about method and style. *Rudos* were brutes. All they cared about was winning. I liked *técnicos*. I was sure Zorrillo would win and take Ruddy down with style.

But the match was dull. From the start Zorrillo was way too predictable. His moves were robotic. He set himself up every time. Ruddy beat the hell out of him.

Zorrillo won, but it was disappointing, like a bad movie. The crowd booed as the two wrestlers paraded around the ring, waving, flexing their muscles and showing off. I ran outside and got more popcorn and a couple of sodas. When I came back Mosca was freaking out. "I shook hands with Zorrillo!"

"For real?"

"I swear. It was all sweaty and everything."

The announcer stepped back into the ring and raised his hands to silence the crowd. But we didn't let up. We were a rowdy bunch. People whistled and mocked him. Eventually everyone mellowed. "Ladies and Gentlemen," he said in a steady tone. "Due to an unfortunate cancellation on the part of his manager, El Hijo del Santo could not make it to tonight's event."

"What?" I yelled.

The crowd jeered. I booed. Mosca threw popcorn. The announcer waved his hands, but it was too much. Popcorn and trash flew into the ring like a storm.

"Please. Please." The announcer covered his face with his arm. "We have an excellent substitute. One of the rising stars in the world of *lucha*."

But we would have none of it. It was a fraud. We booed and whistled and threw so much popcorn, it was a blizzard.

"Tonight's main event pairs two colossus of the ring," the announcer yelled over our ruckus. "Two of the most powerful and aggressive fighters in *lucha* today. These two gentlemen, these two warriors, these two fierce soldiers, promise a fine exhibition for all you good people."

The crowd didn't let up. And neither did Mosca and I. We yelled with everything we had.

The announcer's face twisted in horror. "In this corner," he yelled over the crowd. "Wearing his trademark tricolor mask, the red, white and green of the glorious flag of this splendid nation—and back in Mexico after an extensive tour of Japan—and with only three defeats in his entire career: Ladies and gentlemen,

EEEEL SUUUB-MIN-ISTROOOO FOX!" A spotlight shone on the back of the tent. A powerful bass erupted, thumping and vibrating our ribs and rattling our teeth. A strobe flashed. The thumping morphed into a powerful salsa rhythm. El Subministro appeared from behind the curtain with two girls in skimpy Aztec costumes hanging on each arm.

The crowd went crazy.

Subministro Fox was a *rudo*. He was big—bigger than Zorrillo. And he was big-time. I had even seen him on TV. When he climbed into the ring, the two girls went with him. They removed his luxurious cape and his thick championship belt, gave him a kiss, and climbed down.

Things calmed down enough for the announcer to speak. "And from the working class *barrio* of Tepito—right smack in the historic center of Mexico City—having had a significant career in the United States—with bouts in California, Texas, Nevada, and Florida under his golden belt—the challenger: *EEEEL CHEE-CAAAA-NOOO ESTRADA!"*

There was no music, no applause. From the back of the tent, a *luchador* almost as big as El Subministro strutted like a badass toward the ring. He had on a classic mask, red with little blue stars set along the white trim around the eyes and mouth. His cape was white and red with a large white star like in the American flag. This was El Chicano Estrada.

Suddenly, the silence turned into heckles. The crowd wouldn't cut him any slack. Even Mosca jeered. But not me. El Hijo del Santo had cancelled. It wasn't Chicano's fault. The poor guy had gotten a raw deal. But still he walked up to the ring alone, with his head high, and the dignity of a champion. A sudden gust of pride swelled inside me. He was an undiscovered hero. I took a deep breath and cheered him until my throat burned.

Mosca smacked me. "What are you doing, *güey*?"

"I like him."

He shook his head. Then he dug into his bag of popcorn and

threw handfuls at the ring as Chicano paraded around the arena with his arms in the air. The whole place was a loud, nasty whistle. I was the only one cheering.

Chicano dove into Subministro. But his moves were premeditated. Subministro was always a step ahead. Even I could've done better. It was so disappointing. If the first match had been mediocre, this was worse. After about ten minutes, the crowd began to yell obscenities at Chicano, telling him to go back to Texas. Then it started raining popcorn again.

But despite Chicano's pathetic moves, Subministro was worse. It was as if he was fighting with his eyes closed. He caught everything Chicano threw at him, but he did nothing with it. Totally uninspiring.

"You still rooting for your Chicano, güey?" Mosca asked.

I threw my hands up. "This is ridiculous."

And suddenly, Chicano came back with a vengeance. It was as if someone had insulted his mother. He turned on Subministro with fancy, well-executed moves, one after another. He was on the attack nonstop, charging Subministro again and again. His red mask was all over the ring. He was showing some real heart. He was great.

But Subministro was the favorite. The crowd chanted: "Mexico—Mexico, rah, rah, rah!"

I was Chicano's only fan. He was my luchador. I cheered and screamed like my life depended on it. I needed him to know he had a fan, that he wasn't alone.

Chicano managed Subministro into a full nelson and ran him head first into a corner post. He did it against all four posts. Subministro's mask ripped. Blood gushed from his face. Chicano had him pinned to the ground. He was trying to expose him, unlacing his mask at the back. The crowd went crazy, yelling profanities.

Then someone threw a beer bottle into the ring, nailing Chicano on the side of the face. He turned. Subministro threw him off, then charged from behind. Chicano stumbled, bounced against the ropes and fell back on the canvas with a loud thump. Subministro wasted no time. He jumped in the air and landed with an elbow against Chicano's abdomen. The ring shook like an earthquake.

Chicano curled into a ball. Subministro jumped again and slammed down against Chicano. Then he paused and raised his arms to relish the cheers of the crowd.

Chicano lost his momentum. He pushed himself up and sulked around like a drunk trying to avoid Subministro. But he had nowhere to hide. Subministro punished him without mercy. He slammed him against the floor over and over with moves I had never seen. Chicano was a ragdoll.

Finally, Chicano fell on the canvas. Subministro jumped on him and locked his leg with his arm and pulled it so far it almost touched the back of his head. The ref dropped to the mat and slammed his palm against the canvas: One! Two! Three!

It was over. The crowd went crazy. "Mexico! Mexico!"

Chicano was out. He lay face down on the mat when the first chair flew across the ring.

Subministro strutted around the ring without a care in the world, his hands up in the air, basking in glory while people threw everything: chairs, cans, bottles, popcorn, trash.

Chicano pushed himself up on all fours, but remained on the canvas like a dog looking up at his opponent.

People pushed forward. A chair hit the man in front of us. He fell to the ground. The man next to him grabbed the chair and threw it back. Women screamed. Mosca and I ducked. The crowd moved like a wave back and forth, to the left and right. We were trapped in a riot.

"We gotta get out of here." Mosca pushed me forward.

We crawled on the dirt to the side of the tent. There was no way out. The exit was in the back. People from the *feria* were pouring in and joining the mayhem. Young men and teenagers ran in, swinging sticks and throwing rocks. There was a loud pop, like a gunshot. The lights went out.

People stampeded. I grabbed Mosca's arm. "There." I pointed to a sliver of light in the wall of canvas. It was an opening in the tent. We could see the merry-go-round. We ran.

Outside it was pouring rain. The *feria* was going on as if nothing was happening. People carried umbrellas and plastic bags over their heads. They ate cotton candy and *elotes* and lined up for a turn on the mechanical rides.

Mosca laughed. "That was awesome."

The *lucha* tent moved as if it were alive. People ran out. But once outside, they stopped and looked up at the rain, then walked away as if everything was fine.

"Come on." Mosca tapped me on the back. "Let's go on some rides."

15.

When I got home, the house was dark and quiet. I took off my wet clothes, dried up, and put on my pajamas. Gaby wasn't home yet. I peeked into my *abuela's* room. Her bed was made. Her rocking chair was empty.

"Abuela?"

Then I noticed the closet door. It was open. The dresser drawers were empty. The photos of the family were gone. Even the small crucifix that hung over her bed had disappeared.

"Abuela!"

She was gone.

I ran around the house and double-checked everything. "Abuela!"

But there was only the rain pouring down against the roof. "Jesus," I whispered. "Please help me find her. Please. Let her be okay."

I threw on my father's long raincoat, put on shoes and ran outside.

"Chapo!" I called. He poked his head out from the corner where he slept under the eve of the shed. "Come on, Chapo!" I slapped my thigh. "Come on. We have to go find Abuela."

Chapo stretched and waged his tail.

"Come on." He walked slowly to me. "I need your help." I pulled him by the collar. We walked outside. I wasn't sure what Chapo could do, but it felt right to take him. In the movies the dogs were always helpful.

To the east I could see the glow of the lights of the *feria*. Over the drone of the rain, I heard the sharp crack of fireworks. Or gunfire.

We ran up Avenida de los Recuerdos toward the *panadería*. The street was empty. At every intersection it was the same. No cars, no people, just darkness and rain.

The *panadería* was closed. Everything was closed, rain crashing against the metal shutters. A warm, dizzy wave turned my stomach. Chapo waited in the rain. "Help me," I said. But he just rocked his head from side to side and wagged his tail a couple of times. "*Pinche* Chapo, what good are you? Come on."

We started back and turned south on Calle Lealtad toward the plaza. My best bet was the church. She could be there, praying or lighting candles for my parents. No. She had taken all her things. Maybe she took a taxi, thinking she was in Veracruz. Shit. Or eloping with my grandfather.

There was nothing going on around the plaza. Most everything was closed, dark. A few people had taken shelter from the rain in the arcade of the municipal building and in the nearby *taquerías* that were like small pockets of light in a dark, ugly scene. Zopilote's green Golf was parked in front of Taquería Los Perdidos.

I approached slowly, hoping Joaquín wasn't there. Or Gaby— that she wasn't around. She was the last person I needed to see.

Ximena and Joaquín and two men sat at a table drinking beer. I felt a tap on my back. "Looking for your girlfriend, *güey?*"

It was Zopilote. He looked like shit. He had a black eye that was so swollen it was almost shut. His lower lip had a long cut across the side.

"What happened to you?" I stepped away from the entrance. I didn't want Joaquín to see me.

"Trouble with a couple of *pendejos*." His voice quivered and his one good eye kept looking over my shoulder at the *taquería* where the *taquero* was shaving bits of marinated pork from the *trompo* onto a tortilla. He nipped a slice of pineapple from the top and set the plate on the counter for a waiter.

"You should've seen how I left the other guys. Straight to the fucking hospital."

"Have you been here a while?" I asked.

"What's it to you?"

"Don't be an asshole, Zopilote. I'm looking for my *abuela*."

He looked around as if she might be somewhere in the plaza or down the street. "No. I've been here most of the night. I haven't seen her."

"Shit."

"What happened?"

"I don't know. She's kind of losing her marbles. I think she wandered away somewhere. I can't find her." I looked past him at the street. A car was driving up the road. Zopilote also turned. It was a small Nissan. A family of peasants stood in front of the pharmacy, their backs pressed against the metal shutter, trying to stay out of the rain.

"What about Gaby?" I said.

"What about her?"

"Have you seen her?"

He looked away. The Nissan passed us. "She went on a double date with Regina. Pedro and Francisco were taking them to Coyuca del Río."

I looked up at the rain.

"*Órale pues*." He touched my shoulder. "I have to get back to my post. Good luck finding the old lady."

I walked quickly. Peasants and vendors were abstract shapes warped by the harsh artificial light.

I ran up Avenida de la Merced and stopped at the crossroads. Chapo had abandoned me. The rain didn't let up.

I kept going. A few blocks later, I saw the blue and yellow neon Corona sign blinking in the dark: El Gallo de Oro. There was a big ruckus inside the *cantina*. People catcalled and whistled. A pair of men with cowboy hats stepped out. They stood under the awning. One of them lit a cigarette. Then they looked up at the rain and ran across the street. They got into an old Ford Bronco and drove away. Parked behind the Bronco was Captain Pineda's little patrol car.

In the distance over the low buildings I could see the green sign of the Pemex gas station, all around it raindrops like tiny sparks. I came to the old highway. To my left the gas station glowed white and green and empty like something from outer space. To my right was a long stretch of gravel where the busses and *micros* stopped to load and unload passengers before getting back on the highway. It was deserted except for the small dark figure in the middle of the lot, sitting on a suitcase, back erect, the oval of an umbrella floating overhead.

"Abuela!"

She turned and smiled as if nothing was wrong. "Well, hello, *mijo*. What are you doing here?"

"I came looking for you."

"You're soaked."

I looked down at my pajamas. My father's raincoat had been useless.

"What are *you* doing here?" I said.

"Waiting for the bus. I want to go home."

"You are home."

"Do not be silly. I want to go home to Veracruz."

"No, Abuela. You don't live there anymore. Come on. Let's go home."

She looked at me as if I had broken a promise. I took her arm and helped her up. She didn't resist.

"I'm not crazy, you know?"

"I didn't say that." I grabbed the suitcase and we started back, walking side by side under the black umbrella.

"We should go back to Veracruz, you and me and Gaby."

"We can't go back, Abuela. Please, let's just go home."

We walked in silence. As we came by El Gallo de Oro, we heard a loud ruckus.

"What is going on?"

"It's just a *cantina*."

"No, there." She stopped and pointed to the sidewalk just past El Gallo de Oro. "What are they doing?"

Two men stood against the wall. Another man lay on the ground. When he pushed himself up on all fours, one of the men stepped out onto the rain and kicked him on the side. The man flipped and fell flat on his back.

The men laughed. Abuela squeezed my arm.

The man on the ground rolled over and struggled to push himself up. The other man kicked him again.

I took my *abuela's* hand. "Let's cross the street." Then the Corona sign flickered and I saw the red mask. The man on the ground was Chicano Estrada.

I stopped.

Abuela waited. "Liberio?"

Chicano was alone. He needed help. There was no one around. A taut wire of fear traveled down my throat. I had to do something. I set the suitcase down and handed Abuela the umbrella.

"What are you doing?"

"He needs help."

"*Pero no*." She held me back. "You'll get hurt."

But I had to help him. He was one of the good guys. He had to be. Besides, it was two against one.

I didn't think about it. I ran as fast as I could. Everything I had bottled up inside—my parents, Gaby, Ximena, Joaquín—it all exploded in a flash of rage. I charged from behind and slammed the man on the lower back. His body arched and flew forward. He tripped on Chicano and fell face first on the wet sidewalk.

The other man laughed. Then everything went quiet. Rain.

Chicano raised his head and pushed himself up on all fours. I grabbed his arm and pulled, but he was too heavy.

The other man helped his friend.

I released Chicano and charged again. I hit the other man in the stomach with both hands. He dropped his friend and stumbled back, but didn't fall. He coughed and leaned against the wall for support.

"*¿Qué pasó, pinche puto?*" He shook his head and straightened himself. He wiped the rain from his face. Our eyes met.

I charged again, just like in the Santo movies. I threw punches—right, left, right, left—as fast as I could, one after the other. My fists sank into clothes and flesh. I was a machine at full throttle—left, right, left. Then I was lifted from behind.

"Let me go!" I shouted.

The man in front of me laughed. He picked up his hat, ran his hand over his wet hair and put it back on. "Let's see how you like it, *mocoso*." He stepped forward and threw a long hook. His fist sank into my stomach. Everything went black. Bubbles of light popped in and out of sight. I gasped for air. Pain blasted across my body. For a moment, the world was completely silent.

My face was wet. Everything was a blur. I heard a squeak behind me. It was my *abuela*. I pulled my arms, but one of the men had me in a lock from behind.

The man in front laughed.

The one who held me tightened his grip, pressed his torso against my back. He stank of liquor. He raised me off the ground and shook me. "Give him some more, *tocayo*."

The man leaned in and took a wide swing. It came as if in slow motion: a big curve, a grimace, the flash of his ring. I closed my eyes and flexed every muscle in my body. My head exploded in a flash of light. Sparks flickered like a trail of fireworks and hot pain blasted across my head, up my mouth through the side of my face, my cheek, the back of my head. Silence.

My hands pressed against the wet concrete. The rain burned my face. The wet raincoat weighed on me like a rock.

Laughter. A scream. I opened my eyes and pushed myself up, but my strength was gone. I shook my head. The neon Corona sign flickered upside down. I squinted and pushed up again.

Then I realized the Corona sign was a reflection on a puddle.

I got back on my feet. Dizzy, my legs weak. I stumbled and leaned against the wall. Abuela's distant yelling was overrun with laughter and the loud drone of the rain. The two men stood together, swaying. I charged, but I was moving in slow motion. I saw it happen in advance. The men moved to catch me before I was even close. One of them grabbed me in a half nelson.

"Enough!" A voice cried.

The man released me and I fell to the ground.

"Inside. Now."

"But Efraín—"

"But nothing, *cabrónes*." The voice was a dead echo in the rain. "Get back inside. Let's go."

The men walked past Chicano who was still on the ground. I couldn't see the man with the voice, but I saw his boots. They were the same custom caiman boots I'd polished at La Gloria. I winced and closed my eyes. When I opened them again, they had disappeared into El Gallo de Oro.

Abuela touched my face. "Are you all right, *hijito*?"

"I'm okay, Abuela." She helped me stand.

"Who were those men?"

"Drunks, I guess." I wiped the blood from my mouth with the wet sleeve of the raincoat.

Chicano grunted. He stretched and moved, trying to stand.

I walked over to him. "You okay?"

He didn't answer.

"What are you doing, Liberio? Who is this man?"

"El Chicano Estrada," I said. "A *luchador.*"

"Well, by the looks of it, he's not very good. Why is he wearing a mask?"

He was still dressed in his fighting tights and cape. I grabbed one of his arms and tried pulling him up, but he was too heavy. "Come on, Abuela, help me."

She didn't move.

"Abuela!"

She blinked as if coming out of a trance and took his other arm.

We pulled him to his feet. He leaned over, took a couple of wobbly steps and stumbled. The wall stopped him. He leaned against it and rubbed the side of his mask.

"You okay?" I asked.

He grunted and waved.

"Let's go." I pulled at Chicano. "We have to get out of here."

Abuela held the umbrella over us. "This man is drunk."

Chicano pulled his arm away. "Lemme alone."

"We're trying to help you." My face was throbbing.

"Who are you?"

"Liberio Flores. I'm a fan."

He turned and looked at the entrance of the *cantina.*

"Come on." I pulled at him again. He took a step and placed his giant arm over my shoulder.

Abuela fetched her suitcase and dragged it behind her. "Where are we taking him?"

"Home."

She stopped walking. "No, Liberio. You can't just bring a man into the house like that."

"I have a plan."

Chicano snorted and spat over my shoulder.

"Well, excuse me," Abuela said.

Chicano looked at her with his quivering eyes. Then he shook his head and took another step.

"Take off his mask," Abuela said.

"No. It's his identity."

"What is he supposed to be?"

"A Chicano."

"What's that?"

"I have no idea."

When we finally got home, Chapo was sitting by the front gate waiting. He didn't even come out to greet us. He just stood and wagged his tail under the eve.

"A lot of help you were," I said.

We walked into the patio and propped Chicano against the gate. "Why are we doing this?" Abuela was soaked. She held the umbrella over Chicano.

I opened the door of the shed and pulled out my father's old bicycle, the wheelbarrow and a couple of boxes of old clothes to make room. "Because he's a good guy. And maybe he can help us."

"How?"

I unfolded an old tarp and spread it on the floor. "He's a *luchador*. He's strong. And smart."

"And?"

"I don't know. But no one else will help us. He's a good guy. Trust me."

We led Chicano into the shed and lay him on the tarp.

In a moment, he was fast asleep, snoring loudly.

"Now what?" Abuela said.

"I guess we let him sleep it off." I picked up his feet and pushed them inside the shed. Chapo trotted in and sniffed him from head to toe. Chicano rolled on his side and the snoring stopped.

"Much better," Abuela said. Her hair was drenched and pressed flat against her head, her face pale. She looked tiny.

"Come on." I took her bag and we walked inside. "You dry

up and get in bed, Abuela. I'll get you a *café con leche* after I bring him a blanket." Then I paused and put a finger to my lips. "Abuela, promise me, not a word of this to Gaby, okay?"

16.

The following morning my muscles were sore and stiff. My head throbbed. The whole side of my face felt as if it were on fire. My left eye was black and swollen.

I checked the shed. Chicano lay face up, his arms and legs spread like he'd just been knocked out in a fight. For the first time I had a good look at how massive he really was. His body reached from one end of the shed to the other. I couldn't believe we'd managed to bring him home.

Abuela was sitting at the kitchen table sipping her *café*. And surprisingly, she was tearing small pieces from a *concha*, placing them in her mouth and chewing like a little bird.

"Good morning, *hijo*. Such a nice morning to go out on the boat—*Ay*, Liberio!" She reached for my eye.

"It's fine."

"It looks terrible." She leaned back and studied my face for a moment. Then she smiled. "We had quite an adventure last night, no?"

"You scared me half to death, Abuela. I thought we'd lost you."

"Nonsense, I was only going to Veracruz. Dorian would have been so pleased to see me."

I checked Gaby's bedroom. It was clean. The bed was made. It was Sunday and the *panadería* was closed. An awful chill crawled up my spine. I tried not to think of what Zopilote had said. Or of Joaquín. Or Rocío Morales dead and naked in the weeds, her fingers gnawed to the bone.

"Abuela!" I ran back to the kitchen. "Gaby's not home."

"I gave her permission to spend the night at Regina's. She's a nice girl. I know her family."

But I thought different. I couldn't help it. I thought Gaby never even mentioned anything about going out to Abuela. Not that I didn't trust Gaby or Regina, but everything was changing so fast. And without my parents here, it didn't feel right.

"Abuela." I poured myself a glass of milk and stirred in a couple spoonfuls of Choco Milk. "Why did you want to go to Veracruz?"

She stared at me as if I were one of her memories. "It's home."

"But what about Gaby and me?"

She put another piece of *concha* in her mouth and chewed slowly and said nothing more.

We left Chicano sleeping in the shed and went to church. The morning was dark, gray, ugly. Everything was wet. The storm had washed over the valley and the street was littered with trash and small tree branches that had come rushing down from the top of the hill.

I held Abuela's arm as we walked. Every time we paused at a corner to cross a street, she would protest and pull away. "Please, Liberio. I can walk on my own."

I don't know why, but I wanted to hold on to her.

"I am not going to Veracruz, not right now. I promise."

But it wasn't that. I just wanted her there, with me, at my side. All I could think about was Gaby.

Abuela must have understood because she let me hold her arm for another block. Then she slid her arm down and took my hand and held it the way my mother used to, interlacing our fingers together. I squeezed it and she smiled. For the first time since my parents left for Toluca, I felt safe.

Father Gregorio announced that he had received a request to have mass in Latin, to which he had agreed. "It is up to all of us," he announced, "to make strangers feel like family, to make newcomers feel like neighbors, to open our hearts and our homes in trying times, and not give in to lies, *chismes* and paranoia. Let us not forget Luke 7:44 when Jesus was at the Pharisee's home and Mary the brother of Lazarus came to him and He turned toward the woman and said to Simon, 'Do you see this woman? I came into your house. You did not give me any water for my feet, but she wet my feet with her tears and wiped them with her hair.'"

I really didn't care if Father Gregorio said mass in Spanish or Latin or any other language. Personally, I was fed up with all of it. Church had become a chore. God was walking a thin line with me. My parents had disappeared. Every day that passed, it felt as if their memory faded away just a little more. Hope was dying. No one was doing anything about it. Sometimes I thought Abuela had the right idea. All of us should pile into a bus and go to Veracruz, even Jesusa and Lucio and Mosca. God had to prove to me that he still mattered.

The thing was, I didn't think Father Gregorio had any idea what I was going through. All he ever did was look at the good in everything, always telling us to be patient and trust God. Maybe that's how it worked for priests, but they weren't regular people. They didn't live their lives like the rest of us. They had no idea what suffering was. I imagined Father Gregorio sitting in his office, his feet propped up on a desk and his robe half open, watching television and snacking on wafers and wine. No one lived that way in the real world.

"What is the matter with him?" Abuela whispered. "Nobody here understands Latin. Especially those country folk at the front."

"It's probably just this once," I said.

"I hate Latin mass. It's dull."

"What does it matter, Abuela? It's always the same—we beg forgiveness and God forgives us. The end."

After mass, Father Gregorio waved to me. I took Abuela's arm. "He wants us to wait."

She eyed the altar. Father Gregorio was setting his things in order and giving instructions to the altar boys. "What does he want now? Money?"

"Come on, Abuela."

"Well, that's fine with me." She crossed her arms and sat. "I want a word with him too."

The crowd shuffled out. Father Gregorio stepped down from the altar and shook hands with an old man who had been sitting in the front pew, then came to where we were. "What happened to your face, Liberio?"

"Nothing. Just a little fight with some boys."

"It looks bad." He touched the side of my cheek, but addressed my grandmother. "*Buenos días*, Doña Esperanza."

She nodded.

"Any news?"

"I was hoping you knew something, Father," I said.

"I'm afraid not, *hijo*."

"I did not appreciate the mass in Latin," Abuela declared.

Father Gregorio forced a smile. "It's the original language of the church."

"With all due respect, Father. Ancient Hebrew is the original language of the Bible, but I don't care. I don't understand ancient Hebrew either. And neither do the poor people who come to your church to worship."

I couldn't believe her. It was as if she'd woken from a dream where her only reality had been Veracruz. Now she was here, in the old church, chastising Father Gregorio.

"Doña Esperanza, the Guzmán family are new in town. They had a request. I wanted to make them feel welcome."

"I have wasted my morning."

"Don't say that, Doña Esperanza. God hears your prayers. He knows."

Abuela waved him away. "I doubt he heard anything over that gibberish you were mumbling."

Father Gregorio took her hand. "Have you considered a mass for Alfonso and Carmen?"

"They're not dead," I cried.

Father Gregorio pressed his hands together. "It's been—"

"It doesn't matter. They're not dead." Everyone offered help and condolences, but no one was looking for them. No one was helping us. If they were dead, I would have felt something, had a dream, seen a vision. That's how it worked.

"You misinterpret me, Liberio. I was not suggesting…Your parents were good Catholics. I thought they might appreciate—"

"Indeed." Abuela stood. "But why the past tense, Father?"

"Well, I—"

"You seem quite eager with the new people, perhaps their money is worth more than ours?"

"Doña Esperanza, everyone is equal in the eyes of the church."

"Certainly," Abuela said sarcastically and stepped onto the aisle. "They must have more than the rest of us then. Which is just as well. Either way, I don't believe we're ready to bury my daughter and her husband. Not just yet."

I had never seen my *abuela* sound so tough. It was scary and comical to see Father Gregorio getting a scolding.

"Of course, Doña Esperanza." Father Gregorio gathered his hands at the front of his waist and bowed. "Thank you so much for coming. If there's anything I can do to help, I am always here for you." Then he pointed at my face. "And you should put some ice on that eye."

Outside the deep gray of the rain was breaking up and the sun was struggling to come out.

We paused at the gate. Everyone seemed to hurry away, getting in their cars or just walking home. No one stayed around the plaza. It was weird. Even the vendors seemed lost.

"Abuela, do you think they're dead?"

"I believe what you believe, *mijo*." She took my hand and looked up at the sky and smiled as if it was the first time she had seen the sun. "I would rather have hope than a mass. The problem with the priest is that he does not understand love. He only understands God. And money."

"Where do you think they are?" I said.

"I honestly don't know. But look," she said as if speaking to the world, "this is not a day for sorrow. This is a day for hope."

She was acting so normal it was scary. But I wasn't buying what she said. I had counted too many days on my calendar, and they had all been miserable. Hope was fading quickly.

"It reminds me of Veracruz," she said. "Every day was glorious. Even when it rained, it was beautiful. And we were always happy." She opened her purse and shuffled a few things inside, then she looked at me and smiled. "How would you like to accompany me for a little *botanita*, and a *café* at Los Pinos?"

"Really?" We rarely went out to eat, especially to Los Pinos. It was the fanciest restaurant in town. It faced the church on the opposite side of the plaza. In the days before independence, it had been the bishop's mansion. It had a sprawling garden. Tables with colorful embroidered tablecloths were set under the shade of big pine trees. From there you could admire the tall cliffs surrounding the valley. There was a big fountain and a swimming pool. Eduardo Zúñiga's father was a waiter there.

I had only eaten at Los Pinos once—for my parent's fifteenth wedding anniversary.

We took a table near the fountain. A waiter in black slacks and white shirt came to our table and bowed apologetically. He said we couldn't come in.

Abuela drew back. "Why not?"

"There is a private function," the waiter said. "We're closed to the public."

Abuela looked around. The restaurant was almost empty. The people sitting at the two tables by the swimming pool were the same ones that had taken up the front pews at church this morning.

"But why do they need the whole restaurant?"

For a moment, the waiter looked confused. He adjusted his shirt cuff and then gestured to the large open gate. "I am awfully sorry, *señora*."

Abuela stood. "But this makes no sense."

We walked out. I looked back at the people sitting at the tables. I recognized the older man. He'd been in Pineda's office when Gaby and I went there for help. I saw Pedro and another man whose name I didn't know. And sitting at the back table was Joaquín.

"If you like"—I took my *abuela's* arm and we crossed the street to the plaza—"we can go to El Venus. You can have a coffee there."

She shook her head and continued walking without looking back. "*Gracias*, but I am no longer in the mood. Besides, it looks like more rain is coming."

17.

When we got home, Chicano was sitting on the front step, hunched over, his masked head buried in his large hands.

"Well," Abuela said. "He's alive."

"Did Gaby see you?" I asked.

Chicano massaged his temples and followed us inside. "What am I doing here?"

"You're in our house." I offered him my hand. "I'm Liberio Flores, and this is my *abuela*, Esperanza Solís. We rescued you."

"From what?"

"From the bad guys."

He stared at me. "Looks like the bad guys did a number on you."

"We saved your life," Abuela said proudly. "But there is no need to thank us. We rescued the dog two years ago. Now he refuses to leave."

"Please." Chicano sat on the couch.

"It's true, Chicano. Two men were beating you up outside El Gallo de Oro."

He looked at the ceiling and tugged at the side of his mask.

"I'm going to my room." Abuela pinched her nose and waved. Chicano stank of sweat and tequila. It was all over the room.

"What time is it?" Chicano asked.

"Just after noon."

"*Chingada madre.*" He stood and looked around the room. "Where's my bag?"

"You didn't have one."

"Yes, I did. It was black with yellow tiger stripes. My ticket's in there."

"Maybe the bad guys took it."

"What are you talking about? There were no bad guys. No good guys and no bad guys, just stupid drunk *pendejos.*"

"Is that what you are?"

"Don't get smart with me, *mocoso.*" He waved his finger at me. "I'm older than you. Respect."

"Are you hungry?"

He nodded and touched the side of his mouth where the mask met his lip. Then he adjusted his cape. It was dirty and had a small rip along the side and was frayed at the edges.

I warmed up some tortillas and leftover stew. Chicano came into the kitchen and sat, his huge body slouched over the little wooden table. "What's on the menu, *hijín?*"

"Pork stew."

"You have any beer?"

"Isn't it a little early?"

"You're not my mother, *chamaco.* Hair of the dog. Fixes me right up."

I shook my head. "We have milk, *agua de limón.* I can make orange juice."

"Coffee?"

"Nescafé."

"That's good."

I boiled water and made coffee. I took a cup to my *abuela,* and then I sat at the table with Chicano.

He ate quickly, shoveling the stew into his mouth with a tortilla. His mask was dirty. The white trim around the corners of the lips was stained yellow and one of the little blue stars was peeling off. The left cheek had a bloodstain in the shape of the state of Zacatecas. Behind the opening for the eyes, I could see his small beady bloodshot eyes.

"You make this?"

"No." I laughed. "Jesusa made it."

"Your grandmother?"

"Our maid. She's off today."

He took a long drink of coffee. "That's nice."

"She's in Coyuca del Río."

"Good for her."

"I almost missed the wrestling because of her and my sister."

"Really?"

"Yeah, Gaby had to go out."

"How old's your sister?"

"Seventeen."

"She went out on a date?"

"With a friend."

He nodded and scooped stew into his mouth. I don't know if he sensed there was something wrong. He seemed more interested in the food. "So you were at the *lucha*. What a fiasco, no?"

"They said El Hijo del Santo was going to be there."

He laughed. "That's what they do. They bill it as one thing and give you something different. If you really paid attention, you'd know El Hijo del Santo's on the Todo X Todo tour with Blue Demon Jr."

"Really?"

"Besides." He shrugged. "He's too big for a little country *feria*. In Toluca, yes. But here?"

"They did it on purpose?"

He nodded and continued with the stew.

"And you knew?" I asked.

He smiled, stood and sucked his fingers.

"Why do they do that?"

"For the same reason everyone does what they do: money."

"But that's cheating."

"Welcome to the glamorous world of *lucha libre*."

How could they do this? And El Hijo del Santo, there was no way he would allow someone to use his name to rob good people. But maybe Chicano was right. On TV wrestling had gotten too fancy. The moves were unreal, the outfits too crazy. Sometimes it looked more like a costume show. It was not *lucha* anymore. It was a joke.

"Tell me," —We went to the living room. He dropped his large frame on the couch— "why did you help me out there?"

"I don't know." I sat on my father's big chair. "When I saw you at the match everyone was against you. I guess I felt sorry for you, so I took your side."

He smiled. "You like underdogs, eh?"

"I like Santo."

"He's dead."

"I know, but he was a good guy."

"You're hung up on ghosts, *hijín*. You're not seeing the world in front of you for what it really is."

"Oh, yeah? What makes you such an expert?"

"I'm a realist. I survive." He stretched and lay back on the couch just as if he was at home.

"What are you doing?" I said.

"I'm gonna take a nap."

"But you just woke up."

He placed his hands behind his head and closed his eyes. "I'm a *luchador*," he said. "I sleep during the day and fight evil by night."

"Not in here," I said and pulled his arm. "In the shed."

"You admire me, but treat me like a dog."

"It's temporary." We walked to the front patio. "I promise."

I didn't care what he said about Santo being a relic. He was the one who started it all. If Chicano weren't so selfish, he would see that he owed his career to Santo and Blue Demon and Mil Máscaras. Those guys opened it up for everyone else. They were pioneers.

I called Regina's house, but there was no answer. I was worried about Gaby, but I had to trust that Regina was aware of the danger. She would take care of her like she took care of Ximena. I could only hope.

I grabbed some ice for my eye and went to my room. I leafed though the pages of my latest issue of *Guerreros del Ring* magazine, but it was too disappointing. It was all too flashy. Maybe everything Chicano had said was true. There was something pure about the old days of *lucha*, like Mosca always said, before it turned commercial. I tossed the magazine on the floor and dug out my prized copy of *Punch* (#60) from October 1975 that my father bought for me at La Lagunilla in Mexico City a couple of years ago. It had an awesome portrait of Mil Máscaras on the cover. There was no flash, just good wrestling.

In the old days, *luchadores* were heroes. That's what it was about for me. This business of tricking people made me sick. It was as if you couldn't trust anyone anymore. I set the ice on the side of my face and closed my eyes and thought of Santo and Blue Demon and Mil Máscaras and how they always fought crime and monsters. I wished they were here, helping me find my parents. Maybe Chicano...

When I opened my eyes, it was late afternoon. The ice had melted and left a cold wet spot on the side of my pillow. But at least my face felt better.

I went to the shed. Chicano was gone.

"Abuela?" I cracked opened the door to her room.

"Look." She pointed to the window. "Look at all the

freighters. They say a hurricane is headed our way. They are all coming in to port. Have you ever seen such a stunning sight?"

"What happened to Chicano?"

"They say we might have to evacuate."

I went out. Chapopote came running behind me. There was no trace of Chicano at the plaza. I headed up Avenida de la Merced toward El Gallo de Oro. I'd found him there once. I might find him there again.

Two blocks up, I noticed a crowd outside Paco's Tacos. People were spilling out onto the street, jostling to look inside. My stomach twisted. *Gaby*, I thought, *dead and naked like Rocío Morales*. I ran in and burrowed my way between the people. It was Chicano. He was sitting at a table eating tacos and drinking a beer.

"What are you doing? I said.

He gestured to his plate. "I was told they make the best *tacos al pastor*. Not bad."

"Why did you leave?"

"I had to go."

"Why?"

He set his taco on the little plastic plate. "I missed my fight in Toluca. I went to check on a bus to Querétaro. I have to work, *hijín*."

"But you can't go." I had an idea, an image of Chicano facing Pineda, asking questions and getting answers. Real answers. Behind me, the crowd pushed in. No one spoke. They were like sheep, staring quietly at the *luchador* in his red mask and blue and white cape.

"I know." He took a long sip of beer. "I got rolled last night. I lost my bag with all my cash."

"So you're staying?"

He shook his head. "I need to get my manager to arrange for a bus ticket." He glanced past me. The people pressed forward. "Unless someone gives me some cash."

"But you can't go. I need your help. Please."

"I have a schedule to keep." He dabbed two spoonfuls of salsa on his taco, picked it up between his thick fingers and took a huge bite. "Querétaro," he said with his mouth full. "Then San Luís and Monterrey."

"No, no. Please. What about my parents?"

"What about them?"

"You have to help me find out what happened to them." It came out just like that, without thinking. "Please."

Chicano finished his taco and shook his head. "What are you talking about?"

I told him about my parent's disappearance.

"That's for the police, no?" He leaned back in his chair, sucked the ends of his fingers and wiped his hands with a napkin. "Don't pull me into your fantasies, okay? I'm sorry about your *jefes*. But no one can beat these guys, not the president and his army. Not even the gringos. I can't help you."

"But you can. Santo made a difference—"

"Those are movies, *hijín*. Seriously, you need to get real."

"Please, Chicano. I'll help you. We'll do it together. We'll find my parents and fix everything."

"Liberio!" It was Regina. She broke through the crowd. Ximena trailed her. "What are you doing here? Your sister's looking all over for you. She's really mad. Oh, my God what happened to your eye?"

"Gaby's mad at *me*?"

"You left your grandmother alone in the house."

"Yeah, right. And Gaby never even came home."

"Who's this?" Chicano interrupted.

"Regina," I said. "She's a friend."

"No, no." He leaned back in his chair and glanced past Regina. "The other one."

I followed his gaze to Ximena. She stood like she did—hip to the side, hands at her waist, and that faraway, disinterested look in her dark, cat eyes.

"Nice." Chicano stood. "Very nice." He dug into the waistband of his tights and dropped a few pesos on the table.

I searched the faces in the crowd for Joaquín and his friends.

Chicano reached past me and offered his hand to Ximena. "Chicano Estrada," he said. "*Para servirle, corazón.*"

Ximena shook his hand but said nothing. Then she glanced at Regina and looked around the crowd as if searching for a signal or someone to tell her what to do. When no one said anything more, she crossed her arms and gave Regina a look as if she wanted her to hurry up and finish her business so they could leave.

"Come on," I said and tugged at Chicano's cape.

"Watch it, *niño.*" He slapped my hand and pulled the cape away. "It costs money."

"I'm not a *niño,*" I barked. "My name's Liberio Flores."

"You're not listening to me," Regina said. "Gaby's going crazy looking for you."

"So?" I said. "You think I don't know what you two were up to last night?"

Regina's eyes grew wide. "Fine. Do what you want." She turned and pushed her way out of the *taquería*. Ximena followed her.

"No, don't go, *muñecas,*" Chicano said. Then he smacked me on the chest. "What's your problem?"

"I told you." My lips trembled and my voice cracked. "I need your help to find my parents."

"Listen, I told you once, and I'll tell it to your stubborn face again: I'm a *luchador*, not a superhero."

"But I know you can help me. Even if it's just to find out what happened to them. Just to ask around. Please."

Chicano turned and looked at the crowd as if he were seeing them for the first time. "And you, what *chingados* are you staring at like a bunch of *burros*?"

The people blinked and turned to look at each other as if they'd just woken from a trance. They shuffled and moved without actually leaving.

"I have a fight," Chicano said. "I can't disappoint my fans in Querétaro."

"As if you had any," I cried. Someone in the crowd whistled. "Is that how you want to do it?"

"I'm just asking for a little help. I helped you when you were lying in the gutter. Please, Chicano."

The crowd mumbled. Someone said, "*No sea cabrón, pinche* Chicano. Help the boy out."

"You stay out of it." Chicano waved at the crowd.

"When's your fight in Querétaro?" I said.

"Saturday."

"You have a week. Stay a few days. Please?"

He glanced past the crowd. "So what's that *vieja's* story?"

"Who?" My gut tightened. "Ximena?"

"Yeah, the pretty one."

"She's with one of them."

"You're kidding."

"And he's a real *hijo de puta*."

"And the other one?"

"She's a friend of my sister."

"Right, and they're all seventeen?"

I rolled my eyes. "And?"

"And nothing. Look, maybe I can call my manager, see what I can get away with." I followed him out of the *taquería*. We crossed the street to get away from the crowd. He found a patch of shade at the end of the block and dialed his cell phone.

"Hello?" He held the phone aside and said to me, "Voicemail." Then he spoke into the phone. "Chaparro, it's me. Listen, I ran into a little problem here in...whatever the fuck town I'm in where I fought Subministro Fox. Look, I didn't make it to Toluca. Someone stole my bag with all my cash last night. I need you to wire me some money and arrange for the bus ticket to Querétaro. Give me a call as soon as you get this. And hurry. I'm low on battery and my phone charger's in my bag. *Órale pues.* We'll talk later."

"Don't you have a bank account?" I said.

He spread his arms. "Do I look like I'm rich?"

"You don't have to be rich to have one."

"You know,"—he waved his finger at me—"that mouth is going to get you in a lot of trouble."

"So you're staying?"

He shoved his phone in the elastic waist of his tights. "I'm not sure. I have to run it by my manager. He's a busy man, manages the best wrestlers in Mexico."

"But you can stay for a couple of days, no?"

"Tell me then," he said and grabbed my shoulders, "what's in it for me?"

"What do you mean?"

"Yeah, what's in it for me and my manager? We need to make money. That's how it works, get it?"

"So you won't help unless I pay you?"

"Look, *hijín*. Even in the Santo movies, he was a detective. Someone had to pay him. How do you think he could afford that nice house with the pool and those hot-looking maids. And the nice convertibles and shit? That's how it works."

I tore away from his grip. "Not always."

"Besides," he said, and we started up the street away from the plaza. "If I stay, I'm going to need a place to sleep. I'm going to have to eat."

"You can stay with me."

He laughed. "In the shed, like a dog? I don't think so, *hijín*."

I stopped. "Where you going?"

"To El Gallo de Oro."

"Why?"

"I need to find my bag. If I don't find it and Chaparro Mendoza doesn't send me money or a bus ticket, I just might have to spend the rest of my life in this shithole."

18.

Gaby was on top of me the minute I walked in the house, yelling at me worse than my mother ever had. "I can't believe you would be so irresponsible. Don't you get it? And look at your face. *Por Dios*, Liberio." She paced back and forth across the living room, waving her hands and pointing at me, her fingernails polished pink. Her hair was done up real nice like in her *quince* photo. She wore a shiny blue dress I had never seen before. And high heels. She didn't even resemble my sister. She looked like a woman, eerily like Rocío Morales.

"I was only gone for like half an hour." I didn't know how much she knew—about last night, about Chicano.

"But you left Abuela alone. What if something happened?"

"But nothing happened."

"I need to know that I can trust you, Liberio. It's not easy without Mamá and Papá. We need to be careful or we'll end up living in some orphanage or with tío Jorge in Coyuca del Río. Do you want that?"

Tío Jorge was my father's only living relative. He had a small pig farm outside Coyuca del Río. When my father's mother died, they had a big fight and hadn't spoken since. Tío Jorge was poor. Like really poor. Living with him would be like going back to the dark ages. He didn't even have a phone, and his bathroom was an outhouse. It was disgusting.

"I'm not kidding you, Liberio. And on top of everything, look at your face. Abuela said you got in a fight."

"I'm fine." She said nothing about last night.

"No, Abuela said you got in a fight with some men outside a *cantina.*"

"Yeah," I said sarcastically. "In a *cantina* in Veracruz."

"Come on, Liberio. You need to grow up."

I was tired of people telling me to grow up. I was more grown up than anyone I knew. "Maybe, instead of worrying about what I'm doing, you shouldn't be spending the night with your stupid boyfriend."

"Liberio!"

"It's true. And you know it."

"I was with Regina. And besides, I'm allowed to have a life."

"Papá would never allow you to—"

"Enough!" She waved her hands. "You're not my father."

"And you're not my mother."

She froze. Her lip trembled and her eyes welled up. The space between us shrunk and began to crack and fall away in tiny pieces like glass. My chest hurt and my fear erupted in long, deep sobs.

She touched my hand. "I just want us to be okay."

What came out of my mouth next was not what I had intended. "Father Gregorio thinks Mamá and Papá are dead."

Gaby lowered her eyes.

"But they're not." The truth collapsed around me. "They're not, right? They can't be."

"It's been too long, Liberio." She held me in her arms. Her tone turned soft. "Every night I've been praying and wishing and hoping. But I can't do it anymore. I'm exhausted."

I got a whiff of her perfume, my mother's perfume. I could

feel her chest heaving with sobs, and all the hope I had left seeped out of me like blood.

She pulled away. "We need to be strong and take care of things here. Life has to go on. ¿*Me entiendes*?"

I nodded, but I knew she was just as scared as I was. Everyone was, and that was what made it worse.

She smiled and touched the side of my face. "Does it hurt?"

I shook my head. "But Gaby, honestly, that guy you're dating—"

"Don't believe all the *chisme*, Liberio. People in this stupid town live to gossip. They know nothing."

"But those guys are creepy."

"Not Francisco. He's not what they say he is."

"How do you know?"

"Because I know. He's a businessman. He owns an Internet café. His father has a ranch outside Zitácuaro. They do well. And besides, he's super nice."

"But don't you think it's weird, how they suddenly show up in town, and *el profe* and Rocío, and Mamá and—"

"No! It's not like that. It's just a coincidence. Besides, it's impossible to find a decent man in this town, one who will treat you like a lady."

"And he does?"

She smiled. "He does. He really does."

I followed her to the bathroom where she touched up her makeup. I caught my reflection in the mirror. The bruise on my eye was shrinking. I touched it with the tip of my fingers. I was thinking of the leg they found at the Yonke and the shooting at the *cantina*. "Did you know Ximena is dating one of them?"

"Joaquín's a *compadre* of Francisco. He's nice enough."

"He's the same guy from Pineda's office, remember?"

"Of course I remember. And he said he would help us find what happened to Mamá and Papá."

"Yeah, right. And what has he done?"

"Please, Liberio. Stop it."

"I don't want anything to happen to you. I don't want you to disappear or end up like Rocío Morales."

She turned and looked at me the way my mother used to look at me whenever I did something that made her proud. "*Ay*, Liberio. I won't."

"You promise?"

She smiled. "I promise."

After Gaby left, I went to check in on my *abuela*. She was sitting in her rocking chair, staring at the window.

"Abuelita. Do you need anything?"

She shook her head. "We're fine. *Gracias*. We have everything we need. We have had hurricanes come through before. We will endure this one as well."

I sat on her bed. She had already unpacked her bags. The photo of my father and mother from before they were married was back on her mantle. In the photo, they were sitting, leaning against each other at a restaurant. They looked happy, their heads touching. Maybe that was what my *abuela* liked to do, remember the good old days, which to me didn't seem so long ago. Perhaps one day I would look back on my life and remember the years that came before this when I was with my parents. And those would be the good old days.

I lay back and closed my eyes and imagined my good old days. My parents would drive us out to Las Truchas where we ran in the fields and fished and ate trout in one of the open restaurants. We'd go to the movies or a concert in Coyuca del Río. And vacations. In the good old days, I used to hike El Cerro de la Soledad with my father. We'd be gone all day. He'd point out plants, telling me which ones were good and which ones were bad. He'd tell me stories about Izayoc and how the Indians believed the cliffs around the town had been formed after two gods in the form of giant jaguars battled for the love of a princess. Both gods died in the fight and the princess was left alone to cry for a thousand years. Her tears formed the Lágrimas River that runs by Coyuca del Río. One of its tributaries cuts at the bottom of the cliffs around Izayoc. This was how the town got its name. My father said that in Nahua mythology, jaguars could be both gods and devils. I always wanted to see a jaguar, but we never did. We saw hawks, doves and a lot of tiny songbirds.

We'd pick wildflowers for my mother who existed in different memories of my good old days. It was as if my memories had different rooms where they were kept. In my mother's room of memories, she used to walk me to school when I was little. She would take Gaby and me on her errands at the market or to buy supplies for school projects. We ate popsicles in the plaza on hot days and sang songs together. She loved to sing. We played guessing games and told each other mathematical riddles. We watched *Sábado Gigante* together. My mother. She was always close. If I reached out, my hand would find hers and she would always smile. But now it was all an empty room. Instead of a window, all I could see was a big black vulture eating away at my memories.

When Abuela went to bed, Jesusa came home. The two of us sat together on the couch to watch a Santo movie: *La venganza de las mujeres vampiro*. I had seen it before, but it still scared me a little. I was glad Jesusa was watching with me, although I was pretty sure she was scared too. We sat close together under a blanket. I leaned my head against her shoulder and felt her warmth like the warmth of my mother, and took in her soft clean smell of Nivea.

What scared me most about the movie was how Mayra the Vampiress looked before they gave her the blood transfusion that made her young again. Then she tells her gang of vampires that they have to destroy every enemy that gets in their way. The movie had an interesting fight where Santo is wrestling in the arena, and Mayra hypnotizes him and orders him to lose the fight. In the end, he actually wrestles like a *rudo*. Later, Santo tells the lieutenant that vampires do exist. In the next scenes when the dead start to rise, it made me think of the nightmares I sometimes have—I'm alone and whatever is chasing me is unstoppable and my legs can't move me fast enough.

Near the end, just as Santo began to make his way into the castle, Chapo barked. Jesusa and I jumped. There was a loud thud against the gate. Then a hard knock.

We looked at each other. I turned down the volume on the TV. Chapo quit barking and made whiny noises. Jesusa unlocked the front door. We peeked into the front patio. Chapo was wagging his tail and sniffing at the gate.

"Who is it?" Jesusa called.

There was another hard knock. *Toc, toc!* The hardware on the gate shook. Chapo stepped back and barked.

"Who is it?" Jesusa called again.

"Me." It was a man's voice.

"Me who?" Jesusa said.

"Me, *cabrones*. Chicano!"

I shoved past Jesusa, but she grabbed my arm. "What are you doing, Liberio?"

"It's okay. It's Chicano. I know him."

I opened the gate. Chicano's large frame staggered past me to the front door. He leaned on Jesusa's tiny body. Then he pushed himself away and stumbled inside and dropped on the couch.

"What happened?"

He waved a shaky finger at me. "I couldn't find it."

"He's drunk!" Jesusa said.

"He needs help."

"No, Liberio. I don't like it."

"He needs us," I said. "And we need him."

She stared at his mask, his tights. "Does Gaby know about him?"

Chicano turned on his side and glanced at the TV. "I've seen this one. With the vampires, no? I love that first go-go dancer they kill. She's so beautiful."

Jesusa moved closer to Chicano. She felt the material of his cape between her fingers. "Where are we going to put him, *pues?*"

"*¿Qué hubo, chiquita?*" Chicano reached for her.

Jesusa slapped his hand and jumped back. "He stinks!"

"Come on," I said and took his arm. "In the shed." I pulled him up. He stumbled and almost squished me with his weight.

Jesusa took his other arm and pulled him off me. She placed his arm over her shoulder and we helped him out to the shed.

"This is nice." His words rolled out of his mouth like marbles. He lay on his back and looked at us with red, drunken eyes. "Now all I need is a woman."

19.

Mosca and I were walking by the plaza after school when Father Gregorio waved at us from the steps of the church. Neither of us wanted to talk to him, but there was no getting away.

He placed his hands on our shoulders like he always did. "How are you, *niños*?"

"Fine, Father," I said.

Mosca looked away. He couldn't care less about Father Gregorio, the church and God.

"School's out already?"

I nodded. "We're going to the *panadería*. Gaby's expecting us."

"How is she holding up?"

"Fine, I guess."

He looked past me toward the municipal building. "You should come to confession."

"It's okay," I said. "I've been good since the last time."

"Liberio?"

"I swear."

"Don't swear." He squeezed my shoulder. "I really think you ought to come in and confess."

"Can I come tomorrow? Gaby's expecting me. For real, Father."

"Give him a break," Mosca said. "He needs a little time to sin, no?"

"Don't get smart, Esteban. And you," he said, looking at me, "come and do a little confessing. You need it more than you realize."

Mosca grinned. "Go ahead, Boli. I'll catch up with you later."

The bench of the confessional creaked when I sat. I hated the little dark room. It was like a coffin, and it smelled weird, kind of like the mothballs in my grandmother's closet. I also didn't want Father Gregorio staring at me, smiling his pity-smile. I crossed myself. "Forgive me Father for I have sinned."

"It's okay," Father Gregorio whispered. "You don't have to confess. I only wanted to speak to you in private."

"Is it about my parents?"

"Unfortunately, I have found very little. But I discovered they never made it to Toluca in the first place. So whatever happened to them, happened between here and there. It also gives us a timeframe to work with. Whatever happened must have happened between six and ten in the morning on the day they left."

"Does Pineda know this?"

"Captain Pineda told me he has not been able to find any leads. But I've made my own inquiries. The Archdioceses in Mexico City has agreed to lend their support. I also spread the word among the churches in the vicinity. Your parents didn't just vanish."

"Yes, that's what I've been saying. You think they're still alive?"

"I am not sure what I believe, Liberio. We have to be very careful about how we proceed."

"Because of those people?"

"No. But it is best to be discreet."

"I've seen their guns, Father. I swear. And this guy, Joaquín—"

"Don't swear, Liberio."

"But it's true. I don't trust them. At the *feria* I saw Joaquín—"

"These families were forced to flee their homes to get away

from the violence in their own state, Liberio. The people of Michoacán are facing a horrific situation. Have some empathy. Don't jump to conclusions."

"So they're not—"

"Captain Pineda said he checked them out."

"*El profe* always warned us of what the new highway might bring."

"Progress is not to blame," he said. "Tell me, have you heard anything in the streets?"

"Nothing." I stared at the pattern of the wooden grate that separated us. I couldn't make out Father Gregorio, but in the low light my imagination played tricks. I saw a face that kept changing. Sometimes it looked like Father Gregorio, sometimes like my father. Sometimes like the man in the truck outside La Gloria. "People are scared. They're suspicious of everyone. And Gaby's dating one of them, Francisco…I don't know his last name."

"This town has always been insular. When I arrived from Mexico City, I faced the same resistance. We must learn to temper our fear of outsiders. Your own father told me about the difficulties he faced when he first came to Izayoc. And if I remember correctly, your grandparents were not welcome here either. With the new highway, there will be more visitors. The sooner we get used to it, the better."

"What about my parents?"

"I really don't know, *hijo*."

I hadn't expected Father Gregorio to help. But I still wasn't sure about him. He was getting really cozy with the new people. But if he was reaching out to the other priests… My voice quivered. "I don't want them to be dead."

"It's in God's hands. Trust Him."

When I left, a group of workmen with shovels and carpentry tools were arriving at the church. I walked toward the *panadería*.

Then I noticed a crowd of children in their school uniforms across the street. At the center was a bright red circle like a giant Christmas bulb. Chicano.

"What are you doing?" I said.

"What are you, my boss?"

The kids touched his cape and his dirty tights. They reached for his mask and offered him their notebooks and pens, begging for autographs.

"I was only asking because if you're staying, I need to tell Jesusa to make enough for dinner."

Chicano signed an autograph and then waved the kids away. "Go on now. I'll catch up with you *cachorritos* later on, okay? Come on. *Ándenle.*"

Then he looked at me. "What's the matter with you?"

"Nothing. I was just talking to Father Gregorio about my parents. He keeps telling me not to jump to conclusions."

Chicano rubbed his chin and around the stitching at the opening of the mouth. "That's always good advice."

We started toward the *panadería.* "I thought you were going to Querétaro."

"I was." He waved. "But the event got postponed. The syndicate of the arena is in dispute with the organizers. Money. You know how it is. I figure I might just as well stay here for a week or two. Then I can go straight to Monterrey."

"For real?"

He nodded and placed his heavy hand on my back. "But we need to strategize. We can't just go at this without a plan. We should go check out your sister at the bakery. Find out what she knows. And maybe talk to that other girl Ximena."

"That's great. Thank you, Chicano!"

"But let's be clear on something, I'm a *luchador*, not a superhero. I don't believe all the shit in the Santo movies."

"*Ay*, Chicano. I know it's not real. But you can't tell me they're not fun."

"I suppose. But I just want that out in the open."

"Sure, but it doesn't make you any less strong or brave. Here everyone's afraid of their own shadow."

"Well, we'll see what we can do." He ruffled my hair, and we turned on Calle Juan Escutia. That's when we saw Mosca. He was running toward us with Junior and a couple other guys from school.

"Boli!" he called. "Come on, let's go."

We met at the corner. They were out of breath, excited. They studied Chicano up and down.

"He's staying with me," I said. "We're going to find out what happened to my parents."

"We're going to try," Chicano added.

"Well, you better come with us," Mosca said. "They say there's a couple of people hanging from the pedestrian overpass."

My parents. My dead parents hanging like laundry from the overpass. "Did you see them?" My voice trembled at a high pitch like a girl. "Did you recognize them?"

"No. We're on our way now. Come on."

We ran up Avenida Porvenir, my legs pushing me forward faster than I'd ever run. All I could think of was my mother, my father, ropes around their necks, dead. My legs were like electric wires. I was flying ahead of everyone. My chest was burning.

After a few blocks, I looked back. Chicano had slowed down.

"Come on," I said, "hurry!"

He waved me on. "I'll catch up." Then he stopped and leaned forward, resting his hands on his knees.

We rushed between the food stalls by the side of the old highway and pushed through the big crowd that had gathered at the foot of the overpass. There were people on both sides of the highway. I stopped. Two men hung from the bridge, one beside the other. But they weren't hanging from their necks. They hung from a foot, their heads at the bottom so they looked like a pair of tilted Ys. And they were naked. The bridge itself was deserted except for a dozen vultures waiting at both ends. A dozen more circled the sky.

They were not my parents.

A couple of cars sped past on the highway. And then silence.

Mosca tilted his head as if trying to look straight at the cadavers. Their faces and bodies were swollen out of proportion. Mosca shook his head. "Why won't anyone bring them down?"

"You think they're dead for sure?" Junior asked.

"Of course they're dead," Chicano said. "You can't be deader than that. Where's the police?" He grabbed an old woman by the arm. "How long have they been like this?"

The woman flapped her hands. "Since this morning, I think."

"Did you see who did this?"

She shook her head. Then she tore from his grip and pushed her way through the crowd and disappeared into the maze of stalls.

"Did anyone see anything?" Chicano said in a loud voice.

People stared at him. No one spoke. Another vulture landed on the overpass.

"You have to do something," I said.

Chicano looked at me. "Me?"

"There's no one else. This is why you stayed, no?"

"I'm sorry, *hijín*, but this one's for the authorities."

"We don't have any," Mosca said.

"Take them down, Chicano. Come on," I said.

"No, not me." He shook his head and took a couple of steps back, away from the bridge.

"Don't be like that, Chicano." The people around us heard me say it. Everyone stared at him, waiting. I could see the pleading in their eyes. We all needed someone to take charge, to do something.

"I suppose," he said. "But it's not my place. Where are the fucking authorities?"

"Sleeping," Mosca said. Then he turned to me. "Maybe you and I can take them down, no Boli?"

"They're someone's relatives. Maybe someone's father, someone's son." I kept thinking of my parents. The whole run to the bridge I had been thinking of them, praying it wasn't them hanging like *piñatas*. Now I was relieved it wasn't them, but I also felt guilty. No matter who it was, it was always someone's parents, someone's children. And the way they were hanging, with their legs open, it was gross. Disgraceful. It was the same with Rocío's dead naked body, and even with *el profe*. It wasn't just murder, it was so much more. It was grotesque, humiliating. It angered me more than death.

"Go," I cried and pushed Chicano. "Take them down. You have to. No one else is going to do it."

He looked at me. He looked over the crowd. Another vulture floated past and landed near the middle of the bridge, closer to the bodies.

Finally Chicano nodded. He took a deep breath and adjusted the eyeholes of his mask. The crowd parted and he marched up the steps. The vultures on our side of the overpass skipped away and then took flight only to land on the other side of the bridge. On the highway, cars and semi-trucks zoomed by, barely slowing down to look.

Chicano reached the first person. He knelt, grabbed the rope and with his giant strong arms, pulled him up, hand over hand like a sailor. He stood, still holding the rope, and raised the body over the rail. It was a struggle. Then he took the dead man in his arms and laid him gently on the ground.

Everyone on both sides of the bridge kept silent. It was just cars passing and an occasional dog barking somewhere. Chicano did the same with the other body. He pulled the rope and then grabbed the body and knelt as he laid it next to the other one. When he stood, everyone at the bottom of the bridge cheered.

I nudged Mosca. The people moved forward and climbed the steps. It was as if they had been released from a spell. Someone yelled that they needed to get an undertaker for the bodies. A group of workmen broke through the crowd. "We'll take them to

Monroy's," one of them said. They picked up the dead men and carried them away.

A woman ran up to Chicano and hugged him. Men shuffled and lined up to shake his hand. He looked at me and smiled.

"See?" I grabbed his arm. Mosca and Junior joined us and we walked across the bridge. Everyone was reaching out for Chicano, thanking him and blessing him for what he had done. He held his head up high like he'd just won a match against Santo or something.

"You're a hero," I said.

"For real!" Mosca was ecstatic.

We made our way down the steps. Then I saw Pepino. He was with Kiko and Chato. They stood alone at the end of the crowd, looking straight at us. I thought they were after Mosca because of the devil's fire. Then I realized they weren't looking at us. They were staring at Chicano.

Pepino said something to Kiko who ran off along the side of the highway and disappeared between the food stalls. When it was clear to the both of us that we had seen each other, Pepino tapped Chato on the shoulder. They turned and walked behind a *vulcanizaroda* where two men were working to patch up a flat tire.

20.

Gaby slammed her hand against the table.

"It's just for a week," I said. "Please."

"No." She even refused to make eye contact with Chicano. "He can't stay, and that's final."

"You're not the boss of the house. When Papá was here, I was allowed to have friends over."

Jesusa said, "It's true, *señorita* Gaby." We were eating supper at the dining room table. Jesusa was going around serving the reheated tamales our neighbor Viviana had given us over a month ago when my parents had first failed to return from Toluca. It seemed so long ago, like time had sprinted forward and then stopped completely.

"And who's talking to you, *metiche*?"

"He's staying," I said.

"No, he's not. We know nothing about him."

"We do." I pushed my plate away. "He's a *luchador*. He helped take the people down from the bridge. He's a hero."

Gaby sighed. "*Ay*, Liberio. Stop it."

"But it's true."

"And how do you know he's not the one who killed Rocío Morales?"

Chicano coughed.

"Because he's not. He wasn't even here when that happened. God, Gaby, you can be such a jerk."

Abuela glanced across the table at Chicano. "He can stay," she said suddenly with so much authority, everyone froze.

Gaby's jaw dropped. "¿Perdón?"

"I said he can stay. It's the Christian thing to do. It's not as if he's moving in forever." She smiled at us. Then she turned to Chicano. "Are you?"

"No, señora. Just a week, I think. I have an event in Monterrey coming up in two weeks."

Abuela leaned back on her chair and placed her hands on the table. "So it's settled."

"Abuela," Gaby cried. "We can't afford to feed every stray Liberio drags into the house."

"Por Dios, niña, don't be rude. Your parents raised you better than that. The luchador can stay so long as he doesn't drink."

"No." Chicano coughed. "That won't be a problem. I only hit a rough patch every so often. I'm good now."

Abuela turned to Gaby. "You see?"

"What's this about the drinking? What is going on here?"

"Nothing," I said. "He's a good guy, Gaby. Really."

"We could use a man in the house," Abuela added. "He can help fix things, no?"

Chicano nodded.

"Dios mio. What is the matter with you people?" Gaby said. "Don't you see what's happening?"

"Please, you don't need to act so self-important," Abuela said.

"Válgame," Gaby cried. "When did you get back from Veracruz?"

"Leave her alone," I said.

"And another thing," Abuela said. "It would be decent of you if you brought the young man you are dating by the house so he can introduce himself. Just because your parents are absent does not mean you can go running around town like a common tramp."

"Oh, I'm sure you'd like that," Gaby said. "The way you've all been acting lately, I'm afraid you'll crucify the poor man."

Chicano tugged at the side of his mask. "There's a lot of crucifying going on in this town."

"We're going to find out what happened to Papá and Mamá," I said.

Gaby rolled her eyes and pushed her chair out. "Please. Don't do us any favors."

"It's no trouble," Chicano said. "But like I told Liberio, it's not—"

"*Por favor.*" Gaby stood and held up the palm of her hand to stop him. "Spare me. I can see right through you and your ridiculous outfit." Then she marched out of the dining room.

Abuela reached across the table and laid a dainty hand over Chicano's giant one. "I heard about that business on the bridge. Welcome to the house, *mijo*. You can stay in Liberio's room. And please, take a shower."

That night I lay awake in the dark listening to Chicano snore. Jesusa had prepared him a comfortable space in the corner of my bedroom with cushions from the couch and a few extra blankets. He slept with his mask on and his mouth wide open. I could see the outline of his shoulder, his chest and stomach faint and colorless rising and falling in rhythm with his breathing. He snored deep and long like a truck climbing a steep hill.

When I was nine, my father took me with him on a business trip to Mexico City. It was just the two of us on a four-day weekend. I went with him to visit distributors in different parts of the city. We purchased the big industrial mixers for the *panadería*. He also bought the computer we still use.

When he finished with his business, he took me to the Museum of Anthropology. The history of Mexico, as it was laid out in the museum, was like a long tale of overcoming adversity. From the cavemen hunting giant mammoths to the Aztecs fighting the Spanish during the conquest and then fighting the Spanish for independence and then the North Americans and the French—it was as if we always had to fight someone. Mexico always fought for freedom. All through school we learned the stories of Miguel Hidalgo, Benito Juárez and Emiliano Zapata, but seeing it all at once, one war after the other, it all fit into a pattern. We were tough. We were proud.

I was in awe of the statue of Tlaloc, the Aztec God of water and rain that stood at the entrance of the museum. He looked unstoppable. He was the original *luchador*—strong, imposing. Yet there was a quiet mystery to his features. It was amazing to think this was all Mexico.

At the Castillo de Chapultepec, I looked down the cliff where the Niños Héroes jumped to their deaths, their bodies wrapped in the Mexican flag after the North Americans had taken the city and were making their way up the hill. Those six teenagers were the bravest Mexicans in history. I shivered at the thought that some of those cadets had been as young as me. I stood on the same ground and looked down over the city, wondering if I would have had the guts to do it.

We stayed at a small hotel in Insurgentes Sur. I don't know if it was the city—or Tlaloc and the Niños Héroes—but the last night we were there, I couldn't sleep. I lay awake and listened to my father's strong steady snoring. He was in a deep sleep. It was as if his snoring was telling me everything was going to be okay. Tlaloc was Mexican. He was ours. He was there to protect us. There was nothing to be afraid of in the great city that smelled of iron.

Now, in my own bedroom, with all the horrible things that had been going on around town, I felt a soft easiness as I listened to Chicano snore. I thought of Tlaloc and how, in the end, the good guys win. The Aztecs did not lose to the Spanish. It took them three hundred years to defeat them. All those years, there was resistance. It was the same with the Niños Héroes. They did not die in vain. Mexico regained its sovereignty. Zapata was assassinated, but the Revolution triumphed and the large haciendas were broken up. I knew all this trickled down to us. We had to fight whatever obstacle arose against us. We had to fight for justice, just like Zapata and everyone else.

I closed my eyes and felt safe in a way I hadn't felt since before we discovered *el profe's* head. I knew we could win this war. Chicano was more like Santo than he realized. Together we would fight whoever was destroying the town. And I knew, like all the great heroes of Mexican history, we would win. We were predestined to do this. When Chicano took down those men from the overpass, I got a glimpse of what we were meant to do. Tlaloc and the Niños Héroes and Zapata were with us. I fell asleep with a smile that night. I knew everything would work out.

When I woke up the next morning, Chicano was gone.

Later, when Mosca and I walked out of school, we found him waiting for us across the street from the *secundaria*. He was in the shade, leaning against the wall, surrounded by a handful of kids and the street vendors and parents.

"I thought you'd left," I said.

He ruffled my hair and smiled. "I went for a run. I'm an athlete."

"Really?"

Mosca smacked me on the chest with the back of his hand. "He has to stay in shape, right Chicano?"

"That's right. If we're going to do this thing, we have to be sharp." Then he raised his gaze past us to where Ximena and Regina were walking out the school gate. "Maybe we should make sure those two *pollitos* get home safely."

I could see his eyes behind the mask, black and round, and focused on Ximena.

"*Muy buenas tardes*," he said when the girls crossed the street. Ximena looked away.

Regina glanced at Chicano and back at me. "What do you want?"

"Nothing," I said. "We were just getting ready to go."

Chicano's attention was all over Ximena. Regina rolled her eyes. They walked away. Mosca and I followed.

"I found Gaby," I said. I liked Regina. She had always been so nice. I didn't want her angry at me. It didn't feel right. "Everything's fine."

She slowed so Mosca and me could walk with her. Chicano caught up with Ximena who was walking ahead toward the plaza, her books pressed against her chest.

"And nothing on your parents?" Regina said quietly.

I shook my head. "I haven't given up hope, but I guess I'm prepared for whatever God gives us."

"You sound like Father Gregorio."

"It's not that. Chicano's going to help me find out what happened. Did you hear about the men hanging from the overpass?"

She nodded and walked quickly.

I grabbed her arm and pulled her back. "What's the matter?"

She shook her head.

"Chicano took them down. Pretty heroic, no?"

"And brave," Mosca added.

"I just don't want you to get hurt," she said.

"Why would we get hurt? How?" I knew she might know something because she hung out with Ximena and Joaquín, but she just kept walking, looking ahead to where the road narrowed and the asphalt turned to cobblestone.

We caught up with Chicano and Ximena. Zopilote's green Golf was parked in front of Taquería Los Perdidos. Mosca and I looked at each other. We slowed down, but Chicano kept in step beside Ximena as if there was nothing to fear.

"Don't be that way, *corazón*," Chicano said, turning his head to the side so Ximena could hear him. "I can take you places. Next week I'm off to Monterrey. You could come. Have you ever been there? Those *regiomontanos* really know how to party. You'd love it. *Ándale*, you and me in Monterrey. Unforgettable."

Regina looked down and pressed her schoolbooks tightly against her chest like she was trying to protect them. "What's with your pet wrestler?"

"Nothing." I didn't see what Chicano was after or that any of it had to do with our investigation, although Ximena was our link to Joaquín. "So why do you guys hang out with Joaquín and his friends?" I asked.

Regina raised her chin. "You jealous or what?"

"I've heard the rumors."

"*Estás loco.*" Her tone was cold, short. "To you anyone who makes more money than your parents is a criminal." Then she stopped and covered her mouth. "I'm sorry. I didn't mean that."

"Whatever. I'm going to find out what happened to them. And if someone did something to them, they're going to be sorry. Chicano and I are going to fix this place. Whoever is doing all this is going to regret ever setting foot in Izayoc."

"*Uy*, look at you. How *macho*, no?"

"Don't you want things back the way they were before? Aren't you afraid of ending up like Rocío Morales?"

"I'm not afraid of anything."

Mosca laughed. "You're the only one in town then."

We stopped across from Los Perdidos. Ximena moved to cross the street to the *taquería*, but Chicano grabbed her arm and pulled her to his side. "What's wrong, do I make you nervous?"

Ximena stared at him for a moment. Then she looked at her arm where Chicano was holding it. And as if by magical powers, without a word, Chicano released her.

Zopilote was checking us out from across the street. He wore white long pointy boots, jeans, a polo shirt and a colorful jacket that reminded me of an old Michael Jackson video. When our eyes met, he pulled back the side of the jacket. Tucked into his belt was a chrome-plated automatic pistol.

We all saw it.

"It's not bullets I fear," Chicano said in a tone that was so calm and confident, my own fear vanished. His eyes were locked on Ximena. "It's the pain you inflict in my heart that's killing me."

Ximena's eyes grew wide for an instant, and she smiled. I was thrilled and hurt at the same time.

"Why do you hang out with those *pendejos*? They're nobodies." Chicano took her arm again.

Ximena tossed her head to the side, her long mane of hair flying past Chicano's face. She said, "At least they don't hide behind a mask."

Chicano laughed. "I'm not hiding. I'm just waiting for the right woman to come along so I can reveal myself. You know, you could be her, *corazón*. You never know."

Ximena smirked. "No. I do know."

"He's working real hard, no?" Regina said.

"He's trying to piss off her boyfriend." I said it more to convince myself because I didn't like it either.

"You better be careful, Liberio." Regina's face twisted. "They have money, and yes, they have guns."

"What about Gaby's boyfriend?" I said.

"I don't know."

We followed Ximena across the street, but Mosca stayed behind talking to an old lady who was a friend of his aunt.

Zopilote stepped away from his car and blocked the entrance of the *taquería*. "El Chicano Estrada," he said, and then looked at me. "I see you got yourself a bodyguard, eh Boli?"

"What's with you, *pinche* Zopilote?" I said.

"I don't think I like him flirting with Joaquín's girl."

"So you're *her* bodyguard?" I asked.

"I'm everything, so don't get smart with me. I've acquired a short temper. You don't want to see me when I'm angry."

"Yeah?" I said. "Was it that temper that gave you a black eye last week?"

Zopilote laughed. "You're one to talk. Don't tell me you ran into a wall." He brought his hand down, close to his belt where he had the gun.

A car honked. Mosca crossed the street and waved at the car. An old lady shoved past us and went inside the *taquería*. Then Zopilote moved aside to allow the girls to pass. Ximena looked at Chicano, then at me. She raised her head and walked past Zopilote and went inside.

"Nice place," Chicano stepped forward to follow Ximena, but Zopilote put his hand on his chest and stopped him.

Chicano looked down at the hand. "I'll count to three, *cabrón.*"

Zopilote dropped his hand and glanced at Regina. "You going inside or what?"

Regina glanced around as if she wasn't sure what to do. Then, without a word, she walked past Zopilote and into the restaurant.

"They didn't even say goodbye," Chicano said.

"That's how these bitches are." Zopilote turned and followed them into the restaurant.

"*Pinche* Chicano." Mosca laughed. "You didn't even have to count."

Chicano tapped the side of his head with his index finger. "Strength is an illusion."

21.

Chicano went into the municipal building to see Captain Pineda while Mosca and I waited in the plaza. Except for a couple of vendors who had set up in the arcade and the taxi drivers on the opposite side by the church, there was no one around, just a couple of *niños pobres* sprawled on the floor of the gazebo, sleeping.

We sat on one of the iron benches under a patch of shade and watched the workers coming in and out of the church. They moved quickly, carrying long wood planks and metal bars for scaffolding, wheelbarrows, shovels.

"Check it out," Mosca nodded.

It was Kiko. He was standing by the taxis, looking up and down the street like he'd lost something. Then he walked the long way around the side of the plaza to where we sat.

"What are you two up to with that wrestler?" he asked.

I looked around. "I don't see a wrestler, do you?"

Mosca shook his head. "Where's Pepino?"

Kiko was jittery. His wide, red eyes moved quickly from side to side. "With Chato. They had errands."

"Everyone's real busy these days," Mosca said.

"*No chingues.*" Kiko wiped his nose with the back of his hand and hacked. "Look, you wanna go to the side of the church and shoot a game of marbles?"

"What do you have to lose?"

"Don't be a *pendejo*, Mosca. Let's go to the church and play. Come on."

Kiko led the way, his head turning at all angles, looking everywhere. When we reached the side of the church, he drew a wobbly circle in the dirt with the heel of his boot.

"Look." He shot a marble. "You guys need to be careful."

I laughed. "Not if you keep shooting like that." His marble had landed on the side of the circle.

"That's not what I'm talking about," Kiko said. "It's the wrestler."

"Chicano?"

"He's doing the wrong thing. He's gonna get in trouble. If you two *pendejos* keep hanging around him, they'll mark you too."

"What do you mean, mark?"

Mosca laughed. "Like with a magic marker?"

"Listen to me. That thing the *luchador* did, taking down the bodies from the overpass, it pissed the fuck out of them."

"Out of who?" I said.

Kiko lowered his head and whispered. "You know who."

"Joaquín?"

Kiko grinned. "He's nobody."

"Then who?"

"Duende."

"Who the fuck's Duende?" Mosca looked at me. We moved closer to Kiko, but he stepped away from us.

"Play marbles." He kneeled and took a shot even though there were no other marbles in the circle. "They're always watching."

"Who's this Duende, *güey*?" I asked.

Kiko stared past the wall to the municipal building. From where we stood, we could only see the second floor. The windows were open, probably Pineda's office. "The boss. *El jefe de plaza*," he said. "All the new guys are with him. They're his people."

"What about you?" I asked.

He swooped the marble from the ground and held his hand up for me to take it. "You win."

Kiko's eyes were shiny, ugly, scared. He walked quickly away to the front of the church where the workers had gathered around a well-dressed man and Father Gregorio. When Kiko saw them, he turned and headed in the opposite direction toward the municipal building. Then he disappeared around the corner.

Father Gregorio and the well-dressed man looked at us. They both smiled. Then they looked at the street where Kiko had gone and back at the workers.

Mosca and I walked out of the churchyard, but just as we reached the steps, Father Gregorio called my name.

Mosca ran to the plaza. I walked back and met Father Gregorio. The workers and the well-dressed man had gone inside. He placed his hand on my shoulder. "How do you like it? It seems business is good for everyone. Ramiro Contreras is building a hotel, and Don Ignacio is expanding his store."

"Some kind of progress, no?"

"So it seems." He didn't smile. "It's the new highway. One day we might even get a Wal-Mart."

Father Gregorio led me to the steps, away from the church, then he dropped to one knee so his eyes were level with mine. "Liberio. I have some news from Father Elíseo in Huizachal. Your parents drove a blue Jetta, is that correct?"

"What did he say?"

"One of his parishioners told him he saw a car fall into Devil's Ravine last month."

"But that's right there. How come Pineda—"

"Never mind him. That's precisely why your father went to seek help in Toluca."

"So you think my parents are down there? Dead?"

"I don't know."

"Maybe we can get Pineda to—"

"Listen to me, *hijo*. Forget Pineda. He's a sloth and a good-for-nothing. If something nefarious is going on, Pineda's probably in someone's pocket already. I don't trust him, and neither did your father. We need to keep quiet about this until we find evidence of some kind. Then we can go to the proper authorities. So. Not a word to anyone. Is that clear?"

I ran across the street and met Mosca and Chicano outside the municipal building. The street kids who had been sleeping in the gazebo and the children of the vendors gathered near Chicano, but no one approached him. They just stared as if he were a saint and whispered among themselves.

"Did you find anything?" I asked.

Chicano took a deep breath and raised his hands as if he were about to preach a sermon. "I found out your Captain Pineda is a first-class *pendejo*. The men under him are worse. The whole department is useless. How this town manages to exist is beyond me."

Mosca laughed. "Please, Chicano, tell us something we don't know."

He threw his cape over his shoulder and marched on, his masked head held high.

We crossed the plaza and walked on Calle Lealtad. Once we were out of sight of the church and the plaza, Mosca nudged me. "So what did the priest want?"

"Nothing." It wasn't that I didn't trust Mosca, but I'd given my word to Father Gregorio.

"You and him seem to have a lot to talk about lately," Mosca said.

"He's helping me find out about my parents."

Chicano stopped walking. "And?"

"And what?"

"What else?" He glared down at us, his hands on his waist like

Superman. "Mosca told me what the kid said while I was wasting my time with Porky up there. I'm in this now. My own hide's at stake here, so spill it, *hijín*. No secrets. This is too dangerous."

I kicked the ground and told them what Father Gregorio had said.

"For real?" Mosca said. "You think it's really them?"

"I don't know." I shrugged. "I hope not. That would mean they're dead for sure."

Mosca slapped me on the back. "We should go see."

"I don't like it." Chicano rubbed his chin. "I mean, Devil's Ravine? This is starting to sound like a Santo movie."

"It's no big deal," I said. "Mosca and I've been down there a million times. It's after the big curve—"

"Devil's Curve," Mosca said.

"There's nothing down there, just forest."

Chicano looked at the sky. "It's going to be getting dark soon. Let's sleep on it. We'll go tomorrow after school."

"We have at least two hours," I said. "We can make it."

"No," Chicano said. "I don't want to get caught down there in the dark. Besides, you have homework. I don't want your sister ragging on me about keeping you away from your schoolwork."

"But Chicano—"

"Listen to me. If your parents are really down there, they'll still be there tomorrow."

Mosca placed his hand on my shoulder. "Maybe he's right, Boli."

We heard the loud bass from a stereo. Zopilote's green Golf cruised slowly along Calle Lealtad toward the plaza. As it passed us, the tinted window on the driver's side went down real slow, blasting reggaetón all over the block. Zopilote wore dark shades. He raised his right hand just over the open window and pointed his silver pistol at us. He pulled it back three times in slow motion as if he were shooting at us, his ugly mouth forming little O's with every kick of the weapon.

22.

Later that evening, Chicano and I sat at the kitchen table watching Jesusa cook dinner. I was still stunned about Zopilote's display, but Chicano seemed fine. He sat back on his chair teasing Jesusa about the work she did at the house.

"You don't know work if you haven't lived in the Sierra," she said. "That's work. Hard work, *pues*."

Chicano laughed. "You make it sound as if the Indians are the only ones who work."

"What would you know about work? Your hands are soft. Your muscles," she said, and smacked his back with a wooden spoon, "are built from exercise, not from working the *milpa* and carrying lumber and water."

She stirred the pot of stew. "Every morning before it was light, I had to walk down two mountains to fetch water in the creek."

"Leave it to the Mixtecos to build a village in a place without water." Chicano winked at me. "Who does that, Liberio?"

But what about Zopilote? Would he really kill us? What if

someone gave him the order or he lost his temper. Would he do it? Had he already killed someone? And what about Duende?

"Down and up the mountain three times in a single day," Jesusa went on. "I had to gather wood and make a fire and cook for my aunt and her father and cousins."

"How dramatic, *chaparrita*." Chicano rolled his eyes and tapped his fingertips against the table. "If you were as poor as you say you were, all you did was eat bugs. What's the big deal?"

"*No, pues.* I had to make the masa for the tortillas. And who do you think had to clean the house?"

"Wait." Chicano crossed his arms and leaned back on his chair. "You mean *jacal.*"

Jesusa ignored him and continued her monologue. "In season I had to go to the *milpa* and plant or harvest the corn. I took care of the goats, cooked dinner. Everything,"

"And now, nothing's changed, no?"

"What do you say? A lot has changed. But *el Indio* always works, *pues.* There is no way out. When you are born Indian, you are born condemned to a life of work and poverty. And if you're a woman, it's worse. That is the truth."

Chicano agreed. "Being born poor in this country *es de la chingada.*"

"You're not poor," I said.

"But I'm not rich."

"I would rather be poor and happy than rich and sad." It was something I'd heard my mother say a thousand times.

"That's easy for you to say because you've never been poor," Chicano said.

"Well, I'd rather be poor and have my parents back."

Chicano fell silent. Jesusa stopped chopping onions and chiles. She looked at me for a moment as if trying to find something in my eyes. Then she turned back to the stove and placed the diced onions and chiles in a pan that sizzled and popped with hot oil and infused the house with a sweet and peppery smell. She stirred it, lowered the heat and when the sound mellowed, she said, "There's nothing wrong with work. Money is not the friend of good people, *pues*."

"Please," Chicano said. "Tell me you wouldn't want to be rich."

"I don't waste my dreams on it."

Chicano laughed.

"It's true, *pues*." She waved the spoon at him. "And since I have worked in this house, life has been better. That is the truth."

"Yeah." Chicano kicked me under the table and smiled. "Taking care of this *mocoso*." He stood and signaled for me to follow him to the front patio. Chapo came to us, wagging his tail and sniffing at our legs. We didn't give him any attention, so he made a long circle around the patio and went back to his corner by the shed and lay down.

"Listen to me, Liberio. I'm going to duck out for a moment to chase a couple of leads I picked up from that joker Pineda."

"Can I go with you?"

"No. I have to do this alone. Besides, you have to finish your homework."

"Please, *Chicano*—"

"No."

"God, you're worse than Gaby."

"Liberio."

"But what if something happens?"

"I can take care of myself, *hijín*."

Chicano got cleaned up and walked out of the house smelling like my father's cologne. I followed him to the street. It was dark out. A couple strolled past on the sidewalk across the street. Chicano waited for them to get some distance. "Tomorrow after school meet me by the Pemex. We'll check out this business at Devil's Ravine."

"Where are you going now?"

"Don't worry about that. I just want to see a couple of *güeyes*. Ask some questions."

"Did Pineda give you names? Maybe I know them."

"Look, I told you I'm not a detective. I'm just feeling things out as I go."

"At what time will you be back?"

"What are you, my mother?"

I stared at him, trying to see his eyes behind the mask, but it was just darkness.

He stepped onto the street. "I'll be back when I'm back. That's it."

"Chicano," I said, my voice cracking. "Please…don't go to the *cantina*."

He smiled and tilted his head like Father Gregorio. "Don't worry about that. I gave my word to your grandmother."

Gaby didn't come home for dinner. After Jesusa served, Abuela gestured toward the empty setting. "*Niña*, why don't you sit and eat with us."

"No, I'm fine, *pues*," Jesusa said.

"Do not be shy, *niña*. We are family now."

Jesusa smiled and took Gaby's place.

"So you see," Abuela said. "On the evenings and weekends, bands play at the gazebo in the Plaza de Armas and at the Plaza de la Concordia. Everyone dresses up and comes out to greet each other. The whole town comes together like a family. And everywhere you go, you can hear someone playing a marimba."

I noticed Abuela was describing Veracruz differently. Before it was always about Dorian. It was as if we were eavesdropping on her conversation with someone unknown. Now, she talked to us about what Veracruz was like.

"You really like it there," I said.

"I have been away a very long time. I miss my family. I miss my youth."

"Did you ever go back to visit?" Jesusa said. "I go back to

Coyuca del Río, but never to my *pueblo* in the *sierra*. I don't miss it there. Besides, I have no one there that I care to see."

"Sometimes we leave behind a place and people we think we never want to see again. The last thing you expect is a nostalgia like this one to poison your heart the way it has done mine. When I was young, I detested Veracruz. I resented my father for his old-fashioned ways."

"I was so happy to leave my *pueblo*. I hated it there."

"You don't miss it at all?" I asked.

Jesusa stared at her plate of *albondigas* and rice for a long time. "There is nothing to miss, just work. Monte de Cocula is an ugly, cursed place."

Abuela touched Jesusa's hand. "*Niña*, the whole country is cursed. Life never turns out the way you think it will." She pushed her plate away and rested her hands on the table. "All your life you think you are going somewhere special, but in the end you discover no such place exists. There is no paradise."

"Is that what you and Abuelo were looking for when you came here?" I asked.

Abuela laughed. "No, *mijo*. We were running away. This is just where we ended up. Your grandfather was an idealist. I suppose when it's all said and done, I am one too. He believed that getting away from the city would solve our problems. We thought life in a *pueblo* would be free of the cheating and corruption of the city."

"And it wasn't?" I asked.

"When we first arrived in Izayoc, the people didn't want us. We were outsiders. It was so isolated. Eventually we worked ourselves into society, but it took a long time. To be honest with you, I would have been happy in Coyuca del Río or Toluca. Anywhere. But your grandfather had his dreams. To him, this was the perfect colonial town, with the cobblestone streets, the old church and all the old architecture and the cliffs. I think it was the *gringo* in him that made Izayoc so attractive. In his eyes, this place was Mexico. But the people?" She glanced at Jesusa. "They could be terribly vindictive, secretive. *Gente de pueblo.* We went through a lot. But we stayed and made it work."

"You make it sound just like Monte de Cocula, *señora.* No wonder the country is in such a mess."

"Life is never what you think it will be." Abuela's thin fingers traced the rim of her cup. "Would you mind so much making me another *café con leche, niña?*"

I couldn't sleep that night worrying about Chicano. And about Gaby too. I knew Chicano could take care of himself as long as he didn't get drunk. But I couldn't understand why Gaby was dating Francisco. I didn't understand that about girls. Like why Ximena was with Joaquín. Maybe she bought into his act, the guns and the money. Maybe that's all it took. Maybe that's why everyone wanted to be one of *them.*

If Ximena ever gave me a chance, I'd show her. If I were old enough, I'd marry her right away. I'd love her forever. I knew that deep down, behind those sad eyes and those quiet lips, was a misunderstood girl. No one else got that. She was sad because no one gave her the opportunity to be who she really was. Like in the story of the ugly duckling—only she wasn't ugly. Besides, I knew that despite her beauty, she had troubles. Regina told me Ximena's father was a drunk and that he beat her. In a way, that fueled my love for her. She needed to be saved. And I knew I could do that. But I also knew it was impossible. I desperately wished I were older, just a little, enough so I could do something about it.

And what was worse was that Ximena didn't know I understood her the way I did. If she'd only give me a chance, I would show her what it was like to be with someone who really respected her and loved her and took care of her. She would never have to suffer again. God, I could make her so happy. If she would only dump that Joaquín and give me a chance, we would be happy forever.

‡

Just past midnight Chapo barked. Then it was quiet again. A moment later the front door opened and closed. The steps were soft and careful. It was Gaby. I recognized her every move: getting a glass of water from the kitchen, going into the bathroom, then coming out, looking in on Abuela, checking the locks on the doors, and finally going into her room.

Hours later, Chapo barked again, then whimpered. The front door opened and closed. There were noises in the kitchen, fumbling for utensils, chair legs scraping the floor.

A short while later Chicano came into the room.

I sat up.

"You should be asleep." He arranged the blankets in his corner and lay down.

"What'd you find out?"

"Nothing, really."

"Tell me, please."

"What are you so damn happy about?" he said.

"I don't know. I guess I'm happy you came back."

"Why wouldn't I?"

I didn't answer. I was happy he hadn't gotten drunk. He had come back. And he was helping me.

"Look," he said. "I know you're worried about your parents, but I think you need to know something. I'm going to be straight with you, *hijín*. I don't think they're alive. I have no idea what happened to them, but you need to know there are bad people in this world. People don't disappear just like that without it ending in tragedy."

"What did you find out? Tell me!"

"It has nothing to do with your parents."

"It has to do with something, no?"

"It has to do with this town. It's infected like the rest of the fucking country. This shit's everywhere. There's no way to fix it."

"What are you talking about?"

He waved and turned on his side. "Everyone's giving you hope, telling you there's a chance, that everything's going to be okay. It's all lies. We are a country built on lies. Listen, forget the illusion that the world is a good place. It's not."

"I don't believe it," I said. "There's good out there. I know there is. My father was a good man. And Lucio and Father Gregorio. And you too. You just don't know it."

"Keep thinking that way. One day your heart will break into a million pieces. That will open your eyes real wide."

"My heart's already broken. I lost my parents, remember?" My lip quivered. I couldn't hold back the anger. I turned away so Chicano wouldn't see my tears. I didn't want to give him the satisfaction.

"Gimme a break, *hijín*. It's not as if you're the only one who suffers in this world. You know nothing of life."

"I know enough," I yelled. "I know you didn't want to help me, but you stayed and now you're helping me. I know you took down those poor people from the bridge. That makes you a good guy. It makes you the best and bravest person in Izayoc."

"Do me a favor—don't put me on a pedestal." Then he whispered, "I'm just a guy, okay?"

"You're more than that, Chicano. You have to give yourself credit for the good you're doing here."

"And what if we don't find your parents?"

As much as I had thought of that, of finding them hanging from a bridge or stuffed into the trunk of my father's car or chopped into pieces, it was that there wasn't anything I could do that ripped at my gut. It was the helplessness. My voice broke. "Even if we never find them, at least I'll be able to say we tried."

He was quiet for a long time. Then he turned on his back and set his hands behind his head and stared at the ceiling. I did the same.

"I lost my mother when I was eight," he said. "My father was a drunk. I grew up in the streets of Tepito, in the city. By the time

I was your age, I was a pretty good pickpocket. I stole cars, held up people riding in taxis. I raped a woman when I was seventeen. I did drugs, sniffed glue. I've injected myself with just about every substance, legal and illegal. I lived in the sewer and did a year in prison. I was a lost cause until I walked into the Nuevo Jordan Gym.

"There was an old man there who offered to train me. He charged people a few pesos here and there for his boxing advice, but with me, he did it for free."

"To become a boxer?"

"Yes. He taught me to box. But he also taught me about myself. He taught me to dream and not to give up on those dreams. He taught me that I could be someone better. I didn't have to live in the streets like trash. He became like a father to me."

"How old were you?"

"Nineteen, twenty."

"But how did you become a *luchador?*"

He smiled. "People said I had what it took, that if I stayed with it, I'd have a chance to try out for the Olympics."

"As a boxer, for real?"

"Yeah." He turned on his side to face me. "Well, the Olympics don't really pay. So I took my trainer's advice and went pro instead. In a few months, we were doing pretty well, making a little cash here and there. I worked my ass off, won some fights.

"Then one day I'm on a ticket at the Arena Coliseo against Willy Mendoza, a Puerto Rican with a real reputation." He lay on his back again and stared at the ceiling. "It wasn't a title fight, but it was big. From there, I could climb up to the title. But my trainer, the old man, he told me to take a dive. Lose the fight."

Chicano fell quiet for a long while. He moved his hands in the air and then pulled the blanket up to his neck. "It was all about money, *hijín.* That's what everything's about."

"So you did it?"

He didn't answer.

"Chicano?"

"I'm not proud."

He touched the trim around the side of his mask and stared up at the poster of Santo I had on the wall. I thought of my father lecturing me about the importance of integrity. To be a person of one's word was the most important thing. He'd said that money would always come and go, but if people knew they couldn't trust you, you had nothing. He'd said that to be someone in this world you had to have integrity.

I looked at Chicano lying quietly on the floor. He probably still felt broken about what he did then. But I knew he would regain his pride when we found my parents, when we finally ran Joaquín and his pals out of town. "But then you became a wrestler, no?"

"Some of the guys at the gym got me into it. *La lucha's* just as rigged as boxing, but at least everyone knows it. The fraud is out in the open, plain as day. And sometimes the pay's better."

"But things could've been worse," I said. "You could've died or gone to jail again."

He laughed softly. "You don't get it, *hijo*. It's about reality. Everything out there is rotten. Everything. The sooner you admit it to yourself, the sooner you can get on with the rest of your life. Life is shit."

No. He was wrong. He had given up hope, but not me. Even if we never found my parents, I was not going to change. I was not going to give up on life. I bit my lip. I didn't want to hear my own voice. I didn't want to cry. I turned on my side and stared at the calendar and the little empty squares cut into triangles by diagonal lines. Every one of them empty of my parents.

"Liberio?" His voice was dry and low.

"Lemme alone."

"Listen," he said. "I'm sorry. Don't listen to me. I'm just a bitter old has-been. I don't know what I'm talking about. I never even made it past third grade. Your life doesn't have to be like mine."

I closed my eyes and prayed to God that something good would happen tomorrow, that we'd find my parents and that they'd be alive, that it had all been a misunderstanding, and that Chicano would stay and live with us forever.

23.

Devil's Ravine was a steep fall on the side of the mountain below what we called Devil's Curve, a sharp and long turn on the old highway into town from the east. There was nothing sinister about the place. It was just like any other ravine or mountainside around the valley, but since the old highway was really just a narrow two-lane road, and there was only a small metal guardrail at the edge of Devil's Curve, a crash there meant certain death. We had all heard stories of accidents, but I had never met anyone, ever, who knew someone who had actually died in a crash there.

Chicano, Mosca and I walked up the narrow path between the road and the edge of the mountain. Chicano had finally ditched his tights and cape. He now wore a pair of my father's pants and a shirt, which were way too small for him. We passed a few peasant women carrying plastic mesh bags loaded with goods, their barefoot children trailing behind, staring at Chicano's red mask. Then we passed five men heading into town with loads of firewood on their backs. No one said anything. They stared at the ground and kept clear of Chapo even though I had him on a short leash.

Every few minutes a car or truck would speed down the hill towards town. The ones leaving town climbed slowly up the hill in low gear. It made me wonder because Father Gregorio had said my parents had never made it to Toluca. The real danger of Devil's Curve was if you were driving down the hill on your way into town and came to the curves, one after another, and ended with the biggest curve of all: Devil's Curve. After that the highway flattened out as it came to the Pemex station. There was no way to speed uphill. Sometimes big trucks climbed so slow, peasants riding donkeys could pass them.

When we reached Devil's Curve, we paused to catch our breath. Mosca sat on the metal rail and wiped the sweat from his brow. I looked out at the ravine. It was wooded and green from the rain. Past the ravine and the next low hill, I could make out the church bell tower and the top of the municipal building and the rest of Izayoc in the distance.

"I don't get it," Mosca said. "Why didn't your parents take the new highway?"

I had been wondering the same thing. Chapo sniffed at trash on the side of the road. Chicano leaned forward and studied the asphalt from the bottom to the top of the curve and back. "It's an old rail," he said. "They didn't go down around here, that's for sure."

I glanced at the top of the curve where there was no rail. "What about up there?"

We walked to the start of the curve. Chicano knelt on the narrow shoulder and ran his hand over the loose gravel. He looked just like a real detective, like Santo in one of the movies.

He stood and dusted his hands on the sides of his pants. "I don't see any skid marks."

"Maybe it was down there," Mosca pointed in the opposite direction, past the rail.

Chicano shook his head. "I've been looking. This would be the place." He pointed up the road. "If they came down this way, this is where you would begin to skid. That's why they put the rail down there and not here."

Mosca said, "Unless you were distracted or you fell asleep, no?"

"I guess." Chicano looked down the curve and then up where the road disappeared into another curve. "Come on."

We followed him a few feet up to the next curve.

"No marks," I said.

"Nothing." Chicano shook his head. "No skid marks, broken branches."

"It's true." Mosca walked down to where I was. "Last year I came with Junior after a truck went down. You could see all the trees broken. It was as if a bulldozer had torn through."

"So what do we do?" I asked, but Chicano had walked further up. He was about eighty feet ahead of us at the very top of the curve.

Mosca and I walked to the edge of the ravine and looked down. It was all green treetops. It got darker further down, where the trees were taller. I glanced at Chicano. He was starting to come our way. Then he stopped. He turned and looked back up the hill. Then he turned and waved at us. "Go!"

Mosca and I looked at each other.

"Jump!" Chicano yelled. Then he took two quick steps and jumped into the ravine. A second later, a black double cab pickup appeared speeding around the curve. It rode on the shoulder, tires screeching. Chicano was in midair when we heard the popping like a string of fireworks.

Mosca's face turned white. He ran. I blinked, and he was gone. The pickup was coming head on, fast. I jumped. Below me, the blue of Mosca's jacket rolled down the mountain like a giant marble.

Tack, tack tack, tack. I hit the ground and rolled down the cliff. The popping was softer. Then it was gone. Silence. Twigs and bushes slapped and scraped against me. Every time I tried to regain my balance, gravity pushed me. I rolled until I hit a tree. Pain shot up the side of my leg.

I lay on my side for a minute. The ravine was dead quiet. I shook my head and looked around. Mosca was standing further down the ravine, waving at me.

Above it was just trees and bushes and small bits of white sky. My thigh was throbbing. I couldn't feel a bump, just pain. I moved my toes, my foot.

Mosca climbed toward me. "You okay?"

"Where's Chicano?"

"Are you hurt?"

"My leg."

He helped me up. The ground was at a steep incline. I leaned against the tree until I regained my balance.

"Good?" Mosca's face was scratched up, eyes quivering with fear.

I nodded. "You?"

"The fuck was that?"

A twig snapped. We jumped and looked back. Chapo. He trotted toward us. Mosca grabbed the leash and petted his head. I raised my shirt and looked at my side. No scratches, just pain. I leaned my weight on my injured leg. Pain traveled up my calf and across my hip.

I took Chapo's leash from Mosca.

He pointed to the side. "He must have gone down there, no?"

I looked up the mountain. "Those *hijos de la chingada* shot at us."

Mosca laughed. "They fucking tried to kill us, no?" His laughter morphed into uncontrollable sobs. "They tried to kill us, Boli. They shot to kill us."

"Take it easy."

"It was fucking Zopilote. It had to be." His eyes were big and round. He was on the verge of hysterics.

I put my hands on his shoulders and shook him. "Come on, Mosca. We're okay."

"You think he'll come after us? You think—"

"There's no place for them to pull over up there. Keep it together. We have to find Chicano." His face was pale, his eyes cutting through me like I wasn't there. "We're gonna be okay." I shook him again. He blinked and our eyes locked for a moment. Then he nodded and we started down the mountain.

I pulled Chapo's leash. Mosca followed. We had to be near the bottom of the ravine. I could hear the creek. There was no path, so we zigzagged, walking sideways, holding onto trees and saplings for safety. As we descended it got darker, colder, quiet.

We'd advanced only a few dozen feet when I saw the red of Chicano's mask. He was below us, climbing up.

I called to him.

He stopped climbing and waved to us. "You all right?"

I gave him thumbs up.

We continued, zigzagging and slipping down the steep mountain.

"Someone doesn't like us," he said when we reached him. His pants and shirt were torn, muddy.

"Did you roll all the way down?" I said.

He nodded. "To the bottom."

"What are we gonna do?" Mosca was shaking. "They tried to kill us."

I put my arm around his shoulder. "Relax, *güey*. We're okay."

Chicano leaned forward and petted Chapo. Then he placed a hand on our shoulders. "We're here now, so let's do what we came here to do, no?"

We started single file along the muddy path that ran alongside the creek, a tributary of the Lágrimas River. The bottom of the ravine was lush with tall trees and huge plants. The light was soft and misty. The whole scene had an eerie feel, like an enchanted forest or something from a horror movie. The creek stank a little like a sewer. In parts where the creek swelled, we had to manage by jumping on rocks until we found the path again.

After about fifteen minutes, Mosca stopped. "This is fucked up. We have to do something."

"Look, we were lucky," Chicano said. "It would have been worse if they'd actually killed us."

"It's not a joke!" he yelled. "They shot at us. With guns!"

"Come on," Chicano said. "Take it easy, Mosca."

"They might be waiting for us at the end of the ravine."

Chicano gestured for us to calm down. "We'll be okay. But we can't just stay here, so let's keep going." He took the lead. Mosca shook his head. He trailed behind.

"Maybe they don't want us to find what's down here," I said.

"Look!" Chicano pointed. It was a car wreck.

I ran, my heart pounding against my ribs. It was a mangled mass of metal. But it wasn't a Jetta. It was an old car, a pile of rusted steel. It had been stripped of anything that could be removed and carried away, even the engine. All that was left was the thick metal frame and rusted body panels. Weeds grew through the floor and the engine bay.

Chicano placed his hand on the side of the frame and leaned against it. "It's been here a long time." He looked up and down the creek. "We must be just past Devil's Curve."

"Now what?" Mosca said.

Chicano walked around the wreck. "Where does the creek lead?"

"It goes into town," I said.

"That's what we'll do." Chicano pointed up to the highway. "Who knows what's waiting for us up there."

We started again. Chapo took the lead and trotted ahead of us, his nose low to the ground. As we got closer to town, the stink of the water became more intense. Trash began to appear along the trail: plastic bags, crushed Styrofoam cups, bottles, cans.

Chapo stopped and looked ahead, his head up. He growled low and steady. I grabbed his collar. "What is it?"

The old dog stepped back and growled. The hair between his

shoulders spiked up. He looked at me. He let out a short yelp and pulled forward.

A twig snapped. Chapo barked and jerked hard.

"Let him go." Chicano said.

"Really?"

"Yes."

I released him. He pounced ahead and sped along the trail, disappearing into the foliage. Silence.

We waited, then we looked at each other. Chicano took the lead. Mosca and I followed. We came to a small curve where the creek became wider. We stepped on rocks in the water, our arms extended at our sides to keep our balance. It was a long stretch. In the distance we could see light where the forest thinned before the creek entered a large culvert under the street.

Chapo was nowhere in sight. We could hear trucks cruising on the highway in the distance. When we caught the trail again, Chicano stopped and crossed himself.

I ran to him. "What is it?"

He pointed to the ground. A foot. A single severed bare foot about the same size as mine. It was swollen and pale. The white of the bone was visible at the end where millions of flies and ants were feasting on the raw flesh.

"What the—?" Mosca covered his mouth and turned away.

Chicano shook his head and walked ahead slowly. Then he stopped again. Another foot and an arm lay on the side of the path. The earth and plants were splattered with blood.

"What the fuck is going on?" Mosca was shaking, his hand over his mouth, his eyes bouncing all over place.

It stank of rot, of sewer. I held my breath. Then I called, "Chapo!"

Chicano pulled my arm. "Quiet," he whispered. He looked at Mosca and placed a finger over his lips.

Mosca nodded.

We walked ahead, slowly, close together around the curve of the path. Then Chicano stopped. A boy's naked body lay propped against a tree covered in bugs. It had one arm, a leg, and no head. It was bloated, the skin almost translucent so that it appeared to glow in the darkness of the forest.

Chicano turned to us. I nodded to let him know I was okay, but my heart was beating fast and hard. I wanted to run. We moved slowly, carefully stepping around the body, Mosca and I keeping side by side behind Chicano to where he suddenly stopped again. A head hung from a tree branch.

My knees buckled. "Kiko!"

Chicano picked me up, but my legs had lost their strength. He held me in a hug, my body trembling uncontrollably.

"Kiko. *Pinche* Kiko," Mosca cried and ran up to the head. Kiko's hair was tied to a rope hanging from a tree branch. His eyes had been plucked out. His mouth was slightly open in an expression of sadness. "Kiko." Mosca's voice cracked. "And I thought you were with them, *cabrón*. Look at you now. *Pinche güey*." He walked slowly around the head, his hands gesturing in the air, moving around Kiko but not touching.

Chicano grabbed Mosca's arm and pulled him away. "Come on."

We walked around the tree and ran, Chicano carrying Mosca and me at his sides, my feet dragging, but trying to keep pace. When we reached the end of the ravine where the creek disappeared into the culvert, he stopped and knelt to keep out of sight from the road.

Mosca sat and stared at the empty darkness where we had come from and whispered, "Kiko."

Chicano shook him. "Mosca."

Mosca stared like he was in a trance. "Kiko. Kiko."

"Stop it!" Chicano slapped him.

Mosca's eyes grew wide. Then he turned away and cried. It came out in a long sustained wail that grew and fell with his breathing. It made my skin crawl. I shut my eyes hoping it would all go away. It didn't.

Chicano dropped his head in his hands. When he raised his head again, I could see the panic behind the eyeholes in his mask.

"That was the boy who warned us," I said.

Chicano pulled us in. He held us tight and we huddled, our bodies shivering, my head pressed against his chest. I closed my eyes and felt the quick drumming of his heart against my cheek.

24.

At school, everyone was talking about Kiko. Some peasants walking through the ravine stumbled upon his remains and reported it to Pineda. None of the rumors were an exaggeration. I don't think anyone could have invented something worse. Mosca didn't come to school. I kept to myself and said nothing. As far as I was concerned, I was never in that ravine. I talked to no one. I just did my schoolwork and went home.

I was in such a daze I didn't even notice Chapo hadn't come home. But it had happened before. He often disappeared for a couple of days, off with a pack of street dogs or chasing a female in heat. Who knew what dogs did?

It took a few days for my fear to simmer. I was jumpy, paranoid. It was as if everything had been confirmed. Death was all around us. My worst fear was that my parents had met the same fate as Kiko. And yet something inside me kept hoping. Like maybe I was wrong.

I called Mosca's house. Every time his aunt answered and told me he wasn't home. I didn't believe her. Mosca had been pretty freaked out. I imagined him sitting alone in his room, afraid of leaving the house. And who could blame him? I had never been so scared in my life.

It was then that Gaby decided to bring her boyfriend by the house unannounced. We were sitting at the dinner table when they arrived. Gaby stepped into the dining room wearing a bright red dress, high heels and a lot of make up.

"*Hola!*" She struck a pose, a hand on her hip, her chest out like a model in one of those ads in the back of the newspaper.

"Look how pretty." Abuela dabbed her lips with a napkin. "You look just like your mother when she was your age."

Gaby beamed. "*Ay gracias*, Abuela."

"Someone better call the fire department to put out this fire," Chicano said.

Everyone laughed. Then her boyfriend peeked into the room.

"So," Gaby said in a soft voice, "I brought someone for you to meet." She gestured for him to come into the dining room and took his hand. "This is Francisco Serrano."

He was dressed in black pants that looked as if they were made of leather, a shiny colorful print shirt and black boots with a perfect polish. He didn't wear a hat. And he wasn't ugly or mean-looking. As a matter of fact, he looked like a nice guy.

Abuela smiled politely. "*Mucho gusto.*"

Francisco stepped up and gave her a light kiss on the cheek. "*Encantado, senõra.*"

Abuela blushed a little and turned to Chicano who was still gawking at Gaby.

She pointed at me. "And this is my brother, Liberio. And Jesusa, the maid who I guess has been integrated into the family."

I nodded and glanced at Chicano and then at Gaby. When she didn't say anything, I said, "And this is El Chicano Estrada, the famous *luchador* from Mexico City."

Francisco offered his hand. Chicano took it and held it for like half a minute without shaking it.

"I'm sorry," Gaby said when Chicano released Francisco's hand. "Is that my father's shirt?"

Chicano touched the lapel of the white dress shirt he was wearing and nodded. "And the pants too."

Gaby glanced at me. Her eyes narrowed. "What's going on here?"

"He lost his bag," I said. "He needed to borrow some clothes."

"Now, now," Abuela said, "you're a little late for dinner, but if you would like to join us, I am sure Jesusa can come up with something."

Gaby looked at her boyfriend.

"No, thank you very much, Doña Esperanza." Francisco held his hand up to his chest and bowed politely. "We have a previous engagement."

"Perhaps a little dessert?" Abuela pushed. "¿Un cafecito?"

"I'm so sorry," he said. "Really, we can't."

"My," Abuela said, "a social scene in Izayoc?"

Gaby took Francisco's arm. "It's business, Abuela."

"At this hour?"

Gaby looked at her boyfriend. "Maybe we should tell them now?"

"Tell us what?" I said.

Gaby smiled and took a deep breath. "We're opening an Internet café."

Abuela turned to Jesusa. "What is that?"

"Really?" I said. "Where?" Suddenly things looked brighter. I hadn't seen Francisco around town or with Joaquín's gang. Maybe Gaby was right. Maybe he was just a businessman. Maybe I had been wrong about him, about everything.

"The *panadería*," Gaby announced.

"Cool," I said. "A bakery and Internet café."

"No," Gaby said. "Just the Internet café."

"What about the *panadería*?"

"We're going to change it," Gaby said.

"What is this? You're closing the *panadería*?" Abuela said. "Why, that's Dorian's bakery. He built it. You can't just close it down."

"Abuela, the bakery's not profitable."

"That is of no consequence, *mija*." She spoke firmly, her voice rising. "No. I forbid it. You cannot do that."

"I'm sorry?" Gaby stepped back. She set her hands on her hips and pushed her head forward the way girls do when they're angry. "I'm the one who's been running that stupid bakery. I'm the one who wakes up at four in the morning to go open your dear Dorian's *panadería*. I'm the one who's there all day long working. I'm the one who closes at night and stays up until midnight balancing the books to keep it going. And you're going to tell me I can't do that?"

"*Hija mia—*"

"No, Abuela." Gaby waved her finger. "The time of *panaderías* and *tortillerías* has passed. Ignacio Morales is expanding his store. Did you know he's adding his own *panadería* and a *tortillería*— and even a butcher? Ramiro Contreras is going to build a hotel. There's a rumor that a Wal-Mart might even open in the empty lot by the Pemex station. Who do you think is going to buy bread at poor little Panadería La Esperanza?"

"We've been baking bread for almost"—Abuela paused and counted the decades in her frail fingers—"fifty years. And as far as I am aware, no one has ever complained."

"Abuela, listen to me. The store is deserted. Every day we have too many leftover bolillos and sweetbread. It's not a profitable business. And from what I can decipher from Papá's convoluted accounting, it hasn't been making a profit for years."

"What about Leticia and Lucio?" I said.

"What about them?"

"What's going to happen to them?"

"Listen to you, Liberio. If you really cared, you would have been there every afternoon after school like I've been asking you to. But no, you've been too busy with your friends, playing marbles and prancing around town with this clown—"

"*Luchador.*" Chicano adjusted his mask just slightly.

"Whatever," Gaby cried. "I've been running the bakery by myself. Now suddenly you're all interested? Well, that's not how it works. If you cared, you would have been doing your part. I'm fed up. I didn't go to school to become a *panadera*."

Francisco placed his hands on Gaby's shoulders. "With your permission," he said. "I understand your reservations, Doña Esperanza. Your bakery is a treasure. But Gaby's right. Things are changing in Izayoc. There is only one Internet café here. It's south of town by the *secundaria*. It's very busy with students and with the relatives of the young men who have traveled north to work. I think this is a wonderful opportunity for Gaby. And for all of you."

"It will connect us to the rest of the world," Gaby said.

"I opened an Internet café in San Fernando a couple of years ago, and it's done quite well. I think Izayoc is ready for another Internet café. And with the new highway, there's a lot of change coming to this town."

"What does that have to do with my bakery?" Abuela said. Her lip trembled and her eyes were glassy.

"Francisco and I are partners," Gaby said. "He's getting the computers and helping me set it up. It's going to be a franchise of his place in San Fernando. Our plan is to open a whole string of them across Mexico."

Abuela rolled her eyes. Then she dropped her head in her hands, elbows resting on the table. "It's just one tragedy after another."

25.

By the end of the week, I still hadn't heard from Mosca so
Chicano and I went up to the Barrio Santacruz where he lived.
It was at the top of the cliff north of town. We walked up the
mountain on the dirt road, which at times turned into nothing
more than a path. The rain had washed away most of the gravel,
leaving it muddy and rutted with deep tire tracks and potholes.
How cars ever came and went was beyond me.

Small houses were stacked up on the side of the mountain
in a mess of gray and black wood scraps, cardboard, asbestos and
tarpaper. They seemd to cling to the side of the hill, tiny lots like
caves carved out of the brown earth one on top of the other.
Corn plants grew inside small gardens. Chickens and pigs and
goats wandered the narrow paths between the dwellings, searching
for food scraps. On some of the roofs, television antennas stuck
out like grids and Mexican flags flapped in the wind. A light
breeze came and went with the smell of charcoal fires, corn
tortillas and the stink of open sewers that seemed to exist in the
poor neighborhoods outside town.

A pack of stray dogs followed us. I stopped and picked up a

rock and threw it at them. They scattered, then regrouped and trotted along behind us at a safe distance.

"Why did you do that?" Chicano said, looking back at the dogs. He was wearing a pair of my father's gray slacks and a white short sleeve *guayabera* shirt. His red mask was frayed and soiled like an old rag.

"I don't know. So they won't get too close."

He shook his head and glanced at the climb ahead. "Some dogs bark, some dogs bite, some dogs just want scraps."

We started walking again. Somewhere a television was tunned to a *telenovela*. We could hear dramatic dialogue, music. It made me think of Gaby and Francisco. Maybe they would get married. Maybe that was what we needed. If my parents were really dead, I figured it would be good to have someone like him in the family.

"So. What did you think of Gaby's boyfriend?" I asked.

"Hard to tell," Chicano said. "But I still don't see what she sees in a guy like that."

"What does any girl see in a guy? Just look at Ximena. She could do much better than that Joaquín."

"Oh, yeah?"

"Of course. She could have anyone she wants."

"You mean anyone like you."

"I'm not old enough for her. But why not?"

We walked in silence for a while. Then he said. "Ximena, I could see. But your sister? She's smart. Sharp. Pretty. She's wasting it all on that *pendejo*."

"You think he's up to no good?"

Chicano paused to catch his breath. "I suspect everyone."

"Yeah, me too."

"Ximena told me Joaquín and his pals want to build a hotel with a big restaurant by the plaza." He looked past me at the children who had come running to the side of the road to look at the masked wrestler. They were dressed in tatters, barefoot, snot-nosed, dusty. He waved and they waved back.

"When did she say that?" I asked.

"The other night. She was with her friend."

"Why wasn't I there?"

"It was late."

"You sneak out at night?"

"I don't sneak," he said and started walking again. "I go out. I watch. I ask questions. I'm trying to help you find your parents. Isn't that what you wanted?"

We reached the top of the cliff. Mosca's house was unpainted concrete block with wood and a small front yard. Mosca's father was better off than most of his neighbors because he worked up north. Most of his family lived in Santacruz. Everyone knew everyone. I climbed up the path to the small house, opened the gate and went in. Chicano stayed behind. I knocked on the door. There was no answer.

"Nothing's going on between us," Chicano said when I walked back. "Joaquín's got some kind of spell on her." He followed me across the dirt road to another house.

I knocked on the door.

"Trust me," he said. "She'll never be mine. And probably never be yours either. No offense."

One of Mosca's aunts opened the door.

"*Buenas tardes, señora* Yarce. I'm looking for Mosca."

"He's out," she said. "Goes out all day and night, that one." She waved at the hill toward the big cross. "He might be up that way. If you see him, tell him his father called."

I walked back to the street. "I don't care what you say, Chicano. She's too good for those *pendejos*."

We went to the other side of the cliff. At the very top was a small stone grotto with candles and effigies and a picture of the Virgen, and above it the giant white cross. Big, ugly black clouds rolled in over the mountains to the north.

"I agree," he said. "Unfortunately, it's her choice. Not ours."

"Mosca!" He was sitting on a rock almost at the edge of

the cliff. The fall was straight down like two hundred feet to the bottom. He had a pair of big black binoculars hanging over his chest.

We ran to him. "*Güey*, where did you get those?" I said.

"You'll never guess." He pulled the binoculars off his neck and handed them to me.

They were heavy. The real deal. "Nice."

"Pepino gave them to me."

Chicano took them from me and put them to his eyes. He scanned the landscape from left to right and focused on the highway as it came into town from the west. "*Están rechingones*."

The boys and dogs that had been following us up the hill surrounded us. One of them reached out to touch Chicano, but he slapped his hand away. "

"Where you been?" I said. "Everyone at school is going on about Kiko. I didn't tell them anything."

"I've been busy." He leaned back on a rock. "I got a job."

"*No manches*. I haven't even seen you in the plaza."

"I'm not doing the shoe shining, *güey*. I'm on the lookout for a black Suburban with fat tires and Sinaloa plates."

"What for?"

"Pepino's orders." He showed me a small two-way radio. "I'm supposed to call him whenever it passes."

I took the radio from him and pressed the talk button. "Hello, hello. This is the rubber duck, ten-four, over?"

He snatched it back. "Don't fuck with it, Boli."

"It's turned off."

"I don't care. This is important."

"Oh?" I stepped back. "What's so important about a stupid car?"

"I don't know." He smiled. "But he paid me a thousand pesos."

"For real?"

"I wonder what they want with it?" Chicano said.

"Who cares?" Mosca stood and looked down at the highway.

It was the perfect spot to spy anyone coming in from the west or north in the old highway. Behind the next mountain we could even see the new highway.

"Remember what Kiko—"

"Kiko's dead," he cried and waved a finger at me. "He fucked up."

"*Pinche* Mosca. Why do you want to work for those *hijos de puta?*"

"For money," he said. "I'm only doing this one thing. That's it."

"Yeah," I said. "Suddenly you and Pepino are real *cuates,* no?"

"A thousand pesos worth." His voice was flat, empty. He didn't even sound like himself. "Besides, you're too busy with your personal *luchador.*"

"Stop it," Chicano said, the binoculars still on his face as he scanned the horizon below. "You sound like a couple of girls. Mosca, you know you're dancing with the devil, no? And that little number never turns out well for anyone but the devil. Got it?"

"Whatever."

"Just do this one thing," I said. "Don't get greedy."

Mosca sat up. "What are you now, Santo?"

Chicano lowered the binoculars. "Just be careful, *mano.* I don't want anything to happen to you."

"Don't worry," he said. "I'm cool."

"If you hear anything that might help us find Liberio's parents, let us know, okay?"

"You still beating that dead horse?" he said.

"*Cabrón,* they're my parents!" I couldn't believe it. I moved toward him.

Chicano grabbed my arm and pulled me back. "We don't need to go there."

"I'm just saying. After what happened to Kiko you can be sure—"

"You don't know shit," I yelled.

"Take it easy, you two." Chicano moved between Mosca and me. "We could use your help."

"Well, yeah," he said. "Sure."

"The last thing we need is to fight with each other."

I stepped back. "I wasn't fighting."

"No problem." Mosca smiled. "I'll be like your man on the inside."

"No," Chicano said. "Just finish this job and get out. Don't ask them anything. Just keep your ears open, that's all." He handed Mosca the binoculars.

Mosca brought them to his face and focused on the old highway.

By the houses near the foot of the cross, a woman was setting laundry to dry on a line. Chickens scratched the ground around her. A blond dog slept in the shade under an old Chevy set on blocks. The clouds kept rolling like giant monsters in the sky. It was getting dark.

"So when are you gonna get done with the job?" I asked.

"The end of next week." He lowered the binoculars. "And if the Suburban doesn't pass by then, Pepino said he'd throw in another five hundred for the weekend."

Chicano took the binoculars from Mosca again and scanned the road. Then he focused on the plaza.

"What is it?" I said.

His finger moved over the focusing knob. "The priest. He's talking to Porky the policeman."

"Pineda." Mosca laughed.

Chicano looked to the left and adjusted the focus. "There she is."

"Ximena?"

"The one and only."

"Is she with him?"

"She's with him and another two men. And Regina."

"Poor Regina," I said. "I don't think she likes those guys."

"She's with them, no?" Mosca said.

"Probably because of Ximena."

"Regina doesn't know what she wants," Mosca said and grabbed at the binoculars.

Chicano pulled them back. "It's bad manners to just grab at things." Then he handed the binoculars to Mosca, but kept looking over the town. "We should go to the plaza."

"I really don't want to see Joaquín," I said. "I hate that *pendejo.*"

Chicano slapped me on the back. "You need an attitude adjustment, *hijín.*"

"What, I can't hate him? He's with Ximena."

Chicano waved a finger at me. "You can't blame it all on Joaquín and Ximena. If you'd talked to her, maybe she'd be here with you instead of with that flashy *cabrón.*"

"He's right." Mosca lowered the binoculars and laughed. "You could be lying in the grass feeling her up and squeezing her fine little *chichis.*"

"Shut up."

Chicano laughed. "He's right though."

"Come on. We're supposed to be looking for my parents."

We left Mosca at his post. The children around us parted. We walked through and around the bend past the big cross toward the road. Chicano said, "I have a feeling those guys with Ximena know something about what happened to your parents."

I said nothing. I'd had that feeling from the moment I met Joaquín in Pineda's office.

"It's just a feeling," he said. "But I think it's time to ask them some questions. And who knows, maybe I'll get lucky and get a kiss from Ximenita."

"Is that all you think about?"

"And you don't?"

The gray clouds moved in as we walked down the mountain. Just as we reached the bottom, it started to rain. We ducked under the awning of a shuttered hardware store.

When we finally made it to the plaza, it was deserted. The rain had left the square with a silver-like sheen, like it was made of plastic. Everything looked brand new. But it was empty. There were no people, no dogs, nothing. All the businesses were closed, their metal shutters drawn, graffiti lettering tagging each one like some secret census.

We found Zopilote sitting alone, drinking a Victoria beer at Los Perdidos. When he saw us, he waved us in.

"What the fuck was that shit with the gun the other day?" I said.

"Just goofing around, *pinche* Boli. Lighten up." Then he pointed at Chicano with his beer. "But you, *amigo*, you need to be careful. Joaquín is onto you."

"On to me how?" Chicano sat across the table from Zopilote.

"What you're doing with his girl."

Chicano grinned. "And what is that?"

"Don't play dumb, Super Barrio. He knows you go see her at night. He knows everything that happens in this town."

"She's free to do whatever she wants, no?"

"She was." Zopilote raised his chin. "Joaquín doesn't mess around when it comes to his women."

Chicano stood and took Zopilote's shades from his face. "Tell me something." He examined the glasses and then put them on over his mask. "You heard any talk about what happened to Liberio's parents?"

Zopilote looked at me, then at Chicano. "I already told him. I saw nothing, heard nothing, know nothing."

"Deaf, dumb and blind," Chicano said.

"Better believe it."

"Nice."

"But I've heard a lot about you," Zopilote said.

"All good things, I hope."

Zopilote put his pinky into the mouth of the beer bottle and raised it just off the table, turning it in little circles. He smiled at me and set the bottle back on the table. "If I were you, I'd keep my head low. Maybe go back to Mexico City, crawl back into that hole in Tepito."

"But you're not me," Chicano said.

Zopilote smiled.

Chicano stepped out of the restaurant. He removed the sunglasses and tossed them back to Zopilote.

We walked to the plaza and turned on Calle Lealtad. People were coming out after the rain. A man swept water that had puddled on the sidewalk in front of the small appliance store. All the other businesses were shuttered. A rooster crowed. Across the street, Lucio was walking toward us.

We met him at the corner. He set a large duffel bag on the ground by his feet. It was the first time I'd seen him without *huaraches*. He had on a pair of hard, solid, leather shoes with a good shine.

"Moving on with the times," he announced with a smile.

I glanced at Chicano. "She didn't waste any time, did she?"

"It's no problem," Lucio said. "And don't blame Gabriela. She offered for me to stay and work. She took good care of me. Don't be angry at her."

"But you don't have to leave town. There's other work, Lucio."

He shook his head and gave me his crazy Lucio grin. "I've been around, *hijo*. People like me, we get pushed around from all sides."

"Amen," Chicano said.

"But Lucio, please—"

"I'm going to the coast. I want to spend some time by the water. A nice beach on the Pacific side, the Costa Grande. We'll see."

"But what are you going to do for money?" I said.

"Fish."

"You're not a fisherman."

"Some years ago, I wasn't a baker either."

"I can respect that, *viejo*." Chicano patted him on the back. "It's important to know when it's time to move on."

"The job does not make the man," Lucio said. "Unless you're a *luchador*."

"Stay." I grabbed his arm. "Please. You can stay with us in the house. We'll open another bakery. You and me and my *abuela*. I promise."

He laughed softly and placed his hand on my shoulder. "We all have to move on sometime, *mijo*. If you don't move, you run the risk of getting buried in the past."

"What are you talking about?"

"Life is not about just one thing. In a couple of days, I'll be out on the coast with my toes in the sand. Doesn't sound that bad, does it?"

"I wish I could go with you," Chicano said. Then he raised his head and looked past Lucio. A black Suburban with fat tires cruised slowly toward us. It passed and turned on a side street before it reached the plaza.

I looked at Chicano. "You think?"

Chicano nodded. "Mosca's Suburban."

"*Bueno, pues.*" Lucio picked up his bag.

"When will I see you again?" I said.

"I don't know, *mijo*. But remember to move forward, always. Make new friends, see new places. And don't worry about me."

I had never thought of Lucio being out of my life, just like I hadn't thought of Jesusa or my *abuela* or my parents being out of my life. And Chicano. He would be leaving for Monterrey soon. I felt my throat tighten. I wanted to cry.

We left Lucio and walked in silence for a few blocks. Finally I said, "I'm sorry."

"About what?"

"About earlier, when we argued."

"Forget it. Besides, I was just trying to get a rise out of you. I like how your face gets all red when you're angry."

26.

That night Abuela talked non-stop about Veracruz. We sat at the dining room table, eating a bowl of *fideo* soup and *quesadillas*. She went on and on about some festival and the spectacle of the fireworks. "Look, just look." She waved her hand frantically over the table and pointed to the ceiling. "Is it not beautiful? And that one. Ah, look at them all. You know, José Miranda's father brought them all the way from Atotonilco. They're the best in the country. You won't see a show like this in Mexico City. I know. I've been there. And look how they illuminate Dorian's face. Look how handsome that man is."

Chicano, who had yet to experience one of my *abuela's* episodes, sat with his spoon in his hand, staring at her like she was a ghost. "Tell her something."

"Like what?" It was funny to see him so uncomfortable over something so innocent.

"I don't know, like that she's not in Veracruz for one."

"No, let her dream."

He rolled his eyes and turned to Jesusa for support. "And you, do you dream of your *pueblo* in the sierra?"

Jesusa waved. "Only nightmares."

"That's what I'm saying," Chicano said. "The past is a nightmare."

Abuela stretched her arms out and reached to her sides. "If we hold hands and run to the water we will see better. But we have to go together." She took my hand, squeezed it and smiled. "Thank you, *niño*. You are a prince."

I glanced at Chicano and Jesusa, but they were in their own worlds. Maybe their dreams had faded. Who knew what grownups dreamed about? I was only glad my *abuela* was dreaming of good times and the wonderful things that had happened or that she thought would happen one day. She gave me hope.

After dinner I pulled out a videotape where I had recorded the movie, *Santo contra los zombies*.

"There are some excellent fighting sequences in this one," Chicano said as we settled on the couch. "But I prefer Santo against the female werewolves. The she-wolf, which is also human, wants to eat the men. And that's all the men really want."

"Hush!" Jesusa smacked him on the arm. "The zombies are creepy."

"You think everything is creepy," I said.

"Santo had it made from the start." Chicano stretched his legs and loosened his belt. "With a name like that. And the silver mask. You can't beat it. The man was pure class."

"You could beat him," I said. "I'm sure of it. You could beat Joaquín and Pedro and Zopilote, all of them."

In the Santo movie, Dr. Sandoval's daughter goes to the police because her father disappeared, just like it happened with my own parents. When they can't find any clues, they end up getting Santo's help. I had Chicano's help. The zombies Santo fights in the movie are dead criminals who come back to life. They weren't monsters, just regular people, ugly and invincible, kind of like Joaquín and his friends.

At the end of the movie, after Santo had saved Dr. Sandoval's daughter and eliminated all the zombies, he said something that made me think of Izayoc. "When men defy God's laws," he said, "they fall victims to their own evil."

Early the following morning, as I left the house for school, I discovered a heavy-duty plastic trash bag hanging on our front gate. Our street was deserted except for the neighbor's maid who was sweeping the driveway two houses down. I set my schoolbooks on the sidewalk and grabbed the bag from below. It was too high and heavy for me to lift.

I opened the gate and stepped into the patio. "Chicano, Jesusa!"

Jesusa came out wiping her hands on her apron and joined me on the street.

"Look." I pointed at the gate.

She stared at the bag for a moment, then she looked at me as if I was up to something. The bag smelled foul, like trash.

I grabbed it from the bottom and pushed up. "Help me."

Jesusa reached over me and pulled the top. Together we lifted and unhooked it from the nail. We set it on the ground. Jesusa stepped back, her eyes wide, her mouth twisted with fear.

"What?"

She pointed to my chest. Blood. It was all over the front of my shirt and puddled on the sidewalk around the bag.

I stepped back and stared. I thought of Kiko, my parents. All my fear rushed forward. And then, for a moment I was lifted. I saw everything that had been going on in Izayoc. We were toys, figures in a game. Nothing mattered. I took a deep breath and glanced at Jesusa. She was paralyzed. I leaned over the bag and pulled it open. Jesusa covered her face with her hands.

It was too dark to see. Everything was black. I turned the bag. Hair.

"What is it?" Jesusa whispered like she wanted to know, but didn't.

I tugged at the bag, opened it wider. It stank like puke. I held my breath and reached in. It was tepid, moist. Coarse hair. I thought of Gaby's stuffed toys. I grabbed a handful and pulled. Chapopote's head.

Jesusa screamed.

I dropped the head and turned away. My stomach contracted. I stumbled, fell to my knees. Vomit pushed up my throat in short, violent spasms.

"*Ay, Dios mio!*" Jesusa cried. The neighbor's maid dropped her broom and ran to her aid. They sat on the sidewalk, arms around each other, Jesusa looking away, her cheek resting against her shoulder like she was a child.

I staggered back toward the house. "Chicano. Chicano!"

He came running, shirtless, barefoot. "What's going on?"

"Chapo!" I pointed to the bag. "They killed Chapo!"

He peeked in the bag and turned away quickly.

"They killed him," I cried.

Chicano shook his head and sat beside me. He placed his arm around my shoulder and pulled me close. "I'm sorry, Liberio."

"He never hurt anyone." I leaned my face against his side and cried. It came out of me like rain. Chapo, Kiko, my parents, a nightmare exploding into a million tiny pieces. In that bag were my parents. I could see them chopped up like meat from the butcher, shoved in black plastic bags where no one would ever find them. My body shook. My despair escaped in long painful wails I couldn't control. I kept thinking, why? Why was this happening?

Chicano held me tight. At the end of the block, two boys on their way to school crossed the street as if nothing was wrong, as if my parents had never disappeared, as if Chapo was back in the front patio, wagging his tail, and Kiko was playing marbles with Mosca and Pepino.

After a while my rage simmered and my cries mellowed into sobs. The neighbor helped Jesusa into the house. The sun crested over the mountains and light skimmed the surface of the cobblestones like a sharp knife. Birds sang as if nothing was wrong.

"Liberio." Chicano loosened his hold on me. "I'm sorry." His tone was so soft, he didn't sound like the same man. "I'm very sorry. It's not fair. It's not fair to you or anyone. These *hijos de la chingada*—it's more than a crime what they've done to you, what they're doing to this place."

I took a deep breath and pulled away from his grip and looked at him, his frayed mask. "But why? Why Chapo? And my parents?"

"I don't know." He shook his head and stared down at the pavement for a long while, his hands tracing the cracks in the cement. "We're pissing them off."

"But my parents—"

"They went to Toluca for help. I guess that's reason enough for these *pendejos*."

But then what about Rocío? I didn't get it. What did they have against her? "Why can't things be like they were before?"

"No, Liberio. Life is a fight. It's not a fair fight, but it is what it is. We just have to keep at it. Always."

"Is that why you became a *luchador*?"

He said nothing for a long while. He just stared past me, his dark eyes still and steady. Then he touched the bottom of his mask where it met his skin below the chin. For a moment, I thought he was going to pull it off.

"I became a *luchador* for money. All I could do well was fight. But the few days I've spent here with you and your family—"

"And Mosca."

"Yes, and Mosca." He chuckled. "You have taught me a lot. There are things in life that are worth so much more than just—"

"Money?"

"Until now, I just cared about myself, where my next meal was going to come from. But this isn't right. What's happening here isn't right."

"I know, but you're Chicano Estrada. You have fans all over the country. You have people who believe in you. And you're helping me."

He laughed. "It's not like that. All I ever do is take advantage of situations. I've been selfish. I suppose it's a survival device. But even that's just an excuse. I have no excuse for the way I've behaved. Now I know there's more to life than just me. I'm sorry for taking advantage of you, and of your family's generosity."

"What are you talking about? You stayed here to help. We're making progress, no?"

"Well, I suppose the blade cuts both ways." He took a deep breath. "When I decided to stay here, I was only thinking of my next meal. I have nothing going on. I don't have a fight in Monterrey."

"And Toluca?"

"I had a fight there at a little *feria* in La Unión. But I got drunk at that *cantina* and missed my bus. The story of my life."

"What about your manager, Chaparro Mendoza?"

"I don't have a manager."

"But you called him on your cell. I saw you. You left him a message."

He shook his head. "I was making it up. I'm just a two-bit loser from Tepito. I have no manager, and my cell phone service was cut off months ago. I'm a nobody."

"You can't say that, Chicano. It's not true."

"I needed a place to stay until I made some money, figured out my next move. But when I saw those two bodies hanging on the bridge, and you pushed me to take them down, I understood. I was wrong about good guys, Liberio. You're a good guy. You're the last of the good guys. You make me proud."

We were quiet for a long time. I was angry, but also glad. I wanted to kick him and hug him at the same time. It was at that moment that I knew for sure I would never see my parents again.

27.

I tried getting ahold of Mosca to give him the news about Chapo, but no one answered the phone at his house. He was probably still on stakeout. In the afternoon, Chicano and I went to see Father Gregorio to find out if we could bury Chapo in the cemetery near where my grandfather was buried. But he said it wasn't possible.

"The cemetery is for people," he said quickly. "Besides, your dog wasn't baptized."

"But it's important to me," I said. "Maybe we we could make an exeption, just this once. Please."

"I don't make the rules." He seemed impatient. Workers were all over the church breaking down the scaffolding and cleaning the construction debris.

"What if you came with us and blessed the ground where we bury him? Would that allow him to get into heaven?"

"This is a ridiculous request, Liberio. I'm sorry. We haven't even had a mass for your parents, and you want me to do this for a dog? Seriously, I think you need to reassess your priorities, young man."

"But we don't know if my parents are dead. I can't bury them. Please. It would mean a lot to me, Father."

"What happened at the ravine?"

"It's a funny thing," Chicano interrupted. "We had a real show there. Someone tried to run us over."

"And they shot at us," I said.

"They what?" Father Gregorio's eyes jumped from me to Chicano and back. "I don't believe it."

"Believe it," Chicano said. "And a few days later someone delivered a bag with Liberio's dog chopped up into little pieces like a goat at the market."

"*Dios mio*, but how—"

"It was a set up," Chicano said.

"But who would want to harm you? Did you report it to Captain Pineda?"

"Give us a break," Chicano said.

"Can you come with us to bury Chapo?" I said. "Please?"

"Liberio, I can't. I'm sorry. Besides, I have the workers. I have to get this place cleaned up before Sunday."

"But isn't he one of God's creatures?"

"Liberio, please."

Chicano laid a heavy hand on my shoulder. "Forget it, Liberio. The church won't lift a finger for the poor unless there's something in it for them."

"Excuse me." Father Gregorio gasped. "Who are you?"

"I'm Chicano Estrada. I fight for justice and defend the poor."

I smiled. He was really putting it on for Father Gregorio, but still, it sounded awesome.

Father Gregorio didn't move or say anything, like he didn't get the joke or like he was trying to figure out what to say or what to do. Next to Chicano, he looked small and afraid.

"That's so unfair," I said as we walked back to the house.

"That's why I don't go to church anymore."

"You don't believe in God?"

"Of course I do. But if God is good and powerful, he can see through all this *mierda*. I don't need the church. It cramps my style."

"I can't believe it. I thought he was my friend."

"Priests," he said flatly. "They're vultures."

"Careful, Chicano, that's blasphemy."

He stopped walking and waved a finger at me. "See, that's our big problem. We as a people are too religious. We have too much faith in God. Our answer to everything is that it must be God's will. *La voluntad de Dios*. We're numb. We just sit back and expect God to take care of everything."

We headed to the Flats. I carried the shovel and Chicano carried the black bag with Chapo's remains slung over his shoulder like some kind of Santa Claus *luchador*.

It seemed fit to bury Chapo in the Flats. It was the place where I found him when he was a puppy and where we spent most of our time together. And there was plenty of space. We picked a spot away from the soccer field. It had grass, tall bushes and a few *magueyes* and big *nopales*. It looked peaceful.

Chicano set the bag down, and I began to dig. The rains had softened the earth, but after a while I had to stop. Chicano took the shovel from me and finished digging the hole.

"So. What do you want to do?" he asked.

I glanced at the bundle. "We just put him in, no?"

He picked up the bag and set it in the hole. Then he stepped back and joined his hands together at his waist.

I tossed in a shovelful of dirt and then passed the shovel to Chicano. He did the same and then passed it back to me. As I filled the hole with dirt, I thought of when Chapo was a puppy. I had tried to keep him in my room, but he made such a mess my father forced me to make a place for him in the shed in the front patio. Some nights I would sneak out and lay with him in the bed Jesusa had helped me make for him using old rags. He was a stinky dog. No matter how much I bathed him, he always stank.

But the thing that got me was that after a few weeks, I kind of just left him to his own devices. I took him for granted.

I took my parents for granted too. They were always there taking care of us. I never stopped to think what it would be like if they ever disappeared. We fought and argued about stupid things like homework or having to work at the bakery after school or on the weekends. It had been the same with Lucio and Gaby. Everything we did, we did knowing we would see each other again, as if every day would be the same. I guess for a while it was, but not anymore. As I finished topping off Chapo's grave, my stomach felt queasy with sadness. It felt as if I were burying my parents.

"Any words?" Chicano said.

"I don't know. What can we say?" Everything was stirring inside me. I was afraid if I started talking, I would break down. But I held it in. I told myself I was done with that. I had to grow up.

"Maybe you should just tell God about Chapo, you know, just so he knows."

I joined my hands at my waist like Chicano. I took a deep breath and lowered my head. "Dear God, we are here to bury my dog Chapopote. We hope you will find him a place in heaven. He was a good dog. He didn't know any tricks and sometimes he wouldn't obey me, but he never gave me any trouble. He doesn't eat dog food, just scraps and leftovers. He's afraid of thunder and loud noises. Please take care of him."

I wiped the tears from my cheeks and glanced at Chicano. He was looking down at the mound of earth. "And *Diosito*," I went on, "please excuse the mess. Someone killed him and chopped him up. There are a lot of bad things going on here. Even if we never find my parents, please make a place for them in heaven, and please do something about our little town because we're all sad and scared. Can't you see us crying?"

I pursed my lips. There was so much more I wanted to say, but all the sadness and fear and anger pressed down on me like a big rock. It was too much. Besides, I figured he probably wasn't even listening. "I guess that's all," I said, my voice cracking. "Amen."

"Nice prayer."

I took the cross we had made from scraps of wood and stabbed it at the top of the mound of brown earth. I stepped back. We stared at the grave in silence for a long time. Then I said. "It looks good, no?"

Chicano grabbed the shovel. "Come on. We have work to do."

I followed Chicano to the end of the Flats. Then I paused and looked back at the grave. It wasn't noticeable from the road. I knew someone might eventually steal the cross, but the grave would be fine. If I ever wanted to sit with Chapo, I knew where to go.

We walked up Avenida del Porvenir a few blocks south of the *secundaria* when we noticed a crowd in the street. We ran up and pushed our way through. On a vacant lot between two houses was a black Chevy Suburban with fat tires and doors wide open. It was dented at the front and side. The whole car was riddled with bullet holes. The windows were shattered. There was no one inside, but there was blood and small chunks of flesh all over the upholstery.

"Who's *troca* is this?" Chicano asked.

No one said anything. It looked like all the other Suburbans we'd seen in town, the one Chicano and I had seen near the plaza, the one Mosca might have been watching out for. But this one had plates from Michoacán. On the corner of the shattered back window was a small Tweety Bird sticker.

Chicano faced the crowd. "Who was in this car?"

Everyone looked away. People wandered off slowly, their eyes downcast. Then an old man said, "No one knows. *El gordo de* Pineda and his men took them away." He motioned with his arm to show Chicano the direction Pineda had taken, up the hill, toward the plaza.

"Were they dead?"

"Just look at the car." The old man crossed himself, slung his *morral* over his shoulder and made his way around the car, disappearing between the two houses to the next street.

I stepped closer to the car. It smelled of gasoline and blood. The door panel was splattered with blood. On the handle was a molar. I moved back behind Chicano. The people who remained stared from the car to Chicano with his red mask and shovel and back at the car.

"Did anyone see anything?" he said.

A young man pointed to the road. "This one was coming down like that, when another one just like it came alongside from that street there. Then it unloaded on it with everything. Just look at how they left it."

"What other one? Was it a Suburban or a truck or what?"

"It was just like this one. Black."

"Did you see who was in it?" Chicano said.

The young man shook his head and receded into the crowd.

"I saw it too," a boy said. "It happened late this morning. After they shot it, it crashed into that pole there."

Everyone turned to look at the telephone pole. It had a big chunk torn off its side.

"Then it skidded and turned and ended up here. The other one pulled over there and kept shooting." Everyone's eyes moved from the street to the Suburban.

"And then what happened?"

"Nothing," the boy said. "The other *troca* sped away." He motioned in the direction the Suburban had taken. "Then, *zas*, Pineda came down in a new white *troca*. They pulled the bodies out and took them away."

"How many bodies?"

"I don't know. I think four." Then he raised his right hand like he was taking an oath. "I mean, that's what I saw, *pues*."

"I saw them when they came," a short peasant woman said. "They zoomed in and out, *pues*. Just grabbed the bodies and tossed them in the back of the pickup like they were sacks of corn, just like *el niño* says."

"He didn't investigate or take any casings? Nothing?" Chicano asked.

Everyone laughed, but it was a nervous laugh, as if they all knew it was something plain and obvious. And dangerous: a joke that, if you laughed at it, might get you killed.

"They don't want to find out," someone said. "They don't want to know."

"That's not it," the peasant woman waved. "It's because they already know. That's why they never do anything. Those rats all work together. Let them kill each other, *pues*." Then she adjusted her *huipil* and walked away with short hurried steps.

"That Pineda's been selling himself more than the whores at El Gallo de Oro," someone said. Everyone laughed. But it was that same insecure laugh, as if Pineda or someone might be listening.

"What do you think?" I said.

"I don't know." Chicano swung the shovel over his shoulder. "I don't like it. Let's get out of here."

We made our way to the plaza, but it was a ghost town. All the stores were shuttered. Even the regular vendors were absent. The doors to the municipal building were closed and locked. Chicano knocked and pulled at the handles, but no one answered or poked their head out. Nothing.

"What's going on?"

"Mosca was on the lookout for a Suburban with Sinaloa plates," Chicano said. "It might have been the one that shot up the one we just saw."

The sun slowly disappeared behind gray clouds. Then we heard what sounded like a burst of gunfire in the distance.

"Come on," Chicano said. "This place is giving me the creeps."

We walked quickly across the plaza, keeping to one side, away from the open.

"Maybe they're fighting among themselves," he said.

"You think it was Joaquín?" I was thinking of Ximena and Regina. I hoped and prayed to God they hadn't been inside the Suburban.

"I don't know." We crossed the street, almost running just to get away from nothing.

We took shelter inside the church. The workers had finished cleaning up. The brown spots and the cracks and peeling paint on the ceiling were gone. Everything looked new. It was quiet and dark with the soft orange light from candles reflecting against the sculptured gold leaf wall behind the altar. Chicano took a deep breath. The place smelled of old incense and fresh plaster.

To the right of the altar, hidden from view by a pair of stone columns and a short iron gate, I noticed the glow of candles. A new shrine. It was at the very back of the church. In a small glass case was the bust of a man in a white shirt and black clothes. He had a thin mustache and flat black hair. Around him were paper flowers and a few *veladoras*.

"Jesús Malverde," Chicano said, his voice echoing softly across the church. "The patron saint of bandits."

"I never heard of him."

"If he's here, you know they're here."

"And Father Gregorio built it?"

"He did it for *them*." Chicano looked at the ceiling. "That priest is as dirty as Pineda."

"But he's a good man. He's been helping me find my parents." I walked across the church to his office and lay on the ground. There was no light under the door.

"Maybe it was one of those offers he couldn't refuse," Chicano said.

"You mean like a death threat?"

He nodded. I followed him to the front of the church. He cracked the door open and peeked outside.

"They can't do that," I said. "You can't kill a priest."

"You have a lot to learn, *hijín*. People kill priests all the time."

28.

When we finally made it home, Jesusa was in a panic. "*Ay,* Liberio. Thank God you're here. You have to help me. *Por favor.* She's over the edge. She's packing. She's leaving!"

"I've had enough." Abuela stormed from one side of her room to the other. "She has destroyed everything we worked for. Everything. It was all for nothing." She tore a dress from her closet and shoved it in her suitcase.

"What are you talking about?"

"Gaby!"

"What happened?"

"She destroyed Dorian's work. The *panadería*. It does not exist anymore." She folded a blouse and pressed it into the suitcase with both hands.

"I don't understand," I said. "Calm down. Please, Abuela."

"It wasn't just Gaby," Jesusa said. "Doña Teresa came to say goodbye to *la señora.* They closed the *papelería* and are moving to Houston."

"Texas?"

"I don't know. Houston, Houston, *pues.* But after Doña Teresa left, *la señora* starts about the *panadería* and insists she has to go. She never likes to go, but now she has to go. And then, *újule*, you should have seen. I didn't know Gaby had everything torn up. There's no more *panadería*. Even the sign is gone."

"What did Gaby say?"

"They had a big fight. Your *abuela* yelled all kinds of insults at her and at the workers and everything. Gaby cried. The workers stopped doing what they were doing. They just stood and watched. And who can blame them? It was a real show, *pues*. Right out of a *telenovela*."

"Abuela." I placed my hand on her shoulder. "Please. Wait. Slow down."

"No, Liberio. It's too much for me. I can't take it anymore." She paused her work and looked at me for the first time. Perhaps she had finally realized what was happening. That my parents were gone, that Izayoc wasn't the same place she had come to with my grandfather. "I didn't even have the opportunity to see it one last time," she said. "And you know what she said. She said if I didn't like it, I could leave. The nerve of that girl."

"But Abuela, you can't go just like that."

"And why not? Teresa left. So can I."

I had no answer. After burying Chapo and coming to the realization that my parents were dead, I was ready to go with her to Veracruz or anywhere else.

"Why?" she said again, pleading in a tone I'd never heard her use before. "Why will you not let me go?"

"Because I don't want you to."

And suddenly she stopped. She dropped the dress she had in her hands and stared into my eyes as if an answer existed somewhere in my sadness.

"Please?" I whispered.

She trembled. Maybe she realized we were alone, that we needed to stick together. We were all we had.

"Please, Abuela—"

"You can come too," she said quietly, her energy spent.

"No, Abuela. Not right now." I moved past her and began taking her things out of the suitcase. Jesusa joined me, plucking the clothes from the case and putting them away in silence.

Abuela watched us for long while, her hands resting on the post at the foot of the bed. Then she said, "They never wanted me here, in this town." Her voice was soft. Empty. "It was his dream. I stayed only because I loved him. The other women never allowed me in. They never made me a part of their community. Except Teresa. And now she's gone. I hate it here. I want to go home."

"It's not just here, Doña Esperanza." Chicano stepped into the room. "It's everywhere."

I took her by the shoulders and sat her on the rocking chair. "I understand how you feel, Abuela. But let's wait a little while. We don't even know who's left in Veracruz."

"Everyone is there. The whole family."

"But you haven't spoken to any of them in fifty years."

"But they're there," she insisted. "You will see. Everyone is there, Valentín Valdez and Dolores García and Israel Jacinto, and even Felipe Rosas and Mauricio Ortega." She touched my face. "You would love it, Liberio. I know you would."

"We'll go," I said. "We'll go one day, but not now, Abuela. We can't just abandon Izayoc. And Gaby."

"Yes," she said quietly and bowed. "You're right. There is a protocol."

Jesusa finished putting away the clothes. "How about a little café con leche, señora?"

"Yes. That would be nice. Gracias, niña. With a little sugar the way they serve it at la Parroquia."

I followed Jesusa to the kitchen. She was agitated. Her hands trembled as she went about making the coffee. "Pobrecita, losing her only daughter. Now her granddaughter. It's too much for her. It's too much for anyone."

I was thinking: what about me? I just lost my parents? But I just stared at the tiles, wishing we could leave. All of us. Any place had to be better than this. Izayoc had turned into hell. But we couldn't just leave Gaby. And what if my parents weren't dead. What if they came back?

That night a noise woke me up. Chicano's massive body moved in the darkness. He was dressing.

"What's going on?" I said.

"I'm going out…to investigate."

I turned on my bedside lamp. "Investigate what?"

"Shush. You're going to wake everyone." He put his pants on, sat on the bed and worked his socks over his giant feet. "Let me do my work, will you?"

I tossed the covers aside. "I should go with you."

"No." He stood and buttoned up my father's white dress shirt. "I have to do this alone."

"But—"

"I would never forgive myself if something happened to you, *hijín*. Besides, this is something I have to do alone." He ruffled my hair and walked out of the room.

As soon as I heard the front door close, I hopped out of bed, got dressed, and ran after him. The streets were pitch dark, deserted. When I came to the corner of our street and Avenida de los Recuerdos, I saw his broad shoulders and the slick masked head silhouetted against a streetlight. He walked quickly, then disappeared around the corner toward the plaza. I followed.

He turned on Calle Agustín Melgar and stopped in front of the house with a big black gate where Ximena lived.

He stood in the street and whistled like a bird. Then he picked up something from the street and threw it at the house. He paced for a couple of minutes. Then the gate opened a crack and he walked inside.

I crossed the street and tried the gate. It was locked. I walked a couple of houses down and climbed up a telephone pole. I could see the front patio of the house. It was dark, but I could make out an older Volkswagen Beetle parked in the patio of Ximena's house. Then I saw Chicano, his wide back folding over like he was holding something delicate. Ximena's arm wrapped around his shoulder, her leg around his waist. They moved together around the side of the Beetle and disappeared behind the car.

I told myself he was a *luchador*. I told myself over and over, *Luchadores* always get the girls. I had been the one who had invited him into my life. What did I expect? Besides, he was helping me. He'd come to Devil's Ravine and even saved my life. He helped me bury Chapo. And besides, I was too young for Ximena. There was nothing I could do.

I climbed down the pole and walked home. Chicano, Ximena, they didn't care about me. Nobody did. The streets were quiet. Dogs didn't bark. I was a ghost. I was invisible to the world. I was nothing.

Chicano was a traitor. I hated him. Even if what I felt for Ximena was an illusion—a fantasy—it was something he should respect. I knew Ximena and I could never be together. She was older, beautiful and in control of her life. My life was falling to pieces. I had no parents. What could I possibly offer her?

But maybe Chicano wasn't a traitor. Maybe the best thing for Ximena was for her to be with Chicano instead of Joaquín. That was hopeful. He could save her. I would have to accept that. Even if it hurt.

I lay on my bed and stared at the ceiling. About an hour later, Chicano walked in. He was real quiet and didn't turn on the light. He took his pants off and dropped them in the corner.

"You're back," I said.

"*Ay cabrón*. You scared the shit out of me. I thought you were asleep."

"How did it go?"

"Fine." He pulled his shirt over his head and tossed it in the corner with his pants. Ximena's perfume was all over the room.

"Did you find anything?"

"It's not easy, *hijín*. I can't seem to get a straight answer from anyone."

"Who did you ask?"

He sat on his bed on the floor and pulled his socks off. "Just people," he said and covered himself with the blanket. "But they're scared. Everyone's scared. No one wants to talk."

"Maybe we should ask Ximena, no?"

He didn't move. Then he forced a laugh. "What could she possibly tell us?"

"She's doing that Joaquín, no?"

"Hey, don't be vulgar." His voice was loud. "Besides, they're probably just dating."

"How do you know?"

"I don't. I just don't think you should think of her that way."

"I thought you liked her," I said.

"Who wouldn't like her? And what's with all the questions?"

I shut my eyes and spoke the most difficult words to ever come out of my mouth. "What happened by the white Beetle?"

It was as if I was admitting my parents were dead. Like I was giving up hope. I wanted to know the truth, but I didn't want to know. I didn't want to know about Chicano and Ximena. But I did. I wanted to know everything. I hated it.

"Look, Liberio. Don't feel bad about what you think you saw."

"Don't tell me how to feel."

"But it's not like that, *hijín*."

"You could have any girl in town, but you had to go for Ximena. I thought we were friends."

"Look." He sat up. "It's not as if I planned it. But it's working to our advantage. She's the closest thing to Joaquín."

"So what did she tell you while you—"

"*Chingada madre,*" he interrupted. "Don't be that way, Liberio."

"Tell me."

"Nothing. She wouldn't tell me anything. But maybe she will."

"So you're going back?"

"I don't know." He turned on his side, his shoulder rising like a mountain, like Popocatepetl. "If you don't want me to, I won't. Just say the word."

"I don't want you to see her again. Ever."

He turned to face me. "Look, Liberio. She's not a nice girl. You—"

I jumped on him. I threw punches: left, right, left, right. I threw everything I had, swinging nonstop.

He took me by the wrists and pushed me back. I kicked and kneed, but he pressed his massive weight against me, immobilizing me. I was helpless. Then I did what I'd been trying not to do.

"Liberio, stop. Don't cry. Listen to me."

But I couldn't stop. Everything came crashing out of me. Maybe it was more than just Ximena. Maybe it was about my parents because the emptiness of their presence had become a fixture. And maybe it was Gaby and Abuela arguing. Maybe it was knowing that nothing was ever going to be the same. Ever. It pressed against me, heavier than Chicano's weight. I wanted to die.

"Listen." His voice was deep. His frayed mask hovered over my face like a devil ready to kill. "Women like Ximena are trouble. You understand?"

I took a deep breath. When I exhaled, it came out in short spastic sobs.

"She's not the kind of girl you think she is." I relaxed my muscles and his hands loosened around my wrists. "She's after money. And her own happiness. Whoever ends up marrying her is going to suffer. Big time."

"You don't know her."

"Trust me. I've known a lot of girls like her. She's using Joaquín to her advantage. And she was using me. The only difference is that I knew it. I was willing."

"No." I cried. "You're lying."

"Joaquín's her ticket to a better life. I'm her ticket out of town. She's playing us both. But either way, she gets what she wants. Get it? She gets out of the life she has now. A life she hates."

"I don't believe you."

"She told me."

"Liar!"

"I know you think you love her, but she doesn't love you. She doesn't love anyone. She doesn't even love herself."

I freed my hand and punched him on the side of the face.

He grabbed my arm and pressed down again. "Listen to me, *cabrón*. Ximena is the type of girl who will use men all her life to get what she wants. Maybe if you were rich, you'd have a chance. She wants people to admire her. She's not going to get that with the son of a baker." He shook me and pressed my arms down. "She's trouble, Liberio. Get that through your thick head."

And then, as if an angel appeared before me, I saw Rocío Morales. She was beautiful. She was like that, showing it off like no one else. She had a strange power. People talked about her with a tone and vocabulary that was different. Even my father didn't sound like my father whenever she was around, at the *panadería* or in the plaza. He doted over her. Maybe the man at the Centenario was right. Maybe my father was with her. Maybe he wasn't as good and perfect as I imagined. Maybe none of us are. I closed my eyes and my body went limp.

Chicano released me. "I'm sorry if I hurt you." He sat up and rubbed the palm of his hand with the ball of his thumb. "I went with her because I saw the opportunity. I thought I could learn something about your parents."

It was a struggle for me to speak and not start crying. "But you found nothing."

He shook his head. "She's so wrapped up in herself, I don't think she understands who Joaquín and his friends are or what they're up to."

I didn't care about that anymore. I was thinking of my father. It was all breaking apart around him and Rocío Morales.

29.

Abuela had finally calmed down. She was back to her usual self, drinking *café con leche* and talking in the present tense of Veracruz as if she were there. She seemed to have completely forgotten about all our problems in Izayoc.

"The beach has never been my favorite," she said while we ate dinner. "I cannot stand the sand all over me. But they say it's good for your skin. Hortensia Fernández, the *rubia* whose father owns the Ford dealership, says that when she went to Europe, she had a facial with sand and mud. Can you believe that?"

I didn't listen. And I didn't eat. I couldn't.

"I would much prefer we go to the Hotel Ruiz Galindo in Fortín de las Flores," she went on. "Their pool is covered with gardenias. You cannot even imagine how pretty it smells."

My stomach twisted in a mess of nerves. I just picked at my food while my mind raced in a long loop, trying to sort out this business between Ximena and Joaquín and Chicano. And I was worried about Mosca. I hadn't seen him in days. He still hadn't come to school and was never home whenever I called. The job to stakeout for the black Suburban had to be over. I just hoped he hadn't accepted another job from Pepino.

‡

The following day I stopped by the *panadería* to see what was
going on with Gaby and her new Internet café. It hadn't officially
opened yet, but she was inside, sitting in the corner with her head
resting on the counter. There was no trace of the old *panadería*. A
dozen gray cubicles like the ones they have at the Telmex office
were lined up against the walls. Each one had a nice orange plastic
chair and one of those inspirational posters with a landscape or
scene with words like: achievement, success, imagination.

"Where's your *luchador*?" Gaby said. Her hair was combed back
tight, and her face had a light coat of make-up. Seeing her like this,
I understood what Mosca had said, what men like Joaquín and
Francisco Serrano saw in her. But there was something more. She
looked smart. Her eyes glowed with ambition. I understood now.

"Taking a nap," I said.

"For real?"

"He goes out at night sometimes, searching for clues."

"And has he found anything?"

I sighed. "No. Not yet."

"What do you expect him to find?"

"I don't know," I said. "Maybe who killed them?"

Gaby raised her head and gave me an odd look, as if we'd
been talking of something else, of the color of the walls or the
weather. "*Ay*, Liberio."

I bowed my head. "I know."

We were silent for a moment. Her eyes were on me as I
walked around, my fingers tracing the edges of the cubicles,
the backs of the chairs, the wall. I looked around as if there was
something to look at, but it was just an office space with no
machinery.

She came out from behind the counter. "So, do you like it?"

"I'm sorry you argued with Abuela," I said.

She rolled her eyes. "I really didn't want to upset her, but she just went off on me like everything was my fault."

"I think it's all finally getting to her."

Gaby hung her head and walked around to the side where the only computer in the place sat disconnected and covered with clear plastic. "We'll be operational in a couple of weeks. When she sees the place full of people, I'm sure she'll change her mind."

"What about the computers?"

"Francisco's getting them from one of his friends in Uruapan. He was supposed to come back last night. Not that it matters because we still have to wait for the stupid Telmex people to set up the phone lines."

I looked at the back door. "What are you doing with the bakery?"

"Storage."

"You know, I saw Lucio when he was leaving."

Gaby placed her hand on my shoulder. "I asked him to stay and work for us, but he said he was going to take advantage of the change to go visit his *pueblo* and maybe go to the beach. Leticia's staying. She's going to be my assistant." She moved to the side and looked out at the street. A water truck rumbled passed.

I said, "So you like this guy?"

"Francisco?" She turned and smiled. "That's a stupid question. Of course I like him."

"Do you love him?"

She gave me a gentle slap on the shoulder and turned away. "*Ay*, Liberio, you're so inquisitive. I don't know. Love. It's not that simple."

"Is he nice to you?"

She smiled and pressed her warm hand against my cheek. "You're sweet."

On Saturday evening Chicano and I ventured to the plaza. We'd been avoiding the area since we'd seen the bullet-ridden Suburban earlier that week. The scene had left me with a bad feeling. Now, whenever I thought of the plaza, I thought of death.

I found myself thinking more and more about Abuela's stories of Veracruz. Maybe the magic of her world was working on me. Maybe such a perfect place did exist. Izayoc had been perfect once, so why not Veracruz? And if I actually had family there, even better. In my dreams, I imagined us living in one of those palatial homes she talked about, one with big open windows and a long veranda on the second floor with a view of the ocean. Lucio and Jesusa would be with us, and we would run a new, bigger and better *panadería*.

The plaza was bustling. Christmas lights were strung from tree to tree and *conjuntos* and mariachis strolled around the square looking for customers. It was as if everyone had come to celebrate a *fiesta*, but there was something creepy about the place. Most of the stores were still shuttered. And all the street vendors were new. I had never seen any of these people before. Even the people making their way around the square—they were all strangers dressed up in fancy clothes and hats. This was not Izayoc.

Late model double cab pickups, Suburbans and a black Ford Expedition were parked along the side of the square facing the municipal building.

Chicano walked with his back straight and a badass swagger, just as if he was walking into the ring for a fight. People gawked. They whispered to each other. Girls covered their mouths and giggled. He was special, like royalty or something. We were a team and everyone knew it. Chicano and me. Boli and Chicano Estrada. Chicano Estrada and Boli.

We crossed the street to the plaza. Pineda had parked his brand-new patrol truck, a big white Yukon, on the side of the street. A small crowd surrounded him. As we crossed the street, Pineda leaned back against the hood, pulled the cigarette from his mouth and whistled at us.

"Super Barrio," he yelled, "where's the *lucha*?"

The men around him laughed.

Chicano didn't flinch. He strutted right up to the truck and faced Pineda. "How's the investigation, *jefe?*"

"It's going," he said. "Rest assured, we're digging deep for you."

"That's right," a man said. "Six feet deep."

Everyone laughed. They stank of liquor. Pineda grinned, his brown teeth dull, crooked. Nasty.

"Good." Chicano didn't miss a beat. "I'm glad to hear it. You did an excellent job with that black Suburban on Avenida Porvenir the other morning."

Pineda flinched. Then he smiled and rested his foot on the front bumper of the truck. He was wearing the custom caiman boots, the same ones I had polished at La Gloria, the same ones I had seen outside El Gallo de Oro.

"That's right, *jefe,*" Chicano said. "I hear you're conducting a thorough investigation."

No one said anything. They didn't seem amused.

Chicano smiled. "My contacts in Toluca said you're close to making an arrest."

"What?" Pineda waved. "What do you mean, Toluca?" He pulled the cigarette from his mouth and flicked it onto the street.

"The Federal Police said they're thrilled with your work and the leads you gave them. Keep them coming." Chicano winked at Pineda. "Congratulations."

"No, no." Pineda's face turned pale. "That's a lie." He looked at the men around him. They were staring at him, confused. "There's nothing going on, no clues. I haven't talked to the *Federales.*"

"*Buenas noches, jefe.*" Chicano smiled. We walked away.

"What was that about?" I said.

"Just a hunch. I figure he didn't investigate the shooting because he's in on it."

"And when you mentioned the *Federales*—"

"These jackals don't trust anyone. Now Pineda's going to have to watch his back."

"Did you see his boots? He must have killed the man at La Gloria."

"Don't worry." We looked on both sides of the street. "He'll get what's coming to him."

Zopilote's green Golf was parked two doors up from Los Perdidos. He was leaning against it like he always did, wearing a red Adidas sweat suit and dark glasses. I didn't recognize anyone in his group.

"There you are," Zopilote said. "Long time no see."

"We saw you just the other day, ¿no *güey*?" I could make out Ximena and Joaquín through the dark windows of the Golf. They were in the back seat, abstract shapes moving like a single mass, holding each other, bodies pressed together. I felt nothing. It was all very clear to me now. Everything Chicano had said about Ximena was true. I hated her.

Zopilote stepped away from the car and pushed his chest out. "You still looking for your parents?"

"Tell me something," Chicano said. "How much do they pay you, because I have a big pile of dirty laundry I need washed?"

Some of the men laughed.

"I don't do laundry, Super Barrio." Zopilote's voice was shaky. I guess a coward is always a coward no matter what car he drives.

"I knew a girl," Chicano said.

"Just one?" Zopilote said and his friends laughed.

"Yeah, she was a dancer. She danced at a club like that Gallo de Oro *cantina* you have here, only this place was a classy joint."

Zopilote pulled off his sunglasses. "I like El Gallo de Oro."

"I bet you do," Chicano said. "But let me tell you about this girl. She was a nice girl who dreamed of dancing, just dancing and nothing else. But then a customer asked her to come out with him, right?"

"¡*Pa' cogersela!*" Zopilote said, and rocked his pelvis back and forth. His friends whistled and smacked each other like horny teenagers.

"Yes, but she refused," Chicano said. "She didn't want to be with him. So the man pulled out a wad of bills, right? And he started peeling them off one by one."

One of the men laughed. Zopilote said nothing. He looked confused, as if he didn't know whether to laugh or get angry.

"It didn't take too many bills before she took the man's hand and led him upstairs to a room."

Zopilote stepped forward. "What the fuck's that supposed to mean, *cabrón?*"

"It's just a story about a girl."

"*Una puta,*" one of the men cried out. The others laughed.

"Yes, a whore," Chicano said. "Every whore has a price, don't they, Zopilote?"

The men around Zopilote whistled and catcalled. Zopilote turned red. He reached for his waist and pulled his gun, but Chicano tore the pistol away, cocked it and held it, the barrel inches from Zopilote's forehead.

Zopilote flinched. His hands froze in mid-air.

"How much?" Chicano's voice was like a rock.

Zopilote didn't answer. His hands trembled. No one moved.

"How much, *cabrón!*" Chicano's voice boomed.

"I don't know." Zopilote stuttered. "How...how much what?"

"How much is your life worth, *hijo de tu chingada madre?*"

His friends looked away, at the ground, at Zopilote's feet where a small puddle of urine had formed.

"How much?" Chicano pushed the end of the gun barrel against Zopilote's forehead. Zopilote clenched his teeth and shut his eyes.

Then Chicano flicked his thumb and the magazine popped out from the bottom of the pistol. He caught it with his other hand and put it in his pants pocket. He cocked the weapon again. The bullet in the chamber flew out and fell on the sidewalk with a light clink.

"Don't be a *pendejo,*" Chicano said and waved the silver pistol for everyone to see. "This shit will get you nothing."

Zopilote smiled nervously. He ran his hand over his hair.

"If any of you know what happened to Liberio's parents, I'd like to know. And if you want to keep it confidential, I understand. No one else needs to know."

No one said anything. But in their eyes I could see death. It had been there all the time only I hadn't really looked. I always knew they had killed my parents. Their silence was their confession. Not just Joaquín and Zopilote and their friends, but everyone—everyone who shook their heads and turned away, everyone who kept silent, everyone who told me not to worry, everyone who left Izayoc. They were all guilty of killing them.

Chicano glanced at me. Then he tossed the gun up in the air. Zopilote tried to catch it, but he fumbled and it fell to the ground.

"Come on," Chicano said. The intensity of his anger was all over the street. "It stinks here." Then he turned and smacked the window of the Golf and gestured an obscenity at Joaquín and Ximena.

30.

Despite his protests, Chicano came with us to Sunday mass. "It's just that, where I grew up, the church was very strict," he said as we walked. "If we didn't do what the priest told us, he'd beat the hell out of us."

"Well, then," Abuela said, "if you had done what you were told, there would not have been a problem, no?"

"*Ay*, Doña Esperánza." Chicano was wearing one of my father's suit jackets. It was too small for him so when he raised his arms his hands shot out of the sleeves like Frankenstein. "I'm a freethinker."

"You mean a heathen."

"No, no. I believe in God. *Por favor.*"

"But the church is the house of God. I do not understand what you have against it."

"It's not God or the church, Doña Esperanza. It's the damn priests."

"I agree with you on that particular point. Father Gregorio is not my favorite priest. He is much too liberal and prone to outbursts of passion which are unbecoming in a man of the cloth. But Father Félix Huerta, our previous priest, that was a man of the finest stock—Spanish from Spain."

"You know," Chicano said, "Jesus was a liberal."

"*Por favor.*" Abuela raised her hand to stop him. "Spare me the lecture. Jesus was a good man, but he wasn't perfect."

"No one's perfect," I said, thinking of my father. I thought of what Gaby had said about the bakery's finances. My father never let on that there was a problem. Then there was the man at the Centenario and everything he said. Lies. There was so much I didn't know. I kept telling myself he was a good man, but maybe I was wrong. Everyone lies.

"Jesus is not my beacon," Abuela declared. "La Virgen de Guadalupe. That is who I go to church for. She is the one I pray to."

Chicano nodded his masked head. "I agree, Doña Esperanza. La Guadalupana is my spiritual center."

Abuela smiled. "There. We have something in common."

Father Gregorio's sermon was about the importance of communion and how Jesus' plan was for all of us to get along. Men are men, and we are one family and so on. As usual, it was long and boring.

"The nerve of the man," Abuela announced when mass was finally over. "No priest has ever given me a sermon like that. I will accept whom I choose to accept."

Jorge Bustillo, the carpenter from two blocks down from the *panadería*, leaned forward and tapped my *abuela* on the shoulder. "Neither will I, Doña Esperanza. The sooner they leave, the better."

Without turning, Abuela said, "They are not leaving. That is the problem. We have to either leave or get used to them." Then she looked up at the new ceiling and sighed. "Someone is trying to buy our priest."

People shuffled out of the church. Chicano and I accompanied Abuela to the shrine of the Virgen de Guadalupe on the opposite side of the church from the Malverde shrine.

She lit a candle, picked a few coins from her purse and

dropped them in the box. Then she crossed herself and prayed. Chicano winked at the Virgen. "How's my girl?"

We met Father Gregorio at the entrance of the church. "How did the dog's funeral go?"

"Fine," I said. "I'm pretty sure he made it into dog heaven."

Father Gregorio smiled and ruffled my hair. "I'm glad to hear it, *hijo*."

"That's a nice watch," Chicano said.

Father Gregorio glanced at his wrist. It was a thick gold-colored timepiece just like the one I had seen on the man driving the truck the night of the shooting at La Gloria. It looked heavy, expensive. "An indulgence," he said.

Chicano asked, "Is it gold?"

"I doubt it. Someone left it in the collection basket." Father Gregorio turned to my *abuela*. "What do you think of the renovation, Doña Esperanza?"

"Much better."

"It's been a long time coming," Father Gregorio said proudly. "And I have placed an order for a pair of forty-six inch bells from El Rosario in Tlaxcala. Hopefully in a few weeks we'll be tolling bells to announce mass."

"It's been a prosperous spring, hasn't it Father?" Chicano said.

"I believe the new highway has been a blessing."

"But with prosperity comes greed," Abuela warned.

"Indeed, Doña Esperanza." Father Gregorio nodded. "One problem begets another. But people with strong moral character will always prevail."

Abuela took Chicano's arm. "Thank you for illuminating us, Father."

In the plaza, the vendors were doing a brisk business. Families I had never seen before relaxed in the shade. Poor peasants sat on the stoop of the shuttered storefronts. The fancy trucks and utility vehicles were still parked in front of the municipal building. Behind the cliffs to the north, dark gray clouds threatened rain.

"That man," Chicano said and looked back at the church, "comes about as cheap as your friend, Zopilote."

Every night around one or two in the morning Chicano rose, got dressed in the dark, and walked quietly out of the house. Every night I followed him. Every night he stopped in front of Ximena's house. He'd whistle or throw pebbles at her window, and she would let him in. I didn't climb the telephone pole to see. I knew what was going on.

But then one night, Ximena didn't open the door. I watched Chicano wait in the dark, pacing in front of her house for hours. It tore me up to see him like that. I knew exactly how he felt. Deep down, though, I was glad.

31.

After school I went to the Minitienda to see if anyone had seen or heard from Mosca. Don Ignacio wasn't there. A new girl was working behind the counter. I didn't recognize any of the customers. No one even raised their eyes to meet mine. They just moved slowly about the store, picking out their groceries in silence.

I bought a tamarind Boing and stepped outside. The street was deserted. Everyone that used to hang out was gone. I even missed Zopilote leaning back against the wall drinking a *caguama* and talking trash nonstop.

It started to rain. I finished my drink and headed home. When I crossed the street, I noticed a group of older boys walking out of La Gloria. They huddled under the awning of the *cantina* for a moment and then headed up Avenida Porvenir.

"Boli!" Pepino waved.

He was with Chato, but I had never seen the other three boys. Pepino had on a leather jacket and a Dallas Cowboys baseball cap which he wore sideways. The others were dressed like rappers, baggy jeans hanging down their hips, long t-shirts, dark shades. We met at the corner.

"What's going on?" I said. Chato slapped Pepino on the back. His new friends surrounded him. They were serious, quiet. One of them didn't even look up. He just kept his head bowed, pressing buttons on his cell phone.

"Not a whole lot of nothing, *broder*." Pepino shrugged his shoulders, fingers twisting like a gangbanger in a movie.

"I haven't seen anyone around," I said. "You?"

"I haven't been looking."

"I heard you hired Mosca to keep a lookout for you."

"You heard right, *broder*." He glanced at his friends. "We had that boy on the payroll. *¿Que no?*"

"What do you mean, the payroll?"

"Wise up, Boli." Chato put his arm around Pepino's shoulder. "We're all on the payroll." He pointed at the others, "Franco, Rata, Nacho. How do you see it, *güey*?"

"Yeah, well, I'm not."

"At some point, you'll have to make a choice, *broder*." Pepino shrugged Chato's arm off his shoulder and pushed him back. He gestured, his fingers twisting around his waist and crotch. "You gonna have to decide. You're either in, or you're out."

"What are you talking about?"

"Look at what happened to Kiko," he said.

Chato grinned. "That *güey* made some bad choices."

"You think about it," Pepino said and shook the rain off his hair. "We can't waste time with you right now, *broder*. We're on patrol. We gotta keep an eye on things around here. Report back to Duende, see?"

They pushed past me.

"Pepino?"

He stopped. They all turned.

"Where's Mosca? Is he still on the payroll?"

Pepino smiled wide and shook his head.

"Where is he?" I said.

He stepped forward and unzipped his jacket. He pulled the

sides back. He wore a fancy blue shirt unbuttoned down to his stomach. Hanging over his bare chest on a gold chain was a small red sphere with a bright yellow swirl at the center.

The devil's fire.

I lunged at him. He fell back. I came down at him, throwing punches left and right. He coiled up. The rain pelted down on us. My head burst with pain. I turned. A fist slammed against the side of my head. Twice. I fell off Pepino. Then I stood, dizzy. Two of his friends came at me, kicking and punching like a machine. I stepped back, dodging, folding, fighting. My back hit the wall. They were on me like cats, three of them at once, punching everywhere. I fell to the ground.

Then the kicking started.

I curled into a ball and shut my eyes. Pain shot up my sides, my face, my head.

Suddenly it stopped.

"You don't listen, *cabrón*."

I opened my eyes. Pepino was standing over me. He had a split lip. Blood trickled down his chin. He pulled a switchblade from his pocket and flicked it open. "You're going to end up just like your little *novio*. Maybe you'll get lucky and meet your parents where you're going."

The other boys smiled. Chato smacked his fist against the palm of his hand. I pushed myself back with my feet, but my legs were too weak, my body too heavy.

Suddenly, Pepino was swooped away like he'd been sucked by a vacuum.

His friends turned.

Chicano held Pepino up by the wrist, dangling him like a ragdoll. "What the fuck you doing, *hijo de tu chingada madre?*"

Pepino dropped his blade. "Do something, you fools!"

The other boys pounced on Chicano.

Chicano turned and smacked them with his left as they jumped on him. They bounced back like they were made of rubber. Then he twisted Pepino's arm until it snapped. Pepino howled. Chicano dropped him. The other boys attacked him again. He kicked one in the crotch. The kid dropped to his knees. He punched another in the jaw and he fell beside Pepino.

I tried getting up, but my muscles wouldn't respond.

Chato fell beside me, face flat on the ground, unconscious. Someone screamed. It all became a blur of pain and darkness. Then everything went black.

When I opened my eyes, the ground was moving under me. I turned my head. The street was sideways.

I was draped over Chicano's back. My body bounced. Every step shot a jolt of pain to my ribs. I tried looking back at the road. I wanted to see how he had left Pepino, but I couldn't move. My mouth was dry. I opened it to drink the rain. It was too much effort. I closed my eyes.

When I opened my eyes again, I was lying in my room. Jesusa sat at the foot of the bed, staring at me. The room had a strong smell of eucalyptus. My body, my muscles were like jelly, relaxed, painless. I floated. I closed my eyes and saw my parents. My father was sitting on a bench by the plaza, smiling like when he'd watch Gaby and me playing when we were little. My mother was next to him. They were holding hands. I walked toward them, but I wasn't getting any closer. They kept smiling and waving at me as if everything was fine. I ran. I ran as fast as I could, trying to get to them. But they kept receding. The more I moved forward, the further they moved back, smiling and waving like nothing was wrong. I ran so hard my legs burned with pain. And all the while they kept waving. My chest and arms ached. I couldn't move anymore. And they still waved, floating back until they became little tiny specs in a long black tunnel.

I opened my eyes. It was dark. Figures moved slowly around me. I squinted and blinked. Jesusa, Chicano and Gaby were leaning over me.

"What's going on?" I said.

"You're home," Jesusa said. She touched the side of my face. Someone turned the light on. The room burned bright, hurting my eyes.

"Those boys gave you quite a beating," Chicano said.

"Mosca." My voice came out low and raspy like it belonged to someone else. I took a deep breath and swallowed. "They killed Mosca." My sides burned with pain. "And Pepino took his *diablito rojo.*"

Gaby turned away and wiped her eyes. Then she stood and walked quickly out of the room.

"But she didn't even like Mosca," I said.

Jesusa looked at Chicano.

"They killed Francisco," Chicano said softly. "He was one of the men in the Suburban we saw last week."

Chicano's mask was ripped at the side near his ear. The stitching around the tear-like shapes that outlined his eyes was coming off. The mouth had a long rip and only a few of the little blue stars remained. He smiled. For the first time I noticed he was missing one of his front teeth. "Don't worry," he said. "I got you a present." He held up the necklace Pepino was wearing. The devil's fire.

"Relax." Jesusa's voice was steady, gentle. Her cold hand pressed against my forehead. "You're going to be fine. You just need rest." Her voice was so soothing. My body felt light, like it was levitating. I closed my eyes.

32.

It was almost noon when I woke up. I was still in terrible pain.
When I sat up, a wave of dizziness almost knocked me back.

The house was quiet.

I walked into the kitchen where Jesusa was washing dishes.
"How do you feel?" she asked.

"It hurts."

"They really laid into you, ¿no pues?"

I remembered Pepino, his friends, Mosca's devil's fire. I
hurried back to my room.

Jesusa came after me, wiping her hands on her apron.

I pulled my pajamas off.

"What are you doing?"

"I need to find him," I said.

"No, Liberio, Chicano said you have to stay here until he
comes home."

"Where did he go?" I pulled a t-shirt from the dresser and
caught my reflection in the mirror. My entire left side was a long
black bruise. My face was swollen, black and blue spots at the eye
and cheek.

"He didn't say. But just wait. Please."

I put the shirt on. Then I stepped behind the closet door and changed my pants.

"He said he would be back soon," she said.

"When did he leave?"

"I don't know. Early this morning."

"It's noon," I said.

"Wait for him, Liberio. *Por favor.*"

"What if he never comes back?" I cried as I ran out of the house.

"It's dangerous!"

The plaza was deserted. Everything was shuttered. Three double cab pickups were parked in front of the municipal building. Pineda's Yukon was there. Two men carrying *cuerno de chivo* assault rifles stood by the trucks. Two men and a woman walked into Los Pinos restaurant where another guard stood at the entrance with a black military style machine gun slung over his shoulder.

Across the street, Father Gregorio hurried into the church.

I followed him. He was with a group of men. One of them placed his hand on his shoulder and laughed. Another man gave him a pat on the back. When our eyes met, Farther Gregorio's smile faded. Then he smiled again. It was a lie. The men turned and stared at me, unsmiling. The priest nodded at one of the men and moved toward me with long hurried steps.

"Liberio." His voice was soft, friendly like I had known it all my life. But it was a lie. It was all a lie.

I ran. I slipped on the wet steps and fell. My whole body flexed with pain. I pushed myself up and kept going. I had to keep going.

I ran up to Santacruz. My legs, my sides throbbed with pain. My chest burned. The road was all mud. Every step was an effort. But I had to get to Mosca's house. I kept thinking it had all been a mistake, a bad dream. This could not be happening.

I stopped to catch my breath. There were no street dogs, no kids or old ladies on the side of the road or in front of the houses, hanging laundry. No chickens. Nothing.

I reached the top of the hill. The sun began to peek from behind the rain clouds. There was no answer at Mosca's house. I knocked on his *tía* Yarce's door. No answer. There was no one in the streets, no kids flying kites or playing soccer or mothers sweeping patios. Santacruz was deserted.

I ran to the side where I had last seen Mosca sitting on the edge of the cliff with the big black binoculars. He was gone. Everyone was gone. My parents, Chicano, the people of Santacruz. All gone.

I closed my eyes and asked God for help. When I opened them again I saw two boys running. They disappeared up the path toward the grotto and the giant cross. I ran after them.

Around the bend, at the top of the mountain, a large crowd had gathered, everyone looking up at the sunrays breaking through the clouds and spilling down on the giant white cross where Chicano Estrada's body hung from his neck by a rope tied to the right arm of the cross.

33.

We sat at the center of the bus to Mexico City—Gaby and me with Jesusa and my *abuela* in the seats in front of us. That day there was no first-class bus out of Izayoc, but the second-class bus was comfortable. It had air-conditioning, was quiet and smelled of cherry air-freshener.

I had a window seat. Just after we started, we stopped to pick up two passengers on the side of the old highway. They had a lot of luggage. It took a while for them to get settled and for the bus to start again. Behind us was the Pemex station and El Gallo de Oro.

When the bus finally started, we travelled slowly until we reached the place where the old highway met the new one northeast of town. We passed Zopilote's parent's restaurant. Workers were building something on the empty lot beside it. The parking lot was crowded with big trucks and a black Suburban with tinted windows.

A man walked out of the restaurant. The glint of the silver pistol tucked in his belt caught the sun and reflected like a mirror against my eye. And for some reason I thought of Ximena and the time she blew that kiss at me after we'd won the school's history contest, her lips pressed together as she blew, her eyes bright and full of life and the false promise of the future.

In the front of the bus, the driver had started a movie on the small television above the windshield. It was one of the Scooby Doo flicks.

My *abuela* leaned to the side and touched Jesusa's arm. "You are going to love Veracruz. You will see. It is such a wonderful place. Peaceful like heaven."

I looked at Gaby. She wasn't wearing any makeup. She had her head turned to the side, her eyes downcast, her hands folded on her lap. She looked just like she did when we were little and drove with our parents to Acapulco.

I nudged her with my elbow. "What are you thinking?"

She looked at me and smiled. Then she pursed her lips and her eyes furrowed. "About Veracruz," she said. "I just hope it's like Abuela says."

I lowered my head. Her fingers moved nervously one over the other like the time we waited at Pineda's office. I took her hand. "Relax. It's Veracruz. Everything will be great."

She smiled and wove her fingers between mine the way my mother used to do. "So what's the first thing you're going to do when we get there?"

Gaby's eyes had a terrible sadness. I thought of Mosca and Chicano and my parents and everything that happened in Izayoc. And somehow I knew it would never leave her. It would never leave any of us. Veracruz, Mexico City or any other place in the world could never make the sadness disappear.

"I'm going to find a gym," I said, and brought my hand to my neck and felt the necklace, my fingers rubbing the smooth sphere of the devil's fire. "I'm going to become a luchador. The best ever. El Diablo Rojo."

ACKNOWLEDGEMENTS

I'm extremely grateful and indebted to Rita Ciresi, Ira Sukrungruang and Ylce Irizarry for their feedback on *Playing for the Devil's Fire*, and to my agent Stephany Evans for believing in it. As always, my warmest gratitude to *la familia* at Cinco Puntos, especially to Lee Byrd for helping me make the manuscript sing. And to my wife Lorraine, for everything.

GLOSSARY

A

abuela: Grandmother

agüita: A translucent glass marble

albóndigas: Meatballs

amigos: Friends

ándale: Go on or let's go

B

bolillo: A traditional Mexican bread roll with a hard crust

botanita: Snack or appetizer

broder: Slang, a derivative of the word brother

buen provecho: Enjoy your meal

C

cachorritos: Baby animals like cubs or puppies

café con leche: Coffee with milk

caguama: A large (usually 1 liter) bottle of beer

cantina: Bar

caray: Jeez

cabrón: Billy goat, used as an insult

carnal: Slang, brother

carteles: The posters that advertise an event

chamaco: Boy

chicharrón: Pork rind, usually served with lime and hot sauce

chichis: Vulgar slang, breasts
chingados: Vulgar slang, screw it
chíngatelo: Vulgar slang, screw him over
chingues: Vulgar slang, to mess around with. *No chingues:* Don't mess around
chiquita: Little one. An endearing term
chiras pelas: An expression used with playing marbles when a player knocks another player's marble out
chismes: Gossip
cócteles: Cocktails as in seafood cocktails
colonias: Neighborhood, but it is also used to reference poor neighborhoods that sprout up where squatters take over
compadre: The godfather of a person's child. Also used about a good or best friend
conchas: A type of sweet bread that has the shape of a clamshell
conjuntos: A small musical group
corrido: A traditional style of song or ballad that tells a story of a person or event
cuates: Pals
cuerno de chivo: Goat's horn. *Slang*, an AK-47 assault rifle, referencing the magazine of the rifle that is curved like the horn of a goat
cumbia: popular music style originally from Colombia

D
dios mío: My God

E
efectívamente: An acknowledgement in the affirmative, like saying indeed
el diablito rojo: Small red devil
el dolor del amor: The pain of love
el enmascarado de plata: Silver-masked
el Hijo del Santo: Son of Santo, a Mexican wrestler
el Norte: The north, the USA
elotes: Corn on the cob
enano: Midget. Used either as an insult or endearment
entonces: So, or so then
escuadra: A carpenter's square. *Slang*, an automatic pistol that has a right angle like a carpenter's square
estas loco: You're crazy
estudios Churubusco: Film studios in Mexico City

F

feria: Fair
fiestas: A party. Also refers to holidays
fútbol: Soccer

G

gente pobre: Poor people
gordo: Fat
güey: Alternative spelling *wey* or *buey.* Dude, but has a slightly vulgar connotation

H

hijín: Slang, from *hijo,* which means son. *Hijo* is used in Mexico for a good friend or dude, the same way *güey* is used.
hijo de su chingada madre: Like saying son of a bitch
huipil: A loose brocaded blouse worn by Indian women

J

jacal: Small peasant hut usually made of mud and sticks
jefe: Boss. *Slang,* father

L

limosna: Money you give to a beggar or the church
linda: Pretty
luchador: Wrestler

M

maguey: A type of agave plant with thorns found throughout Mexico
malecón: Seaside boulevard or promenade
mano: Buddy
mantilla: Traditional head and face scarf worn over the head and shoulders
mayordomo: Can mean butler, but in rural Mexico it means the person who works (usually on a volunteer basis) to clean and take care of a church or other community property
metiche: Someone who gets in other people's business
mi amor: my love
mijo: Contraction for *mi hijo,* my son
Mil Máscaras: A thousand masks: a famous Mexican wrestler
milpa: Field planted with crops, usually corn
mis pendejitos: My little idiots, or my little assholes

mocos: An insult. *Mocos* means boogers, but in Mexico the saying accompanies a vulgar hand gesture akin to giving the finger
mocoso: Snot-nosed kid
molletes: Bolillo bread sliced in half, coated with refried beans and melted cheese
morral: Peasant's sack or bag, usually made of woven palm fronds or wool
mosca: Fly
muy buenas tardes: Very good afternoon

N

Nahuatl: the language and culture of the Nahua Indians, descendants of the Aztecs
nalgas: Vulgar, buttocks
naranjas: Slang, no
nieve: A type of ice cream like a sorbet
ni madres: Vulgar, no way
niña: Girl
niños: Boys
Niños Héroes: Boy heroes. Six young cadets who, when in 1847 the invading U.S. forces entered Mexico City and made their way up to Chapultepec Castle—then the military academy—wrapped themselves in the Mexican flag and jumped off the cliff to their death instead of surrendering the flag
no manches: Vulgar slang, don't mess around
nopales: Variety of edible cactus
no, que va: An expression similar to saying, no way

O

órale: Similar to saying, come on

P

pa' cogersela: Vulgar, to screw her
panadería: Bread store where they also bake the bread
pan dulce: Sweet breads
para servirle: At your service
pendejo: An insult similar to idiot, but worse
pepino: Cucumber
perico: Parrot. Also the name of an opaque aggie agate marble that has colors similar to those of a parrot
piloncillo: Raw sugar
pinches putos: Vulgar, fucking assholes

pollitos: Slang, chicks, girls
por el amor de Dios: For the love of God
por favor: Please
procuraduría: The police station
profesor: A male professor or teacher
pueblo: Town
pues: An expression, similar to saying, see or you know?

Q

que Dios lo bendiga: May God bless you
qué hubo: Slang, what's up?

R

regiomontanos: People from Monterrey in the north of Mexico

S

Santo: the most famous Mexican masked wrestler
Secundaria Vicente Suárez: middle school (Vicente Suarez is the name of one of the Niños Héroes)
señora: Woman, but it is also used to show respect. When Jesusa says, *sí señora,* she is saying, Yes, ma'am. Servants don't usually call their employers by their first names
simón: Slang, yes. Derived from *sí*

T

taquería: Taco shop
taquero: Man who makes tacos
telenovela: Soap opera
tocayo: Two people with the same name are *tocayos* and they can refer to each other as *tocayo*
tortillería: Shop where they make and sell tortillas
troca: Slang, truck
trompo: Top, a toy that spins when propelled with a string. The meat for tacos al pastor is stacked in the shape of a large top

U

un perro callejero: Stray dog
Uruapan: A town in the state of Michoacán

V

válgame: Usually people say *valgame dios* (may God save me), but often times people just say *valgame* (oh my)

varos: *Slang*, pesos (Mexican money)
veladora: Religious votive candles
vieja: Old woman. *Slang,* chicks, girls
Virgen de Guadalupe: Patron saint of Mexico
vulcanizaroda: Tire repair shop

Y

ya basta: Enough or stop
ya veras: You'll see

PHILLIPPE DIEDERICH

Phillippe Diederich is a Haitian-American writer and photographer born in the Dominican Republic and raised in Mexico City and Miami. He worked in Mexico for half a decade as a photojournalist, traveling through the country extensively and witnessing the terrible tragedies of the drug wars. He thinks of Mexico as his home. *Playing for the Devil's Fire* is a novel born from his nostalgia and deep sorrow for Mexico. He wanted to put a face to the 80,000-plus deaths in the so-called war on drugs and to address the corruption and the senseless narco violence that is tearing the country apart.

PRAISE FOR PLAYING FOR THE DEVIL'S FIRE

In *Playing for the Devil's Fire*, we ride a young Mexican boy's emotional helter-skelter as he gradually understands the hopelessness of his battle against evil. Philippe Diederich has found a brilliant way of going behind the headlines to show that the Mexican tragedy is about real people. —Alan Riding, author of *Distant Neighbors: A Portrait of the Mexicans*

Phillippe Diederich's *Playing for the Devil's Fire* is a frightening and gripping story of what happens when evil takes control of a small town. Boli, a baker's son, gives us a firsthand understanding about the long plague of Mexico's drug wars, the disappearances of those willing to speak out, and the helplessness common people feel when their leaders choose money over justice. Boli's friendship with El Chicano Estrada, an itinerant masked luchador, recalls the same odd and deep bond Huck and Jim formed in Twain's great book. The stakes are just as high here for a child whose heart is just as good. —Tony D'Souza, author of *Whiteman*